AN APPETITE FOR MURDER

Scrounging around in the refrigerator, Savannah found something that raised her spirits: a chocolate-chip, double-fudge muffin with cream cheese filling. She zapped a cup of stale coffee in the microwave and laced it with Bailey's and Half & Half.

Ah, breakfast.

After sinking into the comfort of her favorite chair, Savannah savored the anticipation of the chocolate cream cheese. But first there was the mail to deal with. Specifically an oversized beige envelope that had no postage or even a return address. But it was sealed, very well, with several passes of cellophane tape.

Savannah ripped open the envelope. Green. At first, that was all she could see. The envelope was stuffed with cash.

On the bottom of the pile was a small note, the same beige stationery as the envelope. On it were a few typed words: *Dear Ms. Reid, I have reason to believe that Kat Valentina was murdered. I would like you to prove this. If you do, there will be more where this came from. Please consider this money a retainer for your services. Begin working right away and I'll be in touch.*

Murdered? The word shot through Savannah's brain, verifying what some part of her had known all along. That was why she had been uneasy hearing of Jennifer Liu's "accidental" ruling. For some reason that was impossible to explain, Savannah knew that Kat Valentina had been a victim of homicide, not just her own carelessness.

And, apparently, whoever had left this in her mailbox knew it, too.

Books by G. A. McKevett

JUST DESSERTS

BITTER SWEETS

KILLER CALORIES

COOKED GOOSE

SUGAR AND SPITE

Published by Kensington Publishing Corp.

• G. A. McKevett •

KILLER
CALORIES

KENSINGTON BOOKS
KENSINGTON PUBLISHING CORP.
http://www.kensingtonbooks.com

Lovingly dedicated to

Carolyn and Joseph Sargent

Rare, precious friends
Through the laughter and the tears

The author would like to acknowledge the following:

Liza Jacobs—for the French stuff
David Jacobs—for the legal stuff
Dr. Ronald L. O'Halloran—for the medical/forensic stuff
Gwendolynn Massie—for the frog joke

Thanks, guys. I couldn't have done it without you.

CHAPTER ONE

"Four-inch high heels should only be worn by a woman who's lying on her back," Savannah mumbled into the tiny microphone that was taped to her left breast, just below the lace edge of the ridiculous red, sequined bustier. The pointed toe of her accursed shoe caught in a sidewalk crack, and she had to perform a quick Highland jig to keep her balance.

"Hey, nobody said it was easy on the stroll," replied a gravelly male voice from the miniearphone stuck in her ear. "They don't call them 'working girls' for nothing."

She glanced across the street at the pseudowino sprawled on the park bench and stuck out her tongue at him. It wasn't quite daylight, and she knew he couldn't see her, so the satisfaction was marginal at best.

"*Working girls* get paid," she reminded him in a down-in-Dixie drawl that was soft as a lilac-scented Southern night. "And as I recall, Dirk, this is a freebie."

"A favor to an old friend," the wino replied.

"You got the 'old' part right. Why didn't you ask someone who's still a real cop to help you out with this?"

"Mike and Jake look horrible in drag. They couldn't pick up a sand flea at a beach party. Besides, you and me ran this scam a hundred times when we were partners. What's the big deal?"

"I was on San Carmelita's Police Department payroll then. Now I'm a private investigator with—"

"With nothing better to do and nobody better to do it with. Otherwise, you wouldn't be out here at five o'clock in the morning with me, strutting your stuff with that Georgia peach waggle of yours."

"Why, sugar . . ." With her hand on her hip, she struck a pose and giggled. ". . . you like my waggle?"

"Savannah, honey, I love your waggle. But right now I'd rather you waggle your butt than your tongue. It could go down anytime now."

Savannah scanned the nearly deserted downtown street of San Carmelita. So far, so good. Nothing stirred but a couple of palm trees, rustling in the predawn ocean breeze. Only one shop was open at this hour on Lester Street in the quaint, Southern California town—Andy's Adult Bookstore.

Dirk had received a tip that the porn shop was going to be the fifth in a string of downtown, late-night business robberies. The small convenience store two blocks over had been hit, as had the open-'til-two service station on Lester and a couple of bars. Andy was open all night; it was his turn by default.

Lonely for a bit of Savannah's verbal abuse, Dirk occasionally invited her to accompany him on a late-night stakeout. It wasn't exactly S.C.P.D. policy. But Detective Sergeant Dirk Coulter lived to snoop, and he had enough dirt on the "suits" to bend the rules from time to time and get away with it.

And Savannah found it difficult to refuse him anything. For five years he had been her partner. Even when she had been ousted from the department, he had risked his own career and defended her. But his most endearing quality was that in all that time he had never noticed that her "waggle" had widened. And if he had observed her increase from a petite size seven to a somewhat-overly-voluptuous fourteen, he hadn't mentioned it. Now *that* was Savannah's idea of a true gentleman.

The door to Andy's opened, and a customer emerged, a guy in his mid-thirties, wearing a city sewer worker's uniform and a sappy, sated grin on his face. Apparently he had slugged a couple of tokens into one of Andy's peep booths. Nothing like getting the day off to a jump start.

Heading her way down the sidewalk, he spotted her, and his smile broadened as he gave her a thorough once-over. "Hey, lookin' good," he said as they met. "Wanna date?"

Great. This was just what she needed. A first-thing-in-the-morning, two-time Charlie. "Get lost," she told him, and kept walking.

He followed. "Ah, come on . . . that's what you're standin' out here for."

"You're not my type," she said.

She heard Dirk snicker in the earphone. He'd pay later.

The guy took a step toward her and grabbed her forearm. "I got money, baby," he said. "That makes me your type."

With one twist of her wrist, she broke his grip, grabbed his pinkie, and bent it backward. She heard and felt something crack. He let out a yelp.

"I said get lost, perv," she told him.

Looking down, she saw the glimmer of a wedding ring on the finger next to the one she had just mangled. "What did you do, tell the wife you were going to work at the sewer plant a little early? Is she still back at home in bed snuggled up with the kiddies while you're in there, jackin' off in one of Andy's booths?"

He winced just a little . . . from conscience or his hurt finger, she couldn't tell. So, she decided to drive the shiv in a little deeper. "What would your mother think if she'd seen you five minutes ago, huh?"

For half a second, he flushed with shame, then he recovered. "Look, sister, you ain't exactly nobody to talk, prancin' around in that getup."

"Yeah, and you're a disgrace to your uniform. Get the hell outta my face before I call a cop."

The guy mumbled a few obscenities as he walked away. And not a moment too soon. An old, blue-green Oldsmobile— early seventies with a bashed right front fender—came around the corner and pulled in front of Andy's.

"Looks like our boys," said Dirk in her ear.

Several witnesses had described the robbers as two Caucasian men, one skinny with short blond hair, one with a dark, stringy mop and a baseball cap, driving a green battleship of undetermined make and model.

"Yep, looks like," Savannah whispered as she leaned nonchalantly against a lamp post and watched in her peripheral vision.

The blond guy exited the passenger's side and glanced up and down the street. For a moment, his eyes met Savannah's, and she did a quick mental estimation of his intelligence quotient. Probably on a par with his shoe size, she decided. He didn't have particularly large feet.

After fifteen years in law enforcement and now as a private investigator, Savannah still hadn't gotten over the shock of seeing how different real criminals were from the ones portrayed on Hollywood screens. Oh, she had met a few cunning, shrewd characters; but, by and large, those who habitually broke society's laws were numskulls. She assumed this was because most rocket scientists knew better than to try to knock over an all-night adult porn shop for spare change.

And one look in this guy's eyes told her that NASA wouldn't be recruiting him anytime soon.

After a two-second, salacious perusal, he dismissed her, turned around, and marched into Andy's.

According to some of the pair's previous victims, Bony-Blondie would enter the store, slip behind some sort of display rack, and don a black ski mask. Then he would pop out with a Saturday night special in his hand and demand their cash and jewelry. Savannah decided to be generous and give him 1.2 points for subtlety, 1.1 for originality.

But the jerk in the car—the one with the long, greasy locks, wearing wraparound shades, had slapped his girlfriend around last Friday night. She had confided in her fellow waitress, who passed the word along to a manicurist, who just happened to live in the same trailer park as Dirk.

Domestic violence didn't pay in a town as small as San Carmelita, where the native crops were avocados, lemons, and gossip. Not necessarily in that order.

Across the street, Dirk had risen from his bench and was drunkenly zigzagging a path in their direction.

"Attagirl," he whispered in her earphone. "Show 'im that waggle."

Employing her best Dixie sashay, Savannah strolled by the parked car, making sure that Creep Number Two had plenty of time to check out the merchandise. She had to work fast; Blondie wouldn't take long.

Once she was fairly sure she had piqued his interest, she meandered closer to the passenger's side. The window was down, so she leaned inside. The stench of stale sweat, cigarette smoke, and rotting fast-food containers prompted her to breathe shallowly.

Number Two was even uglier up close, dirtier, with bad skin, rotten teeth, a baseball cap turned backwards and wrap-around sunglasses that were probably supposed to give him an air of mystery, but made him look like a pathetic Terminator wannabe.

It occurred to Savannah that Blondie might actually be the brains of the operation. Scary stuff.

"Hi there, handsome," she said without choking on her own words. Yes, for this Dirk would owe her . . . big time. "Wanna date?"

"Ah . . . no . . . not now. I'm kinda busy."

She could tell he was weighing his one ounce of common sense against his more urgent needs that were arising, thanks to the abundant cleavage she was displaying in the open window.

"Don't worry, Babycakes. With a girl like me, you won't take long at all."

Ignoring his mumbled half-objections, she jerked open the car door and slid onto the passenger's seat. She allowed her short leather skirt to creep upward, displaying the tops of stockings and garter fastenings. Even through the dark lenses, she could see his eyes bug. Good. He was a stockings kind of guy. They were *all* stockings guys.

He shot a quick glance at Andy's front door, then at her legs. "I don't have a lot of money . . . not yet, anyway."

"Then you're in luck, 'cause I don't charge much. Not for what you need. How about thirty bucks?"

"Well . . . I don't know. I—"

"Twenty."

"Like I said, I'm sorta busy, and you . . ."

"Yeah?"

"And you've kinda got a big butt."

She resisted the urge to feed him his own face, feature by ugly feature. "Yeah, and you got zits and a beer gut. But then, we ain't exactly going on a date to the prom, right? Now, unzip it and let's get this show on the road."

After only a moment's hesitation, he muttered, "All right, I guess," and started to fumble with his fly.

"Not that, sweet thing," she said as she pulled her Beretta from her red, sequined purse and shoved the barrel against the side of his neck. "You can just leave your pants on for this one."

"Wh—wha—what?"

With her left hand, she jerked down the zipper of his decrepit Dodgers jacket. "It's your coat I want, and the cap and the glasses. Hand them over and make it snappy."

When Franky Morick—a.k.a. Frank the Crank, a.k.a. Creep Number One—exited Andy's Bookstore with his pillow-case of loot in one hand and his .22 in the other, he thought

Buzz had taken off without him. The car was gone! That stupid—

But no, it had been moved a few yards down, toward the corner. Why, he had no idea, but he'd have a talk with Buzz about it later. And after they had that conversation, and Buzz got back from the hospital emergency room, he'd hire himself a better driver. Like one with a brain.

He ran to the Olds, threw open the door, and jumped inside. "Go! Go, you asshole!" he yelled.

But the car didn't budge. Neither did Buzz. He just sat there, staring straight ahead, wearing those stupid sunglasses, which were useless as the sun hadn't risen yet.

Frank glanced back at Andy's and saw the shopkeeper's rotund form filling the doorway, taking down the license number, no doubt. Damn! He'd forgotten to switch the plates with his mom's, like he usually did before a job.

"Go, dammit! Don't sit there picking your nose for chrissake! Step on it!"

Still, Buzz didn't budge.

Frank shoved his pistol into the waistband of his jeans and tossed the pillowcase with the cash onto the floor. When he did, something caught his eye.

He blinked, sure he was seeing things in the dim semidarkness of the car's interior. Along with Buzz's lame shades, his baseball cap, and mangy Dodgers jacket, he was wearing black stockings . . . garters . . . and high heels.

"What the hell!"

Frank raised his eyes and stared down the cavernous barrel of a 9 mm pistol. Frank thought he had lost his mind completely. One too many cranks for Frank the Crank.

When "Buzz" lowered his glasses onto his nose and peered

over the top of them, Frank found himself looking into the coldest, bluest eyes he had ever seen.

A soft, feminine voice with a Southern drawl said, "Put your hands on the dash, sweetie, before I rearrange your brain cells for you . . . both of them."

"But you're a . . . who are . . . where's . . . ?"

"Where's your friend?" She chuckled and nodded toward the corner, where Frank saw Buzz standing beside a wino in a rumpled raincoat. Buzz didn't look happy, and Frank assumed it might have something to do with the handcuffs he was wearing.

"What the fuck is this?" Frank turned to the woman with the blue eyes and the gun at his head. "Are you a cop or something?"

"I'm an 'or something,'" she said. "The bum's a cop."

"So, am I under arrest, or what?"

"At the moment, you're 'or what.' If you stick around, you'll be under arrest. And if you move, you're dead. What's it gonna be?"

She looked like she meant it.

Frank the Crank decided just to sit.

Savannah pulled her red 1968 Camaro into her driveway and cut the ignition, but the old car continued to chug, wheeze, and shudder, refusing to give up the ghost.

"Stop, or I'll take a sledgehammer to you," she threatened it, pounding the steering wheel. It responded with a rude honk that grated on her nerves.

"I must be getting old. These all-nighters kill me," she mumbled as she pulled her tired body from the car and limped up the sidewalk to the tiny Spanish-style bungalow that she called home. When she wasn't calling it other, more foul, names because of leaking roofs, sagging foundations, and termite infestation. Actually, she was grateful for the termites. If it weren't for the fact that the little boogers were holding hands and square dancing under there, the whole house would probably cave in.

Halfway up the walk, she paused to pull off the spike heels. Tucking them under her arm, she saw her neighbor, nosy old Mrs. Normandy, peeking out her kitchen window. Once Savannah had tried to explain why she sometimes left the house dressed in strange garb. But Mrs. Normandy didn't seem to grasp the concept of "undercover."

That, or it was more interesting for the old woman to think she lived next door to a part-time private investigator/hooker. Mrs. Normandy was also convinced that aliens had abducted Jimmy Hoffa from her backyard, so Savannah hadn't wasted a lot of time trying to cajole her about the risqué costumes.

Savannah had just slipped her key into her front-door lock, when a cheery voice reached her from across the lawn. "Hey, Savannah! I'm he-e-e-re!" The nasal, Eastern seaboard twang grated on her sleep-deprived nerves.

Glancing at her watch, she saw that it was exactly nine o'clock. Damn, that girl was punctual.

She turned around and saw her trainee-in-private-detection, Tammy Hart, jogging across the lawn toward her.

Savannah loved Tammy to pieces; the young woman was bright, good-hearted, and a whiz with computers—quite the opposite of the ditzy blonde she appeared to be at first glance. But Tammy had one major character flaw. She was a morning person.

Her short, golden ponytail bounced from side to side as she trotted up onto the porch, where she continued to jog in place, bouncing ... bouncing ... bouncing until Savannah thought she was going to be seasick just watching her.

She was wearing a smile that should have been illegal before noon, and a bright yellow short set that made Savannah wish she was still wearing that Buzz creep's sunglasses.

"Hope I'm not too late," Tammy pealed. "My bug wouldn't start, so I decided to just jog to work ... get the old blood flowing ... you know."

Tammy's classic Volkswagen bug was the only car on the planet that was less reliable than Savannah's Camaro. But jogging? It had to be nearly ten miles, and she hadn't even worked up a good sweat ... just this nice, ladylike sheen that looked great on her golden, California tan.

Sometimes, Savannah hated her.

"Neat outfit, especially the shoes!" Tammy continued to bounce.

Savannah thrust the heels at her. "Here, you can have them."

"Gee, thanks. I wonder if they'll fit."

"They'll fit," Savannah growled, not adding the fact that their shoe size would be the only size they would ever have in common. Petite Tammy actually wore a minuscule size zero. Until Savannah had pinned her to the floor one day and turned her shirt wrong side out, looking for proof, she hadn't even known there *was* a size zero.

Savannah unlocked the door and found herself face-to-face with two hungry and unhappy felines. Diamante and Cleopatra were more like miniature black leopards than housecats, with appetites as healthy as their mistress's.

"Oooh, they're so pretty," Tammy cooed as she followed Savannah into the house and bent to pet the cats. "Good morning!"

"There's no such thing," Savannah grumbled.

"Pardon me?"

"I said, there's no such thing as a good morning. It's an oxymoron."

"Oh, you're just grumpy because stupid old Dirk had you out all night."

Minutes after meeting him, Tammy had dubbed Dirk, "stupid old Dirk," and she seldom mentioned his name without the accompanying adjectives.

"I'm not grumpy." Savannah tossed her bag onto a side table and entered what had once been her living room, but was now the office of the Moonlight Magnolia Detective Agency. "I'm just not a morning person," she said. "I hate mornings, and I hate morning people . . . like you."

Tammy laughed, so loudly that Savannah's ears ached. "That's funny. You're a kick, Savannah, even when you're grumpy."

"Tammy, I mean it. Stop with the perky shit. I'm not up to it. We're talking no pulse or measurable brain waves until I have a hot bath and a nap."

Savannah forced herself to go into the kitchen and pour some Gourmet Kit-Kat into the two bowls beneath the counter. She was rewarded by purrs and satiny rubs against her ankles.

Undaunted, Tammy did a samba around the office, turning on the computer and printer, checking the fax machine.

"Don't touch those blinds," Savannah warned her. "If you let one ray of sunlight into that room, you're fired."

She could tell that Tammy was traumatized by her threat; the girl broke into a rousing rendition of "Zip-a-dee Doo-Da."

"And stop singing that stupid song," she told her, "unless some guy's do-da is open."

"What?"

"Never mind." Savannah sighed. There was no fighting optimism and cheerfulness . . . short of murder, and her mood wasn't quite foul enough to warrant homicide.

Scrounging around in the refrigerator, Savannah found something that raised her spirits: a chocolate-chip, double-fudge muffin with cream-cheese filling. She zapped a cup of stale coffee in the microwave and laced it with Baileys and Half & Half.

Ah, breakfast.

But the moment she carried the cup and plate into the office, she got "the look" from Tammy.

"Oh, shut up and drink your pure springwater and nibble your organic carrot sticks," she told her.

Tammy grinned and shrugged. "I didn't say a word."

"Yeah, yeah. I heard every word you didn't say. Not everyone's a Spartan like you." Savannah sank into the comfort of her favorite chair—overstuffed, just the way she liked it, just like her. "Some of us," she said, breathing in the aroma of the coffee and savoring the anticipation of the chocolate cream cheese, "are pure, unadulterated hedonists."

Tammy sat down to the computer and began to type. She shrugged. "Whatever."

"And what's that supposed to mean?"

With a perfectly guileless face, Tammy replied, "If you want to poison yourself with toxins, pollute the perfect body that Nature gave you, it's your personal right to do so. It's just that Ms. Valentina says—"

"Oh, please. Don't quote Kat Valentina to me. She's hardly an expert on nutrition, or anything else, for that matter."

"I like Kat."

The three words were simply, quietly stated, but Savannah could hear the underlying hurt. For some reason beyond Savannah's understanding, Tammy liked her "other" employer, the owner of the notorious Royal Palms Spa that sat on the hillside overlooking San Carmelita.

The resort was a haven for the wannabe-filthy-rich and sorta-kinda-famous. No Oscar-winning actor or critically acclaimed director would be seen inside the complex. Royal Palms was too tacky even for Hollywood.

Back in the late seventies, Kat Valentina had starred in a hit movie, *Disco Diva*. Though the critics had hated it, fans had flocked to the movie, making Kat Valentina a cult phenomenon.

From what Savannah heard, Kat had never quite gotten over the seventies disco scene. She was still stuck in the "Screw Whomever You Can"—literally and figuratively—mentality. By reputation, the Royal Palms was an extension of her own hedonistic attitude. While the club claimed to be a health spa, the guests did more fooling around than aerobics, more hallucinogenic drugs than cleansing herbs, and more scheming than soul-searching.

Savannah hadn't been happy last month when Tammy had admitted to taking a part-time job there as an aerobics instructor. But considering how little Savannah was able to pay her, she could hardy complain.

"I know you like her," Savannah said, cursing her own

insensitivity. "I'll keep my opinions to myself, as long as you keep her nutritional advice to yourself. Deal?"

"Sure. No problem." Tammy brightened instantly. Another aspect of Tammy's personality that Savannah loved: her ability to forgive and forget.

"By the way, speaking of money . . ." Savannah began.

"We were?"

"We are now. Did Mr. Barnett ever pay us the last payment that he owed us for—"

The jangling of the phone cut her off, and Tammy grabbed it, assuming a professional attitude along with a Marilyn Monroe breathiness.

"Moonlight Magnolia Detective Agency," she breathed. "May I help you?"

Savannah listened eagerly. She had the sinking feeling it was Dirk, wanting another favor or inviting himself over for a pizza and beer dinner. Her treat. But one could always hope it was a new client. Lord knows, they needed work if she were to keep Diamante and Cleopatra in Gourmet Kit-Kat niblets.

"Yes, this is Tammy." She looked slightly confused. "Oh, hi, Mr. Hanks."

Hanks? Lou Hanks? Savannah recalled meeting the guy a time or two. He was Kat Valentina's ex-husband and business partner, co-owner of the Royal Palms.

"Yes, I was coming in later this afternoon to lead the step-dance class," Tammy was saying. "Oh, why not? Closed? But what's . . . ?"

Savannah set her muffin and coffee aside as she watched the color drain from Tammy's well-tanned face.

"Oh, no! She did? Oh, Mr. Hanks . . . I . . . I'm so sorry.

I ... of course, I understand. If there's anything I can do, just—"

Tammy hung up the phone and turned to Savannah, her eyes huge with hurt and shock, her hand clapped over her mouth.

"What is it?" Savannah asked. But she knew. She knew the look. It only meant one thing.

"That was Mr. Hanks." Tammy began to tremble all over. Savannah rose, walked to her, and put her hand on her shoulder.

"What did he say, honey?" she asked.

"It's Ms. Valentina. Kat's dead."

Kat Valentina was only in her early forties, and Savannah had seen her at a downtown boutique two weeks ago. She had looked a bit overindulged, maybe some substance abuse, perhaps a tad too much booze, but basically healthy. Certainly not like someone who was going to check out in a matter of days.

"Did he say how she died?" Savannah asked, rubbing Tammy's shoulder, trying to impart a little comfort.

"Not exactly. But he said I shouldn't come to work today because the club is closed."

"That isn't too surprising ... considering."

"Yeah, but he said the police closed it."

CHAPTER TWO

By the time Savannah changed into suitable street clothes, and she and Tammy arrived at the Royal Palms Spa, the appropriate authorities had been alerted, as well as the media. Los Angeles television crews milled around the front gates, seeking entrance and being rejected, as well as the San Carmelita cable station entourage of two. Apparently, Kat Valentina could still create a stir, especially if she died unexpectedly.

Flashing her private investigator's license as though it were a badge, Savannah managed to bulldoze her way through the crowd and even past the gates. "Attitude," she whispered to Tammy, who followed in her wake. "It's all in the flick of the wrist."

Once inside, her past friendships with the local cops enabled her to maneuver through the gauche gold-painted doors and into the reception area. Modeled after Kat Valentina's idea of an ancient Roman villa, the lobby was a nightmare collage of pseudo "artifacts."

Two enormous, white plaster statues dominated the semi-circular room. Nudes, a man and a woman, supposedly the ideal male and female of the species. Muscles rippling, lean machines, they looked as though they were straight off the pages of a superhero comic book. Anatomically correct in every detail, their grossly exaggerated attributes could only have been achieved by plastic surgery.

"Talk about a boob job," Savannah muttered, as she and Tammy hurried past the statues. "And to get a dick that big, you'd have to do a penile implant . . . with a ten-pound Polish kielbasa. The club should be sued for false advertising."

When Tammy responded with wounded silence, Savannah cautioned herself to keep her mouth shut. Heaven forbid that she should speak ill of the dead.

She wondered, who made up that stupid rule about saying only good things about the deceased? Probably someone who was more afraid of being haunted by pissed ghosts than concerned about giving dead people a break.

They passed between Grecian columns, whose paint was peeling, on royal blue carpeting that had seen better days . . . a decade ago. The plastic greenery in the atrium to their left was sun-bleached and yellowed. No one had turned on the fountain this morning, so the "waterfall" was dry. The goldfish in the pool had disappeared long ago.

"How have they been doing financially?" she asked Tammy in low tones as they hurried down the hallway, toward what appeared to be the center of activity . . . the bathhouses.

"I don't know, but Mr. Hanks has been pushing us to

bring in customers and offering lots of special, low prices. So, probably not too good."

A young man and woman met them in the hallway, both wearing gauzy togas that barely covered their assets. The girl was attractive with lots of curly chestnut hair, and the guy looked like a beach bum or lifeguard moonlighting as a Grecian god.

"Brett, Karen, what happened?" Tammy asked them in a tense whisper, even though there was no one nearby.

"We don't know." The pretty brunette looked scared and more than a little shaken. "Mr. Hanks found her this morning in one of the herbal mud baths. She was already . . . you know . . ."

"The cops are here, going over everything and everybody," Brett said. "They won't let anyone in the bathhouses. Not that I'd want to go in. She's still there in one of them. They haven't taken her out yet."

Good, Savannah thought. Maybe she could get a look at the scene before everything was broken down. Of course, she had no official interest in the case, but she couldn't help being curious. Besides, in some probably misguided way, she felt she owed it to Tammy at least to look into the situation.

"How's Mr. Hanks taking it?" Tammy asked. "He must be devastated."

Brett and Karen shared a look that Savannah had to file away as "knowing."

"Not so's you'd notice," Brett whispered. "Mostly, he just seems mad that the detective grilled him for half an hour. The cops are acting like it was murder."

"They have to assume it's murder," Savannah added,

"until they prove it wasn't. I'm sure they're just doing their job by questioning him."

Karen waggled one eyebrow. "Maybe, but this detective is a real slob and an asshole to boot. Not exactly Mr. Hanks's type."

A *slob and an asshole*, Savannah thought as she headed for the bathhouses, Tammy in tow.

She just had a feeling.

Yep. It was Dirk, all right, who was in charge of the scene. He stood outside in the open yard behind the main building, directing traffic, barking questions and orders to the forensic team that was working the area.

Even under the best of circumstances, Dirk made no fashion statement. But he had been up all night, as she well knew, and the lack of sleep hadn't improved his perpetually disheveled appearance. Although he had changed from his wino costume, there wasn't much discernible difference.

The battered, once-white sneakers were the same. His khakis were just as wrinkled, and his token necktie was askew. What little hair he had stood almost on end. *That* was unusual. Slovenly though he might be with the rest of his grooming, Dirk generally made certain that his few remaining hairs were neatly combed across his bald spot.

Long ago, Savannah had theorized: Everyone had his or her point of vanity. Even a guy like Dirk.

Sleep deprivation hadn't sharpened his social skills either, she noticed.

"Get the hell outta here!" she heard him yell at several toga-wearing employees who had crossed the yellow tape that cordoned off the area around one of the bathhouses. The scene of the crime—if, indeed, there had been a crime—was the last in a row of a dozen tiny cottagelike cubicles with white stucco walls and bright blue tiled roofs.

"Each house has its own private tub," Tammy explained. "Some of them are just regular hot tubs, and some have herbal mud baths."

Savannah resisted the urge to tell her that she was quite familiar with the place. Years ago, when she had first arrived in San Carmelita and had pulled a graveyard patrol shift, she had often been called to the club to quell the occasional drunken brawl. At least back then, those cubicles had been used for a lot more private goings-on than just mud baths.

While orgies might be out of vogue, because of fear of social diseases, she imagined that some of the enclosures were still being used for more earthy pastimes than meditation and soul-searching.

"You should probably wait here," Savannah told Tammy before she approached the cordon tape. "He shouldn't even let me cross, let alone both of us. We don't want to push him when he's obviously in 'grouch' mode."

Tammy hesitated only a moment, then her eyes searched Savannah's, asking the silent question.

"Yes, that, too," Savannah admitted. "It's bad enough when it's a stranger. But if it's someone you knew . . . you'll never be able to forget it."

Blinking back tears, Tammy turned and walked over to the tennis courts, where more onlookers congregated and stared, shock and disbelief written on their faces.

Savannah got Dirk's attention. He gave her a curt nod and she wasted no time stepping over the tape. The other civilians would assume she was one of the investigating team.

The other cops knew her and welcomed her presence. The brass would throw a tizzy fit if they knew, but Dirk was the highest-ranking official present.

"If Captain Bloss or the chief shows, disappear," Dirk muttered as he directed her toward the door of the cottage.

"No-o-o-oo problem. Whatcha got?"

"Don't know yet. Doc Liu's here. I suppose she'll figure it out."

"She usually does."

It took a moment for Savannah's eyes to adjust to the relative gloom of the inside of the bath, compared to the glare of the outside sunlight. When she finally focused, she saw the medical examiner, Dr. Jennifer Liu, kneeling on the blue-and-white tile beside the mud-smeared body of a woman.

Savannah never would have recognized Kat Valentina, darling of the disco generation. Her famous long, blond hair was hanging in muddy strings over her once-pretty face. Her body was covered with mud that was beginning to dry, giving her a mottled, rotting look.

Kat Valentina had been a vain woman; she wouldn't have wanted to end up this way. *But then*, Savannah reminded herself, *who would?*

"Hey, Dr. Jennifer," Savannah said as Dirk led her over to the medical examiner, who had just finished making a small incision in the body's abdomen and was inserting a long thermometer into the liver.

"Hi, yourself, sassy." Jennifer's smile was warm as she looked up at Savannah. The two women had become good friends over the years, sharing a love for crime-solving, moderate male-bashing, and German chocolate. The ingredients for perfect female bonding.

Although Jennifer Liu was a stunningly attractive Asian woman with a trim, petite figure and long, flowing black hair—the least likely suspect for a county medical examiner—Savannah had heard her tell some pretty morbid jokes from time to time, and there was that rare, Vincent Price cackle that sent shivers down the backbone. Yes, there was more to Dr. Jennifer than met the eye.

"What does it look like, Doc?" Dirk asked, kneeling on the other side of the body. "Accident, suicide, or . . . ?"

"Can't tell yet." Jennifer checked her thermometer and jotted the results on her clipboard. "Drownings are the toughest."

"Drowning?" Savannah clicked into analytical mode and tried not to think about how this lifeless piece of flesh had been a functioning human being a few hours ago. She hadn't liked the woman, but she hated to see anyone's life end prematurely.

"Don't even know that for sure." Doctor Liu wiped the blood from the thermometer, shook it down, and thrust it into the tub filled with mud. "There's no obvious perforations, other than the one I just made," she said. "No bullet holes or stab wounds. Though we can't be certain until we get her back to the morgue and hose her down. I don't see any strangulation marks on the neck or other contusions. But, it's hard to see anything through the mud."

"What's in it?" Savannah asked, nodding toward the bath. "I smell something like mint and flowers . . . maybe honeysuckle."

"Stinks to me," Dirk said with a sniff. "These people are nuts, sittin' in mud like a bunch of pigs. And they call that a bath."

"Don't knock it 'til you've tried it," Jennifer said with a smirk that bordered on lascivious.

"*You* have?" Dirk seemed genuinely shocked.

"Sure. I've tried everything once, and most things twice," she replied.

Yes, Savannah decided, *the grin is definitely lascivious*. Sometimes Savannah wondered about what lives Jennifer Liu had led before becoming the respectable medical examiner of San Carmelita County.

"I see that rigor has set in, big time," Savannah observed, seeing the stiff, unnatural, outward extension of the body's arms. "I guess that means eight to twelve hours ago, huh?"

"Normally, yes." Jennifer read her thermometer and noted that result, too. "But the mud is over one hundred degrees. The heat would speed up rigor, plus the fact that the victim is so thin. She would set up pretty quickly."

Savannah watched Dirk as he walked slowly around the edge of the bath, taking note of the few items lying on the tiles. "Looks like she was drinking margaritas," he said, pointing to the nearly empty pitcher and the glass with salt around half the rim.

"Yeah." Jennifer slipped a bag over each of the body's hands and taped them. "I noticed that. Alcohol and a hot tub of anything is a bad combination. She may have died of heatstroke. It wouldn't be the first time I've seen the combination turn lethal."

"I drink margaritas in hot tubs any chance I get," Savannah said. Not that she had that many opportunities. In her part of town there weren't a lot of whirlpools and tennis courts.

"Well, stop it, or I'll be doing a postmortem on you someday." Jennifer rose from her knees and nodded to her assistants, who had just entered with a gurney and a white body bag. "You can have her now. Careful, she's slippery."

Dirk held up a tiny bit of black silk and lace that might have been a teddy and turned it this way and that, scrutinizing every stitch. "I guess this is what she wore out here. Sorta skimpy."

"If she's like she was in the old days," Savannah said, "I'm surprised she was wearing anything. She wasn't exactly known for her modesty."

Savannah recalled a night when she had been summoned to the club for some disturbance. She had seen Kat strutting, naked, across the lawn, completely unconcerned with the fact that several police officers were present.

Neighbors of the club had complained continually about her nudity and her impromptu love fests that often occurred in plain sight of the surrounding properties. In this elite area of town where people had more money than they knew what to do with, voted Republican, and went to church every Sunday, Kat Valentina was considered an unwelcome nuisance by those who were most forgiving. The rest deemed her "Hollywood Trash."

The irony of the term crossed Savannah's mind as she saw them load the remains of the unpopular neighbor into the white plastic bag and zip it closed.

No . . . whatever Kat Valentina might have been or done in her lifetime . . . she wouldn't have wanted or expected it all to end this way.

CHAPTER THREE

Savannah looked across the dining table into the most beautiful green eyes she had ever seen. She was madly in lust with Mr. Perfect, otherwise known as Ryan Stone. He was the ideal man in every way. Around forty, tall, dark, so handsome that just seeing him made her ache, romantic, kind, and sensitive. And he adored her; he had said so on many occasions.

But there was always a snag.

Ryan was involved, committed to someone else, heart, body and soul. Oh, yes . . . and he was gay.

His life companion, John Gibson, sat beside Savannah, just as handsome and charming as Ryan. A middle-aged man with thick silver hair, a melodic British accent, dry wit and old-world charm . . . no wonder Ryan loved him.

And Savannah loved them both.

"Thanks for inviting me to dinner. It was wonderful," she

said, savoring the ambience of Chez Antoine, her favorite French restaurant. As always, Ryan had called ahead and asked Antoine to prepare his salmon mousse, just for her. Gibson had brought her a single, perfect, lavender rose that stood beside her wineglass in its sparkling, crystal bud vase.

Maybe she could figure out a way to marry them both.

From behind one of the potted palms, Antoine himself appeared, a tiny man with a gaunt face and too-black hair slicked back from a pronounced widow's peak. He might not be particularly attractive, Savannah had decided upon meeting him years ago, but he made incredible crêpe Suzette. And on Savannah's list of priorities, a great dessert always took precedence over a GQ haircut.

He took her hand and kissed it for the fourth time that evening. "And my lovely Savannah, did you enjoy the food I make for you?" he said, his voice dripping with French mystique. Okay, she admitted, so he spread it on a little thick. She couldn't help lapping it up.

"Very much, Antoine. Everything was perfect."

He sighed, and his smile faded. "Then I fear, your perfect evening is about to be ruined. There is a ... gentleman ... at the door, who says he is a friend of yours. He wants to join you."

Antoine lowered his voice and leaned closer, making the most of the opportunity to peer down the front of Savannah's low-cut evening dress. "This man ... forgive me ... he looks a bit like a ruffian. I don't know that you would welcome his company."

"Dirk." Savannah gave Ryan and John an apologetic look. "Do you mind?"

Of course they minded. Dirk-after-dessert was hardly the

way to end a lovely meal. But they were far too well mannered to say so.

"Show the 'gentleman' to our table, Antoine, and bring him a chair," Ryan said. "Any friend of Savannah's is welcome."

"You're too kind," Savannah said gratefully. She hated to think what a scene Dirk would have made if tiny Antoine had tried to toss him out the front door.

Ryan shot Gibson a quick, but distinctly sour look. "Yes, I am, aren't I."

"It's probably something important, or he wouldn't follow me in here," she said. "He'd be afraid they'd charge him just for coming through the door."

"I'll speak to Antoine about instating a cover charge," Ryan mumbled.

John pasted a mildly pleasant and infinitely patient look on his face.

A moment later, Dirk ambled into the room, winding his way between the sparkling beveled-glass partitions, dodging the palm fronds. He looked even more disheveled than usual and not particularly happy to see her sitting there with two men he had decided long ago to despise.

He gave Ryan and John a curt nod, which they returned, and plopped down on the chair beside Savannah's. Pausing to reorient, he looked her up and down, taking in the French twist hairdo, the pearl drop earrings, the simple but elegant black dress.

"Damn, you clean up good," he said. "Why don't you get dolled up like that when I take you out?"

"I thought the pearls were a bit much for the all-you-can-eat-for-a-buck, happy hour at Joe's Sports Bar."

He glanced around, looking—as Savannah's Granny Reid would say—as nervous as a cat in a room full of rocking chairs. "Yeah, I bet they won't sell you a glass of water here for a buck."

On cue, Antoine appeared. "Good evening, sir. And what will you be having?"

"Whatever you got on draft."

Antoine waited, but when no other information was forthcoming, he lifted his pinched nose a few notches and said, "That will be one . . . beer . . . for monsieur."

"And some pretzels."

Antoine raised one eyebrow. "Pretzels, monsieur?"

"That's right. A bowl full of them and keep 'em coming. I'm starved."

Antoine cast a questioning look at Ryan, then at John. But both men had become fascinated with the hems of their napkins. Savannah didn't know whether to blush or giggle.

"I'm sorry, monsieur," Antoine said, sounding anything but remorseful. "But we have nothing like . . . pretzels."

"You gotta have something around here to munch on. How about Buffalo wings?"

Antoine's eyes widened. "*Buffalo wings*, monsieur?"

Ryan cleared his throat loudly and held up one hand. "Excuse me, if I may," he told Dirk. Turning to Antoine, he said, "I think perhaps the gentleman would enjoy *les cuisses de grenouille* with a nice *sauce piquante*."

"Hey, wait a minute. That sounds expensive." Even the thought of spending money flustered Dirk.

"Everything sounds expensive when it's ordered in French," Savannah told him.

"Don't concern yourself with the cost," Ryan told him. "It'll be my pleasure."

Dirk sputtered for a moment, then muttered a semigracious thank you. "Exactly what is it . . . that stuff you ordered?"

Savannah bit her lower lip to keep from snickering. Gibson's eyes sparkled as he took a sip of his cognac. Ryan looked Dirk straight in the eye and said, "Why, it's French Buffalo wings. That *is* what you wanted, isn't it?"

"I just don't wanna find myself eatin' nothin' like snails and shit. I don't eat crap like that."

Savannah punched Dirk's shoulder. "So, how did you know I was here?" she asked, heading for safer waters.

"I stopped by your place. Miss Prissy-Pot was there."

Savannah turned to Ryan and John. "That's his term of endearment for Tammy. The two of them get along splendidly."

Dirk grunted. "She told me you were over here, chowin' down, and I thought I'd come over here and fill you in on the latest with Kat Valentina."

Savannah perked up instantly. "Did you get the autopsy report?"

"Yep. Dr. Liu wrapped it up a couple of hours ago."

"So, tell us," Ryan interjected, a half smirk on his handsome face, "exactly how did Ms. Valentina . . . croak?"

John Gibson nearly strangled on his cognac. Savannah dabbed furiously at her lips with her napkin.

Dirk studied each one suspiciously in turn before replying. "Dr. Liu ruled the death accidental. She had hyperthermia—that means she got too hot sitting there in that mud bath, plus drinking tequila—and she fainted and drowned herself."

Ryan was on a roll. "And how did Dr. Liu . . . leap . . . to this conclusion?"

Dirk ignored him and turned to Savannah. "Like the doc said at the scene, you shouldn't mix booze and a hot tub. Apparently, Kat had been knockin' those margaritas back somethin' fierce."

"Mmmm . . ." Savannah tapped her fingernails on the base of her wineglass. "That's sorta anticlimactic, don't you think?"

"But it's good news," Gibson said. "At least the poor lady wasn't murdered."

"Of course, it's good news." Savannah wondered at her own reaction. An unexpected death was tragic enough, without the added horror of knowing it was homicide. For those who cared about Kat Valentina—like Tammy—this was the best report possible.

So, why did she feel so uneasy? Had she been petty enough to be hoping for the worst. No, she hadn't disliked the woman that much. Surely . . .

"How do you feel about it?" she asked Dirk.

"One less folder on my desk," he replied matter-of-factly. "Hey, here's my Buffalo wings."

He bent over the plate that Antoine had left behind and peered at the thin, flat pieces of meat, artistically arranged in a half circle and garnished with greens.

"These don't look like chicken wings," he said, darting a suspicious look at Ryan.

Ryan smiled benevolently. "Of course not. They're French chickens."

* * *

Half an hour later, Dirk had devoured his food and downed several more beers. After all, he was off-duty, and, most importantly, Ryan was picking up the tab.

Savannah offered to drive him home.

"Hey, Dirk," she said, as they were leaving the restaurant. "I've got a silly little joke for you, one I heard years ago."

"All right. What is it?"

"How do you eat a frog?"

His expression darkened, his eyes narrowed. "I don't think I'm gonna like this . . . but how?"

"It's easy. You just hook one little leg over one ear, and one little leg over the other and . . ."

When Savannah opened her front door, Diamante and Cleopatra were there to meet her, as always. Their sleek black fur, their pale green eyes, and their rhinestone collars gleamed in the porch light.

They curled around her ankles and purred as she bent over to stroke them, arching their backs as they slid beneath her hand.

"Hello, girls. I'm happy to see you, too. Did any tomcats come prowling while I was out?"

She was about to step inside, when she saw the corner of something protruding from her mailbox beside the door. "Looks like we *did* have a visitor," she said, reaching for the oversize beige envelope. "I distinctly remember getting the mail earlier."

There was no postage or even an address on it. But it was sealed, very well, with several passes of cellophane tape.

Once inside the house, Savannah took the envelope to the kitchen and ripped it open with a steak knife. Green. At first, that was all she could see. The envelope was absolutely stuffed with cash.

Her heart skipped a beat. In the olden days, as a public servant, an envelope crammed with money could only spell trouble, and she sure as hell wouldn't have been able to keep it.

But as a private citizen . . . maybe . . . just maybe . . .

On the bottom of the pile was a small note, the same beige stationery as the envelope.

On it were a few typed words:

Dear Ms. Reid,
 I have reason to believe that Kat Valentina was murdered. I would like you to prove this. If you do, there will be more where this came from.
 Please consider this money a retainer for your investigative services. Begin working right away, and I'll be in touch.

Murdered? The word shot through Savannah's brain, verifying what some part of her had known all along. That was why she had been uneasy at dinner, hearing of Jennifer Liu's "accidental" ruling. For some reason that was impossible to explain, but potent all the same, Savannah knew that Kat Valentina had been a victim of homicide, not just her own carelessness.

And, apparently, whoever had left this in her mailbox knew it, too.

Just the thought of trying to solve the crime, of going

after the bastard who did it, gave Savannah a jolt of adrenaline. Nobody deserved to have their life taken. And everybody deserved justice. Even somebody like Kat Valentina.

Then, of course, there were those other little words: *more where this came from.*

In spite of the stack of overdue bills on her kitchen table and the dwindling savings account, Savannah liked to think that her adrenaline rush had nothing to do with the pile of greenbacks and the promise of more.

Nope. Nothing at all.

CHAPTER FOUR

Not for the first time, Savannah pulled into the Shady Vale Trailer Park and wondered where this nondescript piece of real estate had gotten its name. Without a tree in sight or even a minor indentation that might be considered a ditch, let alone a valley, she couldn't imagine.

Near the beach in San Carmelita was another mobile-home park, one with perfectly manicured lawns and spacious homes that were like miniature mansions inside. But that park had nothing in common with Shady Vale.

Situated on the outskirts of town, the park housed Dirk Coulter, twice-divorced police detective, a few lower-income families with young children, who were starting out in life, and one old codger and his wife who were ending theirs. Not quite soon enough was the opinion held by some at Shady Vale, including Dirk.

Savannah had long held the notion that pure and simple meanness had the power to preserve certain individuals, not unlike pickling vinegar, alcohol, and formaldehyde.

More often than not, when Savannah came here to see Dirk, she had to run the gauntlet of Mr. and Mrs. Biddle's verbal abuse and interrogation. Having lived in the park longer than anyone else, and possessing the first lot on the right near the entrance, they seemed to think that they owned the place—locks, stocks, and trailer hitches.

"Hey you! Who are ya and whatdaya want?" Mr. Biddle hollered across the narrow dirt road as Savannah climbed out of her Camaro and headed for Dirk's green-and-white-striped and rust-streaked trailer.

"Mr. Biddle, don't hassle me," she snapped, not in the mood for his foolishness. "You know darned well who I am."

From his seat on a broken-down plastic chaise in front of his trailer, Mr. Biddle could see everything in his "domain." Or at least, he could if he weren't as blind as a bat with faulty sonar. What he lacked in perfect vision, he seemed to make up in pure nasal audacity, Savannah surmised. Even in her tiny hometown in Georgia, people weren't *that* nosy.

Well, maybe they were, but they were far too well mannered to appear so. If they were going to spy on you, they had the common decency to do it while peeking from behind drawn curtains.

"If you're goin' to see that cop fella, he ain't outta bed yet," Mr. Biddle announced over the top of his beer can . . . the breakfast of champions. Most of the ale he had consumed over the past few decades seemed to have settled around his midriff. The rest of his lanky body was thin, so he looked like a donut stuck halfway down a stick.

"How do you know Dirk isn't up yet?" She couldn't resist asking, because she could never tell herself. Dirk always kept his curtains drawn; he seemed to think it negated the need for dusting. And he seldom ventured outside unless he was in the process of coming or going.

His old Buick was parked in his gravel driveway.

Mr. Biddle grinned a sly, toothless smile. "Ain't heard his commode flush yet," he announced proudly.

Not bad detective work, she mused. If old Mr. Biddle would only use his powers for good.

"He'll get up for me," she said before considering the possible sexual innuendo. No matter; Old Man Biddle probably hadn't even heard her.

Quickly she passed Mr. B., his trailer, his chaise, and his beer. Today, his vision seemed better than usual. His bleary eyes followed her as she walked by, and she could almost swear he was checking her out.

"Yep . . ." He nodded his approval. ". . . I'd say, if *you* can't get 'im up, missy, nobody can."

Savannah did a double take to see if she had heard correctly. Yes, there was definitely a leer on the wrinkled face— toothless, perhaps, but a distinct leer.

"Harry, get the hell in here this minute," screeched a female from inside the trailer. "And stop making a donkey's ass of yourself."

Sweet Mrs. Biddle. It was always such a pleasure to hear the velvet words that rolled off her silken tongue. Like an obedient puppy, the king of the trailer park rolled out of his chaise and trudged across the yard to disappear inside his mobile home.

Snatches of conversation wafted through the torn screen

windows to Savannah—phrases like, "... flirtin' with that hussy ... makin' eyes at ... right in front of God and everybody ..."

Savannah was still chuckling when she rapped on Dirk's door. Judging by the length of time it took him to answer, she knew Mr. Biddle had been right—Dirk hadn't been up and about yet.

"Sleeping in, huh?" she said, as he opened the door and glared down at her, wearing an undershirt, boxers, mussed hair, and a scowl.

"Trying to," he replied. "Did you bring food?"

She held out a brown paper lunch bag, half-expecting him to loll his tongue, roll his eyes, and wag his tail. Dirk was a sucker for sweets ... or food of any kind, for that matter.

"What is it?" he asked, opening the door and reaching for the bag.

"It meets two of your basic food group requirements: edible and free," Savannah replied as she pushed her way past him and into the trailer.

He peeked inside the bag and lit up instantly. "Donuts!"

"More specifically, apple fritters and French crullers. I was hoping you'd share," she added, watching him eagerly dig in.

His smile drooped. "But there's only four."

With a sigh, Savannah walked to his kitchen sink, shoved some dirty dishes aside, and began to make coffee in his old percolator pot. He removed a pair of jeans from a doorknob and slipped them on.

"Now, you don't have to go gettin' dressed up for me, sugar," she said, setting the pot on the two-burner stove and turning up the flame. "It's not like I haven't seen it all before."

He bristled. "You haven't seen it *all*."

"That's true. But not because you haven't offered to show it to me." She squirted some detergent into a couple of mugs.

He grunted, his mouth full of fritter. "Humph . . . that was a long time ago. I've done given up on trying to get you into the sack."

"It wasn't a good idea, and you know it. So don't pout."

"It wasn't a good idea when we was partners on the force. But since you're not a cop no more, what's your excuse now?"

Savannah glanced around the cluttered trailer at the piles of unpaid bills on TV trays that served as end tables, the dirty laundry overflowing from a plastic milk crate in the corner, the kitchen cupboard littered with dishes and crumpled fast-food bags.

Then there was Dirk himself. Chewing his fritter with his mouth open. Slouching in his frayed T-shirt and jeans that been washed in hot, hot water too many times and had shrunk to at least three inches above his bare ankles. He was in desperate need of a pedicure . . . even if it was done with gardening shears.

She loved Dirk. He was a dear, sweet, gruff, teddy bear of a guy who had been her closest friend for years now.

But she didn't want to see it all.

"You're just too much man for little ol' me," she said with an exaggerated Southern lilt and a down-in-Dixie grin that deepened her dimples. "If I were to take you on, you'd spoil me for all the other men to come."

He nodded his head solemnly, continuing to chew. "That's true," he said. "I would. Good point."

As she joined him on the sofa with two clean mugs full of fresh coffee in hand, she decided to jump right in her proverbial, verbal mud puddle with both feet. No matter how much sugar and caffeine he had careening through his blood-stream, he wasn't going to be overjoyed with her news.

Dirk loved investigating a case. But once he had filed it away, he hated nothing more than to have to resurrect it.

He spared her the awkward gambit. "So, why did you show up here at this ungodly hour to bribe me with donuts?"

"Bribe you?" Her blue eyes widened, black lashes fluttered, dimples deepened. "Now why . . . after all the favors I've done for *you* . . . some very recently . . . would *I* have to bribe you with donuts, just to get you to do me one small favor?"

He choked down the mouthful of pastry he was chewing and took a loud slurp of coffee. "Oh, man . . . let me get out my hip boots. It's piling up deep in here."

"Just one itty-bitty favor?"

"How itty? How bitty?"

"Okay, it's a biggy. I want you to reopen Kat Valentina's investigation."

He stared at her, glazed sugar trembling on his chin. "Now, why the hell would I do that?"

"Because last night I found this shoved under my door."

She handed him the note. After he had read it, she shoved the envelope full of money into his hand.

"Damn," he muttered, doing a swift count. "And you get to actually keep this?"

"I guess so, if I can figure out how she was murdered and by whom."

He sat for a long time, fingering the bills and studying the note. Savannah could almost hear those mental cogs turn-ing. Dirk might be a slob, but when it came to criminal investi-gation, the guy was no slouch.

"All right," he said. "I'll talk to Dr. Liu, see if there's

anything we missed. Captain Bloss ain't gonna be happy about it, though. He thought the whole thing was wrapped up nice and neat."

Savannah gave him a saccharine grin. "Now, that's too bad. Because we both know how much that dear man means to me."

Like a true friend, Dirk's eyes glimmered with hatred for the man who had ousted Savannah from the force. "Yeah, I know how much love you have for him," he said. "You'd be happy to see him with an apple in his mouth, roasting on a spit."

Savannah grinned at the fantasy. The apple was a nice touch; sometimes, Dirk had a real way with words. She had always thought of Bloss as a guy with porcine qualities. "Sounds good to me. But only if I can turn and baste him."

Savannah looked into Tammy's eyes, with their long, fluttering Bambi lashes, and thought sadly that the young woman seemed to have lost some of her innocence in the past thirty-six hours. And if she followed Savannah into that autopsy suite, she was going to lose even more.

They stood outside in the morgue hallway with its calm— to the point of depressing—blue-gray walls and gray-blue carpeting. Assorted abstract paintings completed the placid surroundings, studies of blue on gray and vice versa.

"You don't have to come in if you don't want," Savannah told her for the third time in the past ten minutes. "Or we could wait to talk to Dr. Jenny when she's finished this autopsy."

"How long would it take?" Tammy was looking a bit peaked beneath her beach-bum tan.

"Probably about an hour or so. We could go grab a bite to eat and come back."

Tammy shook her head emphatically. "No, as upset as I am, I couldn't possibly eat a thing."

Savannah stared at her, trying to fathom the concept of being too upset to eat. Some things were simply not to be understood.

"Let's just go talk to her and get it over with," Tammy said, squaring her shoulders and hiking her chin up a notch.

"Okay . . ." Savannah pointed to the gleaming double doors. ". . . but promise me you won't barf. Dr. Jenny hates it when people puke or pass out in her autopsy suite."

"You sound like you know what you're talking about."

"I do. I've done both."

"It can't be *that* bad."

"Famous last words."

"I'm really sorry, Jenny. I should have seen it coming . . . what with her turning that nice shade of green and all." Savannah knelt beside a prostrate Tammy, who was splayed across the tile floor.

Dr. Liu walked to a nearby drawer, withdrew some smelling salts, and passed them to Savannah. "No problem. Happens all the time."

Savannah popped the cap and waved the small wand under Tammy's nose. Wheezing and sputtering, she quickly fought her way back to consciousness.

As Savannah helped Tammy to a sitting position, Jennifer Liu returned to the stainless steel table and the body she had recently disemboweled.

Perhaps it had been the dissected liver, lying on a small

table at the foot of the larger one, or maybe it had been the coils of intestines pulled out of the belly and piled onto the pelvic region that had sent Tammy over the edge.

Either way, Savannah positioned herself between her young assistant and the hapless fellow on Jennifer's table. She didn't want to risk losing her again so soon.

"Hey, what happened?" Tammy said as she sat up and held her head in her hands, rocking back and forth. Her face had turned from pea green to a shade of white that was as deathly as the corpse on the table.

"Don't worry," Savannah said, patting her head as though she were a distressed cocker spaniel. "I've seen big guys—rough, tough cops—keel over like felled oaks when they see their first autopsy."

"Autopsy?" Recollection dawned in her eyes. "Oh, god, that's right."

She cast a furtive glance over Savannah's shoulder at the table. Dr. Liu looked moderately amused as she sliced away samples of the liver and placed them into a small specimen jar.

"So, you're a virgin, huh?" Jennifer said. "Come over here, and I'll show you a few things. Once you get over the initial shock, you might find it interesting."

Savannah cringed. Jennifer Liu was obsessed with her work and didn't realize that not everyone shared her fascination with the macabre. More than once, Dr. Liu had shown Savannah "interesting" things that had haunted her dreams for weeks, even months.

And Tammy was one of the most squeamish persons she had ever known. Talk of earthworm farms could put her off a spaghetti dinner.

But she seemed to be rallying as she rose from the floor and walked on shaky legs over to the table.

"Wow . . ." she said, staring wide-eyed at the open chest cavity. She gaped at the flesh that had been peeled back on either side from the large "Y" incision that went from shoulder to shoulder and down the chest to the pubis. "Inside, he looks like . . . like . . . meat."

Dr. Liu laughed. "That's exactly what he is. What we *all* are. A little unsettling, huh?"

"Yeah. Gee, I'm glad I'm a vegetarian."

Savannah sidled up to the table to take a look. "I know what you mean. I don't eat rare steak or barbecued ribs for at least a week after I've watched Dr. Jenny do an autopsy."

"Oooo, gross." Tammy was starting to turn green again, so Savannah decided to cool it.

"Have you ever seen a human heart?" Jennifer asked, shoving the organ under Tammy's nose.

"Ah . . . no." Tammy swallowed hard. "It's so small."

"Only about the size of your fist." With the scalpel Jennifer made a quick, deft slice through the muscle, opening it for closer inspection. "And here . . . is a valve," she added, showing them the thin, pink membrane.

"Really?" Tammy's color was improving as her interest was piqued. "I thought it would be thicker, stronger than that. It's so delicate you can see through it."

Jennifer laughed. "Don't let it fool you. It's a lot stronger than it looks. If this young man hadn't done something so stupid as ride a motorcycle when he was drunk, this heart and its valves would have worked hard for him another fifty years or so."

Savannah looked at the lifeless face, trying to imagine

how he had looked before, animated, with the spark of life glowing in his eyes. She thought of his parents, of the tragic waste. She thought of her own brothers and sisters . . . all eight of them . . . and all younger than she. At times like this, she always sent two brief prayers heavenward: one of thanks that they were alive and healthy, and another that they would stay that way.

"So, what's the cause of death?" Savannah asked.

"Head injury. I took a look in his ears and saw hemorrhaging behind the eardrum. That means a probable fracture through the base of the skull."

"So, why do you have to open up his body," Tammy asked, "if you know it was his head?"

Dr. Liu smiled her soft, mysterious smile that Savannah found so intriguing. "Because I'm thorough, my dear. I take pride in being thorough. I never do anything halfway."

Savannah winced inwardly, wondering how she was going to approach the subject of Kat Valentina's autopsy without sounding as though she were questioning the doctor's conclusions. Dr. Jennifer Liu was a great gal with a charming sense of humor, but she wasn't kidding about the professional pride thing. She took her work very seriously and wasn't open to criticism. Long ago, Savannah had decided that she didn't want to offend Dr. Liu, both because she liked her . . . and because she was more than a little intimidated by her.

"But . . . um . . . some diagnoses are harder to make than others," Savannah said as nonchalantly as possible. "Take drowning, for example."

Both Tammy and Dr. Liu shot suspicious, questioning glances her way. So much for subtlety.

"That's true," Jennifer said slowly . . . deliberately.

"Drowning *is* a difficult diagnosis. It's usually a conclusion reached by exclusion, taking all evidence and circumstances into account."

Savannah decided to push a little harder. "And it's probably hard to tell if it's an accident, a suicide, or homicide."

Jennifer lifted one perfectly shaped eyebrow. "It can be difficult. But most drownings are accidents."

"*Some* are homicides."

"Very few."

The two women stared at each other as Tammy watched, fidgeting and looking miserable. The only sound was the hum of the overhead exhaust fan.

Finally, Dr. Liu broke the tension. "What are you trying to tell me, Savannah? Spit it out."

"I'm not trying to tell you anything. I was going to ask you if there's any possibility that Kat Valentina's death was murder rather than accidental."

"Anything's possible. Especially where drownings are concerned. But I don't think so." She returned to her work, removed a slice of the heart and placed it in a labeled, sample jar.

From the corner of her eye, Savannah could see Tammy watching her anxiously, wondering what she would say next. Dr. Liu had obviously dismissed them and this line of conversation.

Savannah cleared her throat. "I've uncovered some evidence . . . well . . . at least an indication . . . that she might have been murdered."

"Yes, I know. Detective Coulter called me about an hour

ago and told me about your envelope full of cash and its cryptic note."

Jennifer laid her scalpel aside, peeled off the surgical gloves, and dropped them into a nearby biological waste can. "I wish I could help you earn all that money, but there was no physical evidence to support or even suggest homicide."

"It isn't just the money," Tammy interjected. Both Savannah and Jennifer turned to see tears running down her cheeks. "Ms. Valentina was a friend of mine. I liked her; I really did. And if somebody killed her, I want to find out who did it and why. Savannah's just trying to help me."

She wiped her tears away with the back of her hand in a childish gesture that went straight to Savannah's heart.

Apparently, it had the same effect on Dr. Liu, whose expression softened. She reached out and patted the young woman's arm. "I understand how upsetting this must be for you."

Turning to Savannah, she said, "My report will probably be typed by this afternoon and you can pick up a copy at the desk. I don't think you'll find anything there that will help you, but you're welcome to try."

"Thanks, Dr. Jenny. That's all we wanted." Savannah put a hand on Tammy's back and nudged her toward the door.

Jennifer didn't reply until they had nearly left the room. "Hey, Savannah. . . ."

They paused in the doorway. "Yes?"

"If you do . . . find anything, that is . . . let me know, okay?"

"Don't worry, Dr. Jenny," she said with a smile. "You'll be the first to know."

* * *

As they left the building and headed across the parking lot to Savannah's Camaro, Tammy said, "Maybe it *was* just an accident."

She sounded so hopeful that Savannah couldn't bring herself to reply.

"Maybe whoever put that envelope in your mailbox is some sort of nut . . . a *rich* nut, who just wanted to start trouble."

"Maybe." Savannah unlocked the car and they got inside.

"Do you think that's all it was?" Tammy asked, her heart in her big hazel eyes. "Just an accident. Just some rich nut?"

Savannah hesitated, looking into those eyes that were so much like her younger siblings'. Tammy might be an aggravation sometimes, but she really did love the kid. And she could tell she was in a lot of pain over this. Still . . .

"No," she said as gently as she could. "I don't think that's all."

Tammy sighed and closed her eyes. A sob caught in her throat. "I don't think so either."

CHAPTER FIVE

"I'm sorry, Savannah, but I think it was an accidental drowning." Ryan set his cup of coffee on the table, next to the open file that detailed in clinical, albeit gruesome terms, the physical remains of Kat Valentina.

Sitting next to Ryan at Savannah's dining-room table was John Gibson. "I'm afraid I agree," he said. "Sorry, love." He poured himself a cup of Earl Grey from the teapot which Savannah had presented him minutes ago and helped himself to one of the chocolate-coated British biscuits that Savannah had arranged on a small silver tray. She prided herself on giving each of her guests—the charter members of the Moonlight Magnolia Detective Agency—their refreshments of choice.

On the other side of the table sat Dirk and Tammy—as

far apart as the limited space would allow. Tammy had her ubiquitous bottle of springwater, slices of apple, and celery sticks, and Dirk his plate piled high with pecan sandies and chocolate-chip cookies.

No one went hungry on Savannah's turf; it was an issue of Southern hospitality and Georgia pride.

At the head of the table, Savannah sipped her own cup of coffee, fortified with a splash of Baileys and topped with whipped cream and chocolate sprinkles.

Usually, she enjoyed these meetings, her favorite people in the world, gathered around her table, the entire scene lit with the cozy red glow of the Tiffany lamp above them. But tonight, the crimson-tinted light seemed lurid, reflecting on the stark black-and-white of the papers.

And then there were the autopsy photographs.

Poor Tammy. Her eyes were nearly swollen shut from crying. She toyed nervously with the pile of tissues in her lap. The pictures left nothing to the imagination. Her friend, Kat, had been thoroughly bisected, then dissected at Dr. Liu's expert hands.

Dirk shoved another cookie into his face. For him, having a full mouth seemed to be a prerequisite for speaking. "Bloss said, 'No way,' to reopening the case. He's satisfied with Dr. Liu's ruling."

Savannah sniffed her disgust. "Yeah, right. I'm sure Bloss's decision not to reopen had more to do with his precious budget and saving man-hours than anything in this file."

"So, where do we begin?" Ryan asked as he leaned back in his chair and crossed his arms over his broad chest.

"What do you mean . . . begin?" Savannah grabbed a cookie from Dirk's hand, deciding he'd had enough. "You said you agree with Liu, that it was accidental."

"I do. But more importantly, *you* don't. And that's enough for me."

Tammy beamed, gratitude and infatuation shining through the slits of her puffy eyes. Unlike Savannah, Tammy had never given up hope that Ryan might someday be persuaded to join the ranks of womanizers and assorted skirt chasers.

"And for me," John said, toasting her with his Earl Grey. "If I can be of service in any way at all, dear lady, don't hesitate to call on me."

Savannah thanked him and turned to Dirk. "Well . . . ?"

"Well what?"

"Well . . . you're the one who wolfs down most of the goodies at these little soirees. Are you going to earn your keep, or what?"

He sighed and shrugged. "I'll do the cop stuff. Check records, junk like that." Nabbing a couple more chocolate chippers, he added, "And how about *you?* What are *you* going to be doing, Van?"

Savannah looked over at Tammy and saw her friend's pain and desperation, the pleading in her eyes. Reaching deep inside her character, summoning every ounce of self-sacrifice and nobility she possessed, she opened her mouth and spoke those fatal words:

"I never thought the day would come when I would have to do such a thing. But desperate times call for desperate measures. Lady and gentlemen . . . I, Savannah Reid, hedonist extraordinaire, am going to join a health spa!"

"Ms. Reid, your body-fat percentage exceeds the recommended ratio by quite a bit."

"Really . . . imagine that."

"It appears you have been consuming an excess of calories."

"Ah, huh . . ."

"And possibly leading a sedentary lifestyle."

"Hmmm. . . ."

"Here at Royal Palms, we will light the way to a brighter, healthier future for you."

"Yeah, great. . . ."

"You will learn the value of nutrition, of exercise, of becoming one with your body, mind, and spirit."

"Oh, wow. . . ."

"Wholesome food, physical and spiritual cleansing—that's what we're all about here at the Royal Palms Spa. Welcome."

The scrawny, anemic-looking receptionist in the gauzy Royal Palms toga, who couldn't have been a day over twenty, extended her bony hand. Savannah forced herself to shake it, solidifying the contract.

On the office walls hung color posters of other equally skinny bodies, slender to the point of emaciation. Quintessential glamour.

In one area near the water cooler hung a collection of pseudocelebrity photos, pictures of the famous and infamous guests who had frequented the Royal Palms Spa in its heyday. The recently departed hostess, Kat Valentina herself, occupied center stage in most of the shots.

The unspoken promise delivered by such advertising: Royal Palms can turn even *your* flabby, out-of-shape body into one of these lean, mean machines!

Savannah could hardly wait.

For the next two weeks, Royal Palms would starve her, subject her to the physical tortures of a chain gang, deny her every creature comfort that she held dear . . . and for this dubious pleasure, she would pay them a large chunk of the money she had received in the infamous envelope.

Oh, joy.

Where the hell was Tammy, anyway? Savannah wondered, feeling the walls of the office closing in around her. Wasn't this time when she was supposed to provide the preplanned diversion?

Like an answer to prayer, a soft knock sounded on the door, and Tammy stuck her head in. "Hi, Bernadette, can I talk to you for a minute . . . out here?"

"Well, I'm in the middle of my initiation with Ms. Reid but—"

"That's okay, Bernadette, really," Savannah interjected. "I have to read these papers over before I sign them anyway."

Bernadette looked distressed. "They're just standard release forms that say—"

"I know, but I never sign anything without reading every word. See, my cousin's first husband's brother, the one from New Jersey, well, he was a lawyer, and he always told us to—"

"Okay, okay." Bernadette bounded out of her desk chair—everyone seemed to bound or bounce or bop around here, Savannah noticed. Maybe there was something to this health kick after all. "I'll go see what Tammy wants and get right back to you."

"No problem . . . take your time. I read slowly."

Bernadette left the door open a crack, so Savannah could hear the trumped-up question Tammy was asking her in the hallway, something about scheduling problems between herself and another aerobics instructor.

One quick glance around the three-desk office told Savannah that this was a fairly organized establishment. She was sitting at Bernadette's enrollment/initiation station. The other two desks, fortunately unoccupied, were marked by small brass plaques as: Sandra Cummings—Bookkeeper and Louis Hanks—President.

With a quick glance toward the doorway, Savannah hurried across the faded red carpeting to Lou Hanks's desk. No doubt it would yield the juiciest secrets. Or at least, it would have, if it hadn't been locked.

Although she was an expert in the fine art of lock-tumbler manipulation, Savannah decided she didn't have time to pick it. So, she scuttled over to the bookkeeper's desk.

Fortunately, the top two drawers were unlocked. The first drawer contained the usual office supplies. But in the second, she found a pile of unpaid bills. Having gone through a time of financial struggles herself this past year, getting Moonlight Magnolia Detective Agency on its limping feet, she knew grossly overdue notices when she saw them.

Some were from the Internal Revenue Service and threatened dire consequences if large sums weren't paid within the next ninety days. Apparently, some sort of federal lien had already been placed against the Royal Palms Spa.

She would have loved to scour deeper, but she could tell by the tone of the conversation in the hall that their talk was coming to a close.

The moment her rear hit the chair, Bernadette bounced back into the room, toga aflutter.

"Well?" she asked, nodding toward the release forms. "Would your cousin from Jersey approve?"

Savannah thought of the days ahead—the grass-drink concoctions, the unflavored yogurt and tofu, the unnatural and miserably uncomfortable yoga positions, the sweaty aerobics classes at the break of dawn, the agonies of withdrawal she would suffer going cold turkey off Ben & Jerry's Chunky Monkey ice cream.

She glanced over to the door and saw Tammy standing there, gazing at her with doe eyes, begging, pleading.

She sighed, shoulders slumped, a defeated woman. "All right, all right . . . where do I sign?"

Dr. Freeman Ross was a quack. That was Savannah's assessment after he gave her the quickest physical examination in ancient or modern history. Until he pronounced her perfectly healthy—excess fat ratio not withstanding—and then she decided maybe she had judged him too hastily.

"You're in great shape, Ms. Reid," he told her as he lowered himself onto the tiny, rolling stool beside the examination table where she sat, shivering in a blue-and-white paper gown.

"Thanks. I always thought so, too."

"So, why are you here?"

Yes, she liked Dr. Ross, very much. If he kept this up, she might propose. He *was* kinda cute in a Clark Kent sort of way, somewhere in his mid-forties, with perfectly waved dark hair and round, tortoiseshell glasses. He wore jeans and sneakers along with his formal, white doctor's smock. A nice look.

And he hadn't complained about her weight.

"Why am I here?" she said. "That's a good question. It's just that . . . well, you know . . . I've been taking a lot of heat from friends about those extra pounds."

"And which pounds are those?"

"The ones on every chart I read." She sighed. "According to those, I'd be the perfect weight . . . if I were only six-foot-three."

He chuckled as he scribbled notes on her chart, which was lying on his lap.

Nice thighs, too, she decided. They certainly looked hard, muscular, well rounded. Ah, well, maybe this wasn't the best time to think about hard, well-rounded male anatomy.

"What are you hoping to gain during your stay here at Royal Palms Spa?" he asked.

She thought fast, but nothing came to her mind—which still seemed to be occupied with bulging jeans and such.

"Ummm . . . I guess I hope to lose a little and tone up." There. That had been delivered with just the right amount of conviction. She hoped.

Maybe not. He was studying her through those tortoiseshell-framed lenses, a look of serious doubt on his Doctor Hunk of the Month calendar face.

"If you don't mind me saying so, Ms. Reid—"

"Please call me Savannah."

"Okay, Savannah." She liked the way he caressed the

vowels in her name. In fact, she decided he could caress her vowels anytime. Her consonants, too, for that matter.

"As I was saying," he continued, "you don't seem all that motivated to be here at Royal Palms."

Think fast, airhead, she told herself. *You're blowing this on account of some bulges.*

"I'm just a little concerned," she said, venturing into dangerous waters, "about the safety of the spa. You know, with what happened to poor Ms. Valentina and all."

Warm and friendly before, his manner changed abruptly. If an arctic blast had whipped through the tiny office, the atmosphere wouldn't have turned any more frosty.

"What happened to Ka ... Ms. Valentina, was a tragic accident," he said, rising from his stool and snapping her folder closed. "You have nothing to worry about concerning the safety of this facility."

If he was going to have an emotional reaction, she might as well fuel the flame and see how high it would burn. "I just don't want to drown in any mud bath," she said.

"You won't," he said as he turned his back to her and headed for the door.

"But I just—"

"Ms. Reid," he said, cutting her off and demoting her from a friendly "Savannah" with one verbal blow, "there's absolutely no reason to worry. I'm sure you'll enjoy your stay with us. If you have any other questions ... about your own health and well-being, that is ... please feel free to consult me."

He jerked the door open, passed through it, and slammed it behind him, leaving her sitting there in her wrinkled paper gown.

"Hmmm . . . interesting," she mumbled as she pulled the ugly thing off and wadded it into a ball. Tossing it into the nearby waste can, she evaluated the unexpected information that she had just collected.

Dr. Freeman Ross had been in love with Kat Valentina.

Savannah had seen it in his eyes when he had defended her "accident." No doubt about it; a woman could read these things.

As Savannah pulled on her underwear, sweater, slacks and loafers, she considered what this new revelation might mean. Maybe nothing at all. But then, she had learned long ago that if you peeled back layer after layer of a murder, more often than not, you uncovered a love affair or two . . . or at least, some hot sex.

"Don't look at me like that," Savannah told Diamante and Cleopatra as they traced furry figure eights between her ankles and gazed up at her with rapt green eyes.

She scooped spoonfuls of the foul-smelling Pampered Kitty gruel into their matching bowls. They buried their faces in it, as though no future meals would ever be forthcoming. Somehow, they could always tell when she was getting ready to leave for a while.

"I'll only be gone a few days, and Mrs. Normandy is going to come by to feed you and give you pets. Don't worry; you'll get your salmon mousse. It's your mistress who's going to be deprived of culinary pleasures. Do you feel sorry for me?"

Not really, she decided. They lapped and smacked, oblivious and unconcerned.

She thought of the DoveBar ice cream treats in the freezer, the Mrs. Fields chocolate-chip and macadamia cookies in the jar, the stash of Godiva truffles in the pantry. What if an attack of PMS set in?

Maybe she should stick a few truffles and a cookie or two into her suitcase . . . just in case. . . .

The phone rang, and she grabbed for it, feeling a little guilty. Sure enough, it was Tammy.

"I'm here at the club," she said, sounding so encouraged and hopeful that Savannah decided she was doing the right thing after all. "They said you went home to get some things, and you're coming back this evening?"

"Right. I needed to settle my affairs, before I check into Hotel Hell."

"Geez, Savannah, it's supposed to be fun. People pay big bucks to come here."

"That's the real mystery . . . not what happened to Kat."

"Naw, really, you're going to have a good time. But I wanted to warn you . . ." Tammy lowered her voice. ". . . when you officially check in tonight, they'll search your bags, just to make sure you aren't smuggling in any goodies. They've had trouble with contraband in the past."

"Contraband?" Savannah feigned shock. "You mean . . . *drugs?*"

"Oh, no . . . I'm talking junk food. You wouldn't believe the kinds of garbage they try to smuggle in here!"

"Really! I'm appalled!" She reached for the cookie jar, extracted one of Mrs. Fields's best, and took a big bite.

"Go figure," Tammy rattled on. "I mean, why would somebody enroll in a health spa if they were just going to poison their bodies with toxic substances like sugar and chocolate . . ."

"And butter." Savannah chewed, savoring every bite. "Don't forget creamy dairy butter and, of course, macadamia nuts."

"Macadamia nuts?"

"Yeah. I heard they're a common problem." She munched. And smiled. "Macadamia nuts comprise about 10 percent of the overall contraband that's confiscated at health club entry checkpoints."

"Really? I didn't know . . ."

"Oh, yeah, it's true. They're worse than peanuts and cashews."

Savannah walked over to her pantry, gave the phone cord a pull, and disappeared inside. "I read it in some magazine called *Health Spa Beautiful*," she continued, rummaging along the bottom shelf. "An article about 'Keeping Your Spa Nut-Free.'"

"Savannah, I think you're pulling my leg."

"Why, Tammy, honey, would I do that?"

"Every weekday and twice on Sunday."

Savannah cackled with glee as she saw the gleam of a gold foil box behind a cream-cheese brownie mix and a cherry-swirl bundt cake. "Thanks for the tip about the search, sweetie," she said, coming out of the pantry, chocolates in hand. "I owe you one."

Hanging up the phone, she glanced down at the cats, who were gazing up at her as though expecting more salmon mousse.

"Forget it. One bowlful apiece is enough," she told them.

They meowed a protest. "No way! You two are gluttons! You should be ashamed of yourselves."

She left the kitchen and headed upstairs, clutching her truffles to her chest. "Besides, I have to pack," she muttered. "Maybe I can shove these things under the lining."

CHAPTER SIX

"So, what do we do now?" Savannah asked. "Paint each other's toenails, talk about boys, tell ghost stories?"

She and Tammy lay on matching twin beds in the tiny room that was to be Savannah's home away from home for the next week ... or two ... or however long it took her to investigate Kat Valentina's murder.

Like the rest of the Royal Palms, the dorms reflected the faded, gaudy glory of the early seventies. The bedspreads were crushed red velveteen that had long passed their prime. The shag carpeting was the sort that required "raking." Overhead a wrought-iron light fixture represented someone's idea of a Roman torch with flickering bulbs that supplied hardly any light at all.

But Savannah had decided to get into the fantasy of it and enjoy the experience. She was even wearing her Victoria's

Secret toga nightgown in honor of the occasion. Plus, having Tammy spend the night with her helped. She would just pretend they were hanging out in some badly decorated catacombs.

"It is sorta like a slumber party, huh?" Tammy said with a giggle, wriggling her pink flannel pajama–clad legs. "I haven't had this much fun in a long time."

Silently, Savannah filed that information away for future consideration. For all her cheerfulness, Tammy seemed rather lonely at times. Her family lived on Long Island, New York, and Savannah got the impression that they hadn't been that close even when Tammy had lived at home. The only child of a socially prominent father-physician and attorney-mother, Tammy had grown up with absentee parents . . . something Savannah understood.

Savannah had never really known her dad, and Mom had produced child after child, turning them over to their grandmother to raise.

But at least Savannah had Granny Reid. And she wouldn't have traded their relative poverty and the responsibility of eight younger siblings for Tammy's privileged, but solitary, childhood for anything.

At least, Savannah had known without a doubt that she was loved. And she had been taught life's most important lessons by Gran's example.

"Tell me something, Tammy," she said, staring up at the gaudy, flickering fixture over their heads. "Why were you so fond of Kat? Please don't take offense. I'm not implying you shouldn't have been. I'm just asking why."

Tammy was silent for a long time, thinking before answering. "I guess it sounds simple and dumb, but Kat could be really nice when she wanted to be. She was really pretty, and sometimes, when she looked at you with those big golden eyes of hers, she made you feel like you were the only person in the world." She paused. "Does that make sense?"

Yes, Savannah knew the pleasure of receiving someone's undivided attention . . . especially important to a young woman who hadn't received enough of that valuable commodity as a child.

"Yes, it does," she replied. "What else?"

"She was really funny. She would say things that were kind of . . . naughty . . . and make people laugh."

Savannah nodded. "My Granny Reid is like that. That sort of woman sets the rest of us free to be our own sexy selves."

"That's true! I felt more free around Kat than with anyone else. It's like nothing shocked her."

Savannah recalled the infamous Royal Palms orgies back in the seventies, but decided not to comment.

As Tammy continued to enumerate Kat Valentina's qualities, Savannah silently noted that all her attributes fell into the category of "personality" rather than "character."

Kat knew how to entertain people, make them laugh, make them feel special. Those abilities were nothing more than highly developed social talents, forms of acting and interacting. Endearing as those charms might be, they said little about the person inside.

Long ago, Savannah had learned to look beyond those social graces to the actions that defined a person's true character. And although Kat Valentina might have been pretty, witty, and interesting, she had also been known as a liar, a swindler, an adulteress, and a wanton, bent on self-destruction.

Savannah's Granny Reid had told her that although someone might put on a charming facade, it was their actions that more clearly defined who was living inside the pretty package.

But Savannah decided to keep this bit of homespun wisdom to herself tonight, as they lay there enjoying their slumber party. If Tammy hadn't figured out the difference between personality and character, she would. This didn't seem to be the time for life lessons.

"Besides," Tammy chattered on, "Kat had really changed the last two months or so."

Savannah's investigator's ears perked up. "Really? How had she changed?"

"I'm not sure, exactly, but she seemed more serious about things. She said she was changing a lot of her habits. Like drinking, for example."

"Drinking?"

"Yes. She had decided to purify her body, said she needed to do it for her health's sake. She was taking lots of vitamins and good stuff, was watching everything she ate, and she had stopped drinking completely. That's why I was so surprised when she had that pitcher of margaritas there by the mud bath."

Savannah rolled over onto her side, facing Tammy. "I hate to mention this, sweetie, but Kat wouldn't have necessarily been the first person with a drinking problem to fall off the wagon."

"I know. I thought of that. But I don't think so. She seemed so determined to eat and drink only healthy stuff. It was like she was finally practicing what she'd been preaching. She seemed *really* motivated . . . almost scared, like she *had* to do it, or something."

"Hmmm." Savannah digested that for a moment. "Did you mention this to anyone?"

"Yes. I told Kat's husband, Mr. Hanks, I thought it was strange that she was drinking again, when she'd been so good."

"What did he say?"

"He said, 'Nothing Kat did surprises me. I got over that a long time ago.'"

"Maybe he's right. Maybe you're reading too much into something that may have been just a lapse for her."

"Maybe."

Savannah could hear the doubt in Tammy's "maybe." But then, Tammy was a bit too trusting with people, a bit too eager to give them the benefit of that doubt . . . whether they deserved it or not.

Either way, it was something to consider. And something to check out.

"I think I need to find Lou Hanks and have a talk with him tomorrow," she said. "I just have to finagle it without him getting suspicious."

"Too late," Tammy said. "I meant to tell you . . . he was looking for you this afternoon, heard you had checked in. Seems he's already wondering why you're here. I guess he knows you're a detective and all."

"Great." Savannah sighed, plopped onto her back, and stared up at the ugly light fixture. "There's nothing quite like going undercover . . . when everybody and their dog knows who you are."

"What the hell!" Savannah bolted upright in bed, her ears ringing from the rude alarm that was sounding up and down the hallway. "What is that! A fire bell?"

A sleepy Tammy stirred in the bed next to hers. "No, that's just the wake-up call." She yawned, stretched, then bounced off the bed, fully rejuvenated. "We've got ten minutes to get dressed and outside for warm-up exercises."

"What? Who said anything about exercising? Where's my coffee? I need a Danish . . . or two," Savannah grumbled, her heart pounding in her throat.

Tammy hopped around the room, flinging off her flannel jammies and donning a shapeless gray workout suit. She tossed Savannah's to her.

"Act alive!" she pealed. "Shake a leg now, or we'll be late."

Savannah shot her a dark look as she climbed into the ugly uniform. The last time she had gotten up this early and dressed this badly to do exercises, she had been in the police academy. And that had been before the decline and fall of the Roman Empire, give or take a year or two.

"Shake a leg, my ass," she grumbled. "I'll shake *you*, until your teeth rattle, if you start that perky 'morning' shit with me again."

"Ah, Sa-a-v-aaa-nah! Give me just one little good-morning smile. Come on . . . just for me . . . !"

Savannah bared her teeth and growled.

"Now that's better. Let's go. We've only got two minutes!"

Savannah didn't mind the exercises half as much as she had anticipated. Even the cross-country run around the perimeter of the spa's property wasn't so bad, she decided. If only Tammy had mentioned that the exercise session was led by Dion Zeller, Kat Valentina's leading man in *Disco Diva*, she might have jogged to the exercise field more eagerly.

There was nothing to compare with following those cute little bouncing buns around to clean those "nasty toxins" out of her system and make her feel like a "new woman" just as Tammy had predicted.

Yes, there were worse ways to spend a morning than looking at the backside of Dion Zeller. Her eyes were likely to be as sore the next day as her long-dormant, newly awakened muscles.

Their exercise class had boasted only six students, including Savannah and Tammy. This *did* appear to be a slow time for the Royal Palms. Their four classmates were all older people, three women and a man, who had dropped out of the routine soon after the workout. They had declined the joy of the hillside run, leaving only Tammy and Savannah to join Dion.

With a not-so-subtle nod of her head, Savannah had indicated to Tammy that she should make her own exit. Reluctantly, she had, leaving Savannah to run behind Dion with an unobstructed view of the marguerite daisies, the sage scrub, and—most importantly—Dion's electric blue running shorts.

On a wide straightaway across the top of the arroyo, she caught up with him and jogged beside him.

"So, how long have you been working at Royal Palms?" she asked, dryly congratulating herself on the originality of the line. Perhaps she should make her humiliation complete and ask when he got off and if he came there often.

"Since I decided to start earning my keep," he replied with the somber face of a golden-haired Greek god. "I've been living here off and on since the *Disco Diva* money ran out. Kat was kind enough to let me stay."

She had to give him a perfect score of 10.0 for honesty. Long, curly blond hair, a physique to die for, patrician features, turquoise eyes ... and a penchant toward honesty and humility.

Not bad.

"You were a good friend of Kat's then?" she asked.

Their feet churned a lot of dust on the dry unpaved path before he finally answered. When he did, his voice was husky with emotion. "Kat was a good friend to me. I don't know how good a friend I was to her."

"I'm sorry for your loss," Savannah added, meaning it. If she were any judge at all, she could swear she saw genuine sadness in his eyes as she sneaked sideways glances at him.

Chugging along beside him, matching him stride for stride, she was thankful for her sturdy constitution. She was hardly huffing and puffing at all.

For all of Tammy's bitching at her about health, Savannah decided she was in remarkably good shape for someone whose most strenuous form of exercise lately had been hefting forkfuls of Black Forest cake. Compared to police work, being a private detective was pretty soft employment. But she hadn't lost it all. Not by a long shot.

They came to a fork in the path, and he chose the one leading toward a large, sprawling hacienda that crowned the top of a hill.

"Are we still on Royal Palms property?" she asked, beginning to feel the burn in her calves and thighs. Yes, she would definitely be sore tomorrow. Hopefully, he would turn around and head for home soon. The last thing she wanted to do was fall flat on her face with exhaustion in front of this ravishing male specimen.

"It runs right up to that fence, the one near that big

Spanish-style house," he replied, wiping the sweat from his face with his forearm.

A very muscular, tanned forearm . . . she couldn't help noticing.

"Wow, nice place," Savannah observed, as they rounded a corner and still more of the estate was revealed.

The white stucco gleamed in the rose-tinted, early-morning light, as did the red tiled roof and the cobalt blue mosaic accents around the windows and doors. An elegant belfry graced the center of the building, giving it the old-world charm of an adobe mission.

She could see at least three fountains, meticulously mani-cured flower gardens everywhere, and an arbor draped with lavender and white wisteria that ran from the backyard to a huge, modern barn.

"Yeah, that's the Chesterfield estate," Dion said. Savan-nah detected a note of . . . something . . . in his voice when he spoke the name. Was it contempt? Or maybe simple dislike? "Ford and Phoebe Chesterfield own the whole hill. They're brother and sister, and they're a matched set."

"How's that?"

"Old, cantankerous, and richer than God."

"Doesn't sound as though you like them very much."

"They don't make it easy. Ford was always hanging around the spa. He was nuts about Kat—even asked her to marry him. Can you believe that? An old fart like that?"

Actually, Savannah *could* believe it. If Chesterfield was richer than God, an opportunist like Kat Valentina must have at least *thought* about it.

"And his sister, Phoebe . . ." Dion shook his golden head. ". . . now there's one irritating lady."

He paused in the middle of the path and pointed to the belfry. "Phoebe's favorite pastime is to sit up there in that tower and spy on everything that goes on at the spa."

"She must have great eyesight for an old woman."

"Naw . . . but she has a great telescope."

"Ah. I see."

"So does she. Everything. And she complains about it all. To hear her tell it, she's living next door to Sodom and Gomorrah."

"How entertaining. Lucky her."

"Exactly. As you may have heard, Kat and her friends weren't known for their modesty or self-restraint," he said with a chuckle, "and they gave the old lady quite an eyeful."

"They?" she asked him with a mischievous grin that deepened her dimples.

He laughed. "Okay, we. I'm not exactly a saint myself."

A couple of butterflies in her belly fluttered around and did a mating dance. It was an enticing situation, being up here on this beautiful, sun-drenched hill, waist-high in marguerite daisies with an Adonis who admitted he wasn't exactly a saint.

The job did have its occasional perks.

"Hey, I think Miss Phoebe is checking us out right now," he said, waving cheerfully to the tower.

Savannah peered up at the belfry and caught the glimmer of sunlight reflecting off a small, round object . . . a telescope lens? Just for good measure, she waved, too.

A second later, they saw a flash of bright, floral print, then the belfry appeared to be empty.

"She hates getting caught," he said, laughing. "She ducks down and waits for us to be on our way, then she's at it again."

"Why get a life of your own, when everyone else's is so much more interesting, huh?"

"Precisely. The old busybody."

Savannah thought of Mr. Biddle in Dirk's trailer park. Then she remembered her own granny Reid, who was far too busy even to notice, let alone worry about, what others were doing. Not every elderly person was a busybody. And not every busybody was elderly . . . as she knew from having the comfortably middle-aged Mrs. Normandy for a neighbor.

"She was a definite pain in the ass, really got under Kat's skin. I wonder if she'll lighten up now that Kat is . . ."

His voice trailed away, and Savannah saw the sadness return to his eyes as he gazed out across the vista of rolling, chaparral-covered hills to the shining sea.

"Maybe it's time to start back," she said gently.

"Yes," he replied. "Gotta keep moving. No matter what . . ."

Dion's stimulating company had kept her mind off her body—well, most parts of her body—until they returned. But once they jogged into the central area of the club, Savannah began to feel her fatigue and soreness with a vengeance.

"What's next?" she asked him, trying not to sound as though she were on her last leg, even if it was about to buckle beneath her.

"Massage," he replied, pointing to a small white cottage, situated in a copse of olive trees beyond the pool house.

"Don't toy with me," she said. "Really?"

"Absolutely. Not every moment here at Royal Palms is spent working out, you know."

"Thank God!"

A good massage . . . or even a mediocre one . . . was her favorite thing—next to chocolate, of course.

"Josef's pretty good," he told her. "And he'll even give you breakfast first."

"Breakfast, too! What more could a woman want?"

As soon as she spoke the words, she took a last quick look up and down the wonder that was Dion Zeller, former disco king and now exercise coach. Maybe there were a few more things a woman could wish for.

But one appetite at a time. And right now, what she really wanted was some breakfast and to be rubbed the right way.

"This is breakfast?" She held the tiny cup of green juice up to her nose, took a sniff, and nearly gagged.

"Drink it. It's wheat grass. It's good for you." Josef Orlet, masseur and green-gunk drink enforcer, towered over her. What he lacked in good looks and charm, he made up in sheer size and presence. His voice was a nasal monotone that grated on her nerves almost as much as his equally dull personality.

At the peak of her karate training, she might have considered taking him on. But, exhausted from the morning run and weak from caffeine withdrawal, she decided it would be easier just to drink the damned stuff and have it over with.

Maybe not.

The moment the liquid hit her tongue, her throat closed and refused to let it pass.

Josef watched her with narrowed eyes, a scowl on his pockmarked face. "Swallow," he said.

She shook her head vigorously and looked around for a sink or waste can to spit it into. But the tiny "nutrition station," as they call it, had no such receptacle. They had probably learned from experience to remove such temptations from their nauseous guests.

"I said, 'Swallow.'" He reached out and pinched her nose, holding it tightly and restricting her breathing.

As an older sister, she had used the technique herself many times on her younger siblings who had refused to take their medicine. How humiliating to be on the receiving end of such treatment at the ripe old age of forty-something.

He had a firm grip on her nose, and eventually she had to breathe, so . . .

"Aaauuggh! That tastes like shit!" she said, shuddering and shaking her head.

"It cleans the toxins out of your blood."

"So does a good temper tantrum, and that's what I'm going to throw if you ever grab my nose like that again, buddy," she said, shoving her face into his—or at least, as close as she could, considering that he was nearly a foot taller.

He laughed at her, but it wasn't a particularly mirthful sound with any warmth in it.

No doubt about it. Josef was more than a masseur around here; he was the bouncer, the obligatory establishment goon. And she got the distinct impression that he enjoyed his work.

"Now you get your massage," he said, nodding toward the open door and the small room with its sheet-draped table. "I'll rub those toxins out of your muscles, so that you can do more exercise this afternoon."

"Geez," she muttered, dragging her tired body into the appointed room. "You guys are really hung up on this 'toxin' thing. What's wrong with a little sludge in the system to keep things lubricated?"

She glanced back. Josef the Terrible was staring at her, hands on his hips, biceps bulging beneath his white smock. "Get undressed and lie on the table," he said in that flat, computer-like tone that she was quickly growing to hate.

"Yes, sir, Sergeant Orlet! Right away, sir!" she said . . . and slammed the door in his face.

Josef wasn't the best masseur Savannah had ever had, but she had to admit he wasn't the worst either. The oils he used had a pleasant, herbal smell. Although they did remind her a bit of the mud bath that Kat's body had been found in, and that took away some of the romance.

His big hands were gentle, but firm, as they glided over her skin. And, even if she couldn't detect any "toxins" escaping, a lot of her stress was melting away beneath his ministrations.

The New Age jazz playing on the stereo in the corner of the room trickled deliciously along her nervous system, calming and soothing, allowing her to forget that she was a detective on duty. For just a few moments, she was Savannah Reid, pampered patroness . . . a fantasy she wouldn't mind indulging.

But her respite was short-lived, interrupted by a brisk knock on the door. Before she or Josef could even reply, it swung open, and a man barged in, a pale and pudgy guy who looked nothing like what he was: the owner of a health spa.

Savannah barely recognized Louis Hanks, as it had been years since she had seen him, and when she had, he had looked much younger and far more fit. The intervening years hadn't been kind.

"Mr. Hanks," Josef said, obviously as surprised as she at the abrupt, inopportune visit. "Is something wrong?" He stopped the massage and covered Savannah's bare leg with the sheet.

"I need a word with our . . . guest," Hanks said, nodding a curt dismissal to Josef, who seemed to evaporate.

Savannah lay on the table on her stomach, with only a thin sheet to cover her nakedness. She had probably felt more vulnerable at one time or another, but she couldn't readily recall when.

"Excuse me, Mr. Hanks," she said. "But this isn't really a good time for me. Would you mind if I at least get dressed before we have our little chat?"

"That's exactly what I want you to do, Miss Reid," he said, his grayish face suddenly flushing an ugly shade of red, mottled with purple. "I want you to get dressed . . . and then get the hell off my property."

CHAPTER SEVEN

Savannah sat up on the table and clutched the sheet tightly around her. "Excuse me? I just paid a lot of money to attend your charming spa, Mr. Hanks. Are you telling me you don't *want* my cold, hard cash?"

"I know why you're here," he said, taking a couple of threatening steps closer to the table. His fists were clenched at his sides, and he looked as though he were about to explode.

"And why is that?" she asked, deliberately keeping her voice low and even.

"You're a private detective! I recognized your name and face from the newspapers."

"That's true. I am. But even private detectives find themselves in need of some rest and relaxation, not to mention dietary and exercise guidance."

"That's not why you're here, and I know it."

".Do you really?"

She slid off the table, sheet still tucked snugly around her body. But she made certain her legs and feet were free in case she needed to run or land a karate kick in one of Louis Hanks's more vulnerable. areas.

"So, if it isn't to avail myself of your world-renowned spa, why am I here, Mr. Hanks?"

"You're investigating my ex-wife's death."

"The medical examiner's office ruled that Ms. Valentina's death was an accident. What's to investigate?"

He walked up to her and shook a sausage-shaped finger in her face. "Don't play dumb with me. I'm no fool. I know who you're working for."

Really? she thought. *Then you're better informed than I am.* But she decided to keep her thoughts to herself and her mouth shut. Maybe she would find out.

"That damned insurance company hired you! I know it!" he shouted. "They want to trump up some crap about it being a suicide, so they don't have to pay me off. Well, let me tell you, I won't stand for it! I won't!"

"Mr. Hanks," she said, using the conciliatory voice that she usually reserved for hostage situations and rooftop jumpers, "I have no idea what you're talking about. I swear to you that I'm not working for any insurance company."

Insurance companies don't pay investigators with a mailbox stuffed with cash, she thought. *Someone does, but not an insurance company.*

He must have believed her, because he seemed to deflate before her eyes. His crimson coloring gradually subsided and his fists relaxed. He actually looked apologetic.

"You mean . . . you aren't . . ." he stammered. "Oh . . . I'm sorry. I . . ."

"It's all right, Mr. Hanks. I'm sure you've been under a lot of stress lately," she hurried to assure him. "It was a natural assumption to make under the circumstances."

The genuine remorse on his face made her feel a little guilty. After all, he was half-right in his suspicions. Unfortunately, she couldn't salve her conscience by telling him so.

"You're really here to enjoy the spa? To lose weight or—"

She cleared her throat. "Actually, I need to rid my body of its toxins," she replied with a completely straight face.

"Oh, well, we have lots of ways to do that!"

"So I've heard."

He turned and walked to the door, where he paused. "Ummm . . . Miss Reid . . . I hope we can keep this conversation in the strictest confidence."

"No problem, Mr. Hanks. It'll be our little secret." She reached up and "zipped" her lips.

He rewarded her with a nervous smile. "Thanks. Enjoy the spa. If there's anything I can do to make your stay more pleasant, please say so."

A dozen suggestions flooded her mind: New York cheese-cake, sleeping until noon, massages without the obligatory exercise classes, and no green gunk in little cups.

But, instead of stating them, she simply smiled, and said, "Thank you, Mr. Hanks. I'll keep that in mind."

After he had left the room and closed the door behind him, she sat on the table and contemplated her latest revelation.

So . . . Louis Hanks had taken out a life insurance policy

on his now-dead ex-wife. And it must have been a pretty sizable sum, considering how hot under the collar he had been at the thought of having the payment delayed.

He was in financial trouble—she had already known that—and was probably hoping for the insurance money to bail him out.

Yep, she thought. *Very interesting.* That sounded like a motive for murder if she had ever heard one.

Mercifully, the remainder of her first day at Royal Palms went by quickly for Savannah: a morning meditation class in which she learned to sit cross-legged and hum "in harmony with the universe," a lunch of some strange, gray, pulverized drink mixture, a salad and a soup of "purifying greens," afternoon aerobics with Tammy, a sauna, a basket-weaving class "to teach discipline and balance," dinner, which was another blenderized concoction, more veggies, and an evening dip in the pool. Or at least, Savannah had intended it to be a dip, until she found that Josef, the enforcer, expected them to take three laps around.

Exhausted, she climbed the hill back to their dormitory, her body atingle with more oxygen than it had experienced in years.

"What doesn't kill you, makes you stronger," she told herself as she trudged along in her swimsuit and cover-up, her wet hair wrapped in a towel. "And if this doesn't make me stronger, I'm going to kill Tammy for getting me into it."

The sun had set an hour before and she had to pick her way carefully among the overgrown shrubs that lined the narrow rock walkway. Apparently, Royal Palms had been forced to cut their landscaping budget, too.

Although lanterns had been strung along the way to provide light, they were the flickering variety that added more ambience than illumination. And nearly half of them weren't lit.

She stubbed her toes several times on the rocks, her beach thongs doing little to protect her feet from the uneven walkway. Next time, she vowed to return from the pool before sundown to avoid this obstacle course.

Just as she was nearing the long, low building which served as their dorm, she thought she heard something move in the shrubbery off to her left.

Yes, there was a distinct rustling in the oleander bushes. And it wasn't just a rabbit or cat. Whatever it was, it was big. Big enough to cause a problem.

She stopped, ears perked, eyes searching the dark bushes with their pink and white blossoms.

"Who's there?" she asked, instinctively knowing that no one was going to answer. Whoever it was, they were hiding and probably intended to stay hidden. Or was that just wishful thinking on her part?

"I can see you," she lied. "Come out of there right now before I come in after you."

Yeah, good one, she thought. *Half-dressed, without a gun or any other kind of weapon, you're going to go charging in there and drag him/her out by their ear and whop the snot out of 'em. Good plan.*

The bushes were deathly still, but she could feel someone there, watching her, evaluating her.

She stepped out of the feeble light cast by the nearest lamp and into the shadows. Dammit, if she couldn't see them, they weren't going to see her.

"Come on out and show yourself, chicken shit," she said, mentally rehearsing the karate moves she might use if they did.

Just as she suspected. No answer.

Finally, she was tired of the game and beginning to run low on adrenaline. "Okay, just stay there," she said. "I didn't want to look at your butt-ugly mug up close anyway."

She waited a moment longer, thinking she was going to feel like a first-class idiot if somebody's poodle or Labrador came waltzing out.

When no humans, lions, tigers, or bears appeared, she decided the best thing to do was continue on her journey. But she did so with one eye looking over her shoulder.

The door to the dormitory was, thankfully, only a few yards away. She hurried inside, eager to leave the eerie experience behind.

But she didn't really feel safe until she had entered her and Tammy's room and locked the door behind her.

"That was weird, Savannah, ol' girl," she whispered as she flipped on the light and turned around. Her relief at being "home at last" quickly vanished.

Someone had been here before her, someone extremely untidy. Everything in her drawers and Tammy's had been dumped onto the floor as well as their clothes from the closet. The beds were stripped, the linens lying in a heap in the middle of the room. Savannah's suitcase lay open and empty. Her nightcase, too, with her toiletries strewn across the counter.

At first, she thought they had been robbed. But then she saw that the small amount of jewelry she had brought and her wallet were among the rest of her things in the pile. So was her cell phone . . . a pretty toy for any self-respecting burglar.

She hadn't been robbed; she had been searched.

For what, she wasn't sure. But, whoever they were, they hadn't found anything. She wasn't stupid enough to leave anything behind that had anything to do with her investigation.

Lou Hanks came to mind first. But she was pretty sure he had believed her denial earlier that morning. And she had returned to the room after dinner to change into her bathing suit. Everything had been in order when she had left it.

Someone jiggled the knob on the door, and her heart leapt into her throat. A key turned in the lock and it opened.

She positioned herself in a karate stance beside the door, wishing she was wearing more substantial shoes than some flimsy beach thongs. But it was only Tammy.

Walking into the room, she took one look around, her mouth fell open, and her eyes bugged. "Wow! You're a messy roommate," she said, gazing at the chaos. "What on earth happened?"

Savannah sighed and sank onto the bare bed, suddenly feeling the fatigue of the day overwhelm her. "Sorry," she said, "but I guess I just got carried away with the unpacking. I couldn't find my toothbrush."

CHAPTER EIGHT

"I'm scared, Savannah." Tammy sat on the edge of her bed, her hands clasped tightly in front of her, and from the look on her face, Savannah knew she wasn't kidding. "I mean, this is just too spooky. Kat dies like that, and then somebody's watching you from the bushes and now this." She waved her hand, indicating the tornado-struck room. "What are we going to do?"

"I'm calling Dirk," Savannah said, retrieving her cell phone from the heap.

"Oh, good. You're going to ask him to come out here?"

Savannah laughed. "You *must* be scared, if you want me to bring 'dumb old Dirk' to the rescue."

Tammy made a face. "You know what I mean . . . any cop would do."

"We can't call the cops, kiddo. The last thing we want is to draw attention to ourselves. Lou Hanks was all over me today because he thought I was here investigating for Kat's life-insurance company."

"Oh, that's what he wanted with you. I was wondering. So, he had a policy on Kat?"

"Seems so."

"Hmmm."

"My feelings exactly."

Savannah punched in some numbers and waited until Dirk finally answered. "Sorry," she said, "did I interrupt *I Love Lucy?*"

She couldn't help teasing the rough, tough cop about his favorite television show.

"No," he barked. "I was on the john. What do you want?"

"I'm here at Royal Palms getting—"

"Slim and trim?"

"No. Stalked and vandalized. I need you to run a few checks for me: Louis Hanks, the owner of this fine establishment, Dr. Freeman Ross, the spa's physician, Josef Orlet, the resident masseur . . . and, what the hell, Dion Zeller, too. Might as well be thorough."

"Is that enough? Isn't there anything else you'd like me to do for you?"

She heard the sarcasm in his voice, but decided to ignore it. After all, she had stood on street corners in four-inch heels for him. This wouldn't kill him.

"Yes, that's all. Unless you can smuggle me in some Ben and Jerry's Cherry Garcia." She intercepted a horrified look of indignation from Tammy. "Never mind. I'll just suffer . . . in the name of purification."

The instant, radiant smile on Tammy's face was her payment for exercising discipline, she decided as she hung up the phone. Virtue was its own reward.

Besides, there was always the box of truffles in the lining of her suitcase.

"I feel raped and violated."

At first, Savannah wasn't sure she had heard the words correctly. She had just begun to drift off into an uneasy sleep when Tammy spoke to her from the other bed.

"What?"

"I do. I feel raped and violated. Just to think that someone was here in our room while we were gone. And they threw our clothes all around and dumped them on the floor and . . . and *touched* them."

Savannah opened her mouth to say something, then thought better of it and closed it. In her line of work, she had seen rape and violation, the real thing. At least she and Tammy had been fortunate enough not to have been inside those clothes when they were thrown around and dumped on the floor.

But she didn't want to diminish Tammy's sense of outrage; the act *had* been one of violation, and she was entitled to her anger.

"Do you know what I mean?" Tammy continued. "I feel as if I should wash all my clothes before I even touch them, like they've been contaminated or something."

"Yes, I know what you mean. We'll find out who did it."

"Really? Do you really think so?"

"Yeah . . . well . . . maybe."

"Do you think it was the same person who killed Kat?"

Savannah rolled onto her side. In the darkness, she could just make out Tammy's silhouette. "In the first place, we still don't know for sure if someone murdered Kat. And whether or not he's the one who tore up our room . . . there's no way to know that either right now."

"But having someone search our stuff that way makes it seem like maybe she *was* murdered. Don't you think?"

"Maybe."

Savannah heard Tammy snort with frustration as she flounced about on the bed.

"Well, I don't like not knowing," she said.

Savannah laughed. "Me either, that's why we're investigating. That, and because it's why we get paid the big bucks."

"We get paid big bucks?"

"Right now, with my personal economy . . . any bucks at all are big ones."

"I hear you. Well, I was trying to earn mine today. I was asking questions, here and there, doing a little detecting on my own."

Uh, oh, Savannah thought. *This could spell trouble.* "Oh, really? You have to be careful, you know. If we ask too many questions or talk to the wrong people, we could tip our hand before we're ready."

"Savannah! I know that! Geez . . . I'm not a bimbo. I was just 'gossiping' with people, like I would anyway, even if I wasn't detecting."

"Oh, okay. So, what's on the grapevine?"

"Some of the workers think she might have been murdered, too. They're pretty nervous. A couple of them won't go into the mud baths alone."

"That sounds sensible."

"And I talked to Karen quite a while. She's the nutritionist that you met the first day, when you came to see Kat's body. She said Kat was sick before she died. Like, maybe *really* sick."

"Yeah? Why did she think that?"

"She said she overheard Kat talking to Dr. Ross, just a few days before she died. They were arguing about something. Seems Dr. Ross wanted her to go to a specialist to get checked out for some kind of surgery. But she wouldn't do it. Said she'd rather die first."

Savannah sat up in bed. "Tammy! Why didn't you tell me this earlier? That's important."

"It is? Oh, cool."

Suddenly energized, Savannah bounded out of bed and began to throw on jeans and a dark sweatshirt.

"What are you doing?" Tammy asked.

"Getting dressed."

"It's after midnight."

"I know. That's the best time to do a B&E."

"What's that? Are you sneaking out for junk food after promising me you wouldn't."

"No, ding-a-ling, B&E stands for 'Breaking and Entering.' It's a crime."

"You mean, like burglary?"

"Not exactly. I'm not going to steal anything . . . at least, I'm not planning on it." She tossed Tammy some clothes. "Shake a leg, kiddo. You're coming with me."

"But I've never broken any laws before."

"Then it's high time, Miss Pollyanna, that you lost your

virginity." She snickered. "Trust me, it's fun. Unless, of course, we get caught."

"This *is* fun," Tammy whispered as they crept from shadow to shadow, cutting a circuitous path between the dark, silent buildings. "It's sorta like playing Nancy Drew."

"That's why I became a cop." Savannah pulled Tammy between a couple of cars, where they crouched and waited for a night watchman to pass by.

"Because you got to do this sort of thing all the time?" Tammy asked when he disappeared around the corner of one of the bathhouses.

"No, because I *thought* I was going to get to do this sort of thing. Mostly, I tossed a lot of drunks out of bars, broke up domestic disputes, and hauled runaway kids back to homes where they didn't want to be. Exciting stuff like that."

"But now that you're a private detective . . . ?"

"Now I can break the laws I once swore to uphold. Far more liberating, to be sure."

She grabbed Tammy by the forearm and pulled her toward the building that was their destination. Set away from the others, the small cottage was where she had received her medical examination the day before from Dr. Freeman Ross.

"The clinic?" Tammy asked, as they ducked behind some fragrant star jasmine at the side of the building.

"That's right."

"But if we're going to break into somebody's place, shouldn't it be Kat's?"

"I already tried earlier today. She was still living with Lou, and he's got the place locked up tighter than a Sunday-Go-To-Meetin' girdle. Is there a back door to this place?"

"No, just the one in front."

"Shoot. Okay, we'll have to do it out in the open and hope nobody walks by."

"Do what?"

"Pick the lock."

"You know how to do that?" Tammy sounded simultaneously scandalized and impressed.

"I most certainly do. And one of these days, I'll teach you how, too."

"Cool."

Savannah paused and gave her a scornful look. "Cool? Is that your favorite adjective these days?"

"It's better than the one your generation uses. You guys say, 'Neat.' Now *that's* lame."

"What do you mean *my* generation? We're the same generation."

"No way. You're old enough to be my mother."

"No way. How old are you?"

"Twenty-four."

Savannah did the math. Forty-something minus twenty-four. "Not unless I got a really early start. Now, are you going to help me break into this clinic or not?"

"Sure . . . Mom. Lead the way."

With a foot to Tammy's diminutive rear, Savannah gave her a shove, pushing her out from behind the jasmine and onto the walkway leading to the cottage.

A study in nonchalance, they strolled to the front door

of the clinic, paused, and glanced around. The only movement on the grounds was the drifting wisps of sea fog that had made their way from the beach to the top of the hill.

They listened intently, but all they heard were some crickets, a few frogs, and a coyote yipping in the distance.

"Keep your eyes open," Savannah said, before she took her lockpick from her pocket and slipped it into the keyhole.

She jiggled it around, feeling for just the right combinations of pressure and release before she heard the pleasant sound of tumblers falling into place.

"Open sesame," she muttered, and gave the door a push.

A second later, she and Tammy were inside the small office, where she had sat, shivering in her blue paper gown thirty-six hours before. It looked different in the dark.

She promptly smacked her shin on the doctor's stool and sent it skidding across the room.

"Oww . . . shit. Tammy, where's that flashlight?"

"Flashlight? What flashlight? I thought *you* brought it."

"No, I brought the lockpick and my finely honed expertise. *You* were supposed to bring the flashlight. Remember? I handed you the one by my bed . . . the one I keep in case of earthquakes."

"Oh, yeah . . . you did say something about the earthquake; that rings a bell."

Savannah sighed. "I don't call you a ding-a-ling for nothing."

"Sorry, I was just all nervous about the idea of breaking into someplace that I—"

"Don't worry about it. But we can't turn the light on or we'll get busted. And we have to find something to read by. . . ."

She fumbled around in the dark for a moment, trying to remember where the doctor had laid his instruments after examining her. "Pay dirt! Instant flashlight!"

"What is that?" Tammy squinted as Savannah shone the narrow beam of light into her face.

"The gadget the doc uses to look into your ears. Here, you hold it."

"Yuck. It probably has ear wax on it."

"I sincerely doubt that, but take it anyway." She shoved it into her hand. "Some partner in crime you're turning out to be. First you forget the equipment and then you turn squeamish on me."

"Hey, I didn't barf during that autopsy."

"True. I guess you get points for that."

Hurrying over to the file cabinet, she dragged Tammy along. "Oh, goody. More locks," she said as she tried to open the drawer labeled U-V-W-X-Y-Z.

Although this lock was stiff and not as cooperative as the door, she finally got it open. Tammy held the light as she located the file in question.

"Valentina, Katherina," she said as she pulled it out.

Sitting on the floor, she spread the papers across the carpet, and Tammy directed the pinpoint beam.

"Don't you feel a little guilty doing this?" Tammy asked.

"Doing what?" Savannah took the light from Tammy and quickly scanned the forms, one by one.

"Reading Kat's private medical file, when she's . . . you know . . . dead."

"That's just the point, Tammy. She's dead. Taking that into consideration, I sincerely doubt she gives a damn."

Tammy's silence was Savannah's cue that, perhaps, she had been a wee bit insensitive.

"Sorry," she said. "But I guess what I'm trying to say is: I figure the end justifies the means. If Kat was murdered, she deserves justice. And if I have to violate her privacy to get it for her, so be it. How's that?"

"Much better."

"Good. Hey . . . I think we've got something here."

The medical terms were only so much gibberish, but even without an M.D. after her name, Savannah could understand enough to know just how sick Kat Valentina had really been before her death. And Dr. Ross's handwritten notes had left no doubts about his feelings on the subject.

"You were right." She slowly closed the folder and returned it to the cabinet. "Kat *was* sick."

"What was wrong with her?"

How ironic, Savannah thought as she relocked the metal cabinet. Kat Valentina had been the subject of so many male fantasies over the years, and one of her most famous assets had been her generous bustline.

"What was it, Savannah?" Tammy asked again. "What did it say?"

"It says she had a tumor in her left breast."

"Cancer? Kat had breast cancer?"

"They didn't know if it was malignant or not. According to Dr. Freeman's notes, she wouldn't let them biopsy it to find out."

"But why not? If it was cancer, they needed to know so they could . . ."

Savannah could tell by the tone of Tammy's voice that they were thinking the same thing.

Tammy's friend and idol had been so vain that she had

chosen to risk death rather than have her famous body disfigured by surgery.

"Let's go, sweetie," she told Tammy as she gently guided her back to the door. "I'm afraid we found out what we needed to know."

CHAPTER NINE

As Savannah led Tammy out of the clinic and back along the shadowed path they had come, she wondered if "knowing the truth" was all it was cracked up to be. Sometimes, ignorance *was* a blissful, dark, cavelike refuge where one could hide from the blinding light of knowledge.

Judging from the painful silence radiating from her young friend, Savannah decided this had been one of those times.

The problem with "knowing" was that you couldn't "unknow" it. Tammy's image of her glamorous friend would never be the same again. It was one thing to think your idol had died of a tragic accident, but quite another to believe she took her own life.

So much for enlightenment.

"Are you okay, Tam?" she whispered, as they crept along behind the oleander bushes that lined one side of the pool.

"Yeah, I guess so. I just don't understand why—"

"Quiet! Listen."

Savannah grabbed Tammy's shoulder and held her still, straining to hear.

Voices . . . a man's and a woman's . . . coming from the pool area. The woman sounded as though she were in distress.

Or maybe not, Savannah decided when the female uttered another, "Oh, God . . . oh, oh . . ."

"What is it?" Tammy whispered, her lips next to Savannah's ear.

"No big deal. Somebody's making it in the pool."

"Making . . . ? Oh, right." Tammy stood on tiptoe and tried to look over the oleanders. "Who is it?"

Savannah yanked her back down by her sleeve. "It's none of our business. *Now* who's violating people's privacy."

"Yeah, but I want to know . . ." She shook off Savannah's restraining hand and did a little hop, again trying to see over.

"Tammy, mind your manners. Let's go."

She hopped again, a bit higher. "It's Lou! Hey, Savannah, it's Lou and Bernadette."

"That scrawny, self-righteous redhead who checked me in?"

"Yeah. Wow . . . who would have thought that Lou and Bernadette . . . ?"

"Ehhh, who cares? They deserve each other. Come on."

Savannah was about to grab Tammy by the scruff of the neck and drag her away, when she noticed a change in the couple's tone. Apparently, the sex was over, and they were discussing some contentious subject.

"It does *too* matter," she was saying in a tearful, angry voice. "Kat's dead now. That changes everything."

Tammy gasped. Savannah reached over and put her hand across her mouth. "Sh-h-h-h."

"Nothing's changed," they heard him say. "Not between us, anyway. I told you before, I'm not going to marry *anybody*, ever again."

"But you said you loved me."

"What's that got to do with it?"

"If you love somebody, you marry them."

"Only in fairy tales, Bernadette. Get real."

"But you *promised*."

"I promised you a job. You've got it. I don't know what you're bitching about."

Tammy leaned closer to Savannah. "That scumbag! I have a half a mind to go out there and tell him what I think of him."

"You will not! Shut up and listen!"

"But the only reason I wanted the job . . ." Bernadette continued between sobs, ". . . was so I could be close to you."

"So, you're close to me." He gave a nasty little chuckle. "How much closer can you get than what we just did, huh?"

"That's not what I mean, and you know it. You said you couldn't marry me because of Kat. You even said once that you'd be happier if she wasn't around."

"I never said that!"

"Yes, you did. And I thought that since Kat was dead, you'd . . . oh, God . . . you really are a jerk. You've just been using me."

They heard a vigorous splashing of water. Bernadette was leaving the pool in a huff. A second later, wet, splatting footsteps came their way. They pressed into the oleander as Bernadette exited the pool area only a few feet from them. She had a beach towel wrapped tightly around her and a miserable look on her pretty, young face.

"You didn't seem to mind getting used a few minutes ago," Lou called after her.

"Go to hell!" she yelled back as she stomped down the path toward the employees' dormitory.

Savannah and Tammy listened intently as Lou climbed out of the pool, dried off, and left. Thankfully, in the opposite direction.

Tammy turned to Savannah, her eyes wide and shining with excitement by the faint, blue-green glow of the pool lights. "Now *that* was interesting!" she said. "I'm starting to like this Nancy Drew routine."

"No kidding," Savannah replied thoughtfully. "I'll have Dirk add little Miss Bernadette to his list of suspects to check out."

"Ow-w-w-www! Ouch! The pain! Oooo-o-o-o . . . the pain!" Right in the middle of her jumping jack, Savannah dropped to the ground, clutched her ankle, and began wailing.

The small class of five students, with Dion the Magnificent instructing, halted their first-thing-in-the-morning workout and stood, stunned and silent, watching her writhe in apparent agony.

Dion and Tammy were the first to snap out of it and hurry to her aid.

"Are you faking this?" Tammy hissed in her ear. "Because if you are, I have to tell you, I'm very disappointed in—"

"Savannah!" Dion knelt by her side. "What's wrong?"

"I think I pulled something," she said through gritted teeth. "My ankle . . . shooting pains . . . o-o-o-o, it hurts!"

He peeled down her sock and studied the appointed ankle. "Really?" he said.

"Of course, really." She gave an indignant snort. "Do you think I'd lie about a thing like that, just to keep from getting up in the middle of the night and coming out here to jump, push up, squat, and thrust with you fools?"

He cleared his throat and gave her a devilish grin. "It wouldn't be the first time."

"Well, if I say my ankle's sprained, it's sprained, dammit. Now I wanna see the doctor."

She glanced over at Tammy, who seemed to be wearing a new look of awareness.

"Yeah, I think we'd better have Dr. Ross examine her," Tammy told Dion with great gravity. "She slipped on a snow-cone wrapper and fell in a Kmart, and she sued their asses off. She won, too."

"Okay, okay. Can you walk?" he asked, pulling Savannah gently to her feet.

She felt his arms, hard and muscular around her waist. Sliding her hand along his equally developed shoulders, Savannah gave him a deep-dimple smile and donned her silkiest Southern accent. "Why, I don't believe I can. I'm afraid you're just going to have to carry me."

Thrown over his shoulder, like a sack of potatoes wasn't what Savannah had in mind, when she suggested Dion transport her to the clinic. By the time he got her there, so much blood had rushed to her head that she felt like her face was going to explode.

"Gee, thanks," she told him, as he deposited her at the

front door and left with some murmured excuse about having to continue the exercise session with the others.

Dr. Ross arrived moments later, his wavy, dark hair boyishly mussed, his shirttail half-out. He looked deliciously bedraggled.

"I see not *everybody* around here gets up at the crack of dawn," she said dryly. "I guess you reserve that privilege for your guests."

"Of course. Who, in his right mind, would want to get up at this ungodly hour and jump around like a lunatic? That *is* how you hurt yourself, isn't it?"

"Oh, yeah," she said, remembering her supposed injury. "I think it was that last jumping jack that put me over the edge."

He unlocked the front door—quickly, because *he* had a *real* key—offered her a supportive shoulder, and guided her inside the clinic, where she had been only a few hours before.

"Let's set you down right over here," he said, leading her to the examination table. "And we'll have a look at you."

He flipped on an overhead light, then walked by the counter where his instruments were laid in tidy rows.

Except for his ear thingamabob, she thought as she spotted it, lying crooked and on top of his tongue depressor thingamajigs . . . just where she and Tammy had left it.

He noticed, too. He paused beside the counter, looked puzzled and maybe a little irritated, then straightened the arrangement to his liking.

A second later, he seemed to have forgotten all about it, his attention fully on her. She breathed an inward sigh of relief.

"A wayward jumping jack, you say?" He grabbed his stool, rolled it over to the table where she was, and sat down on it.

"Yep. That was the culprit."

"Would you say it's more of a throb or a sting?"

Was this a trick question? The mercury in her paranoia thermometer rose.

"Maybe a bit of both."

"A bit?"

"Okay, a lot . . . of both, that is."

"Sounds serious. We may have to amputate."

"How about if you just write me a note, excusing me from P.E. class for about a week while it heals?"

He gave her a searching look with those great eyes that were the same rich amber as his tortoiseshell glasses. She felt herself melting. In fact, if he kept holding her ankle like that and looking at her that way, she might just turn into a big, warm, wet puddle right there on his examination table.

"Is that what you want from me, Savannah?" he asked, every word, every syllable, dripping with sexual innuendo. Or was it just her hormone-stimulated imagination? It was hard to tell. "You want me to write you a note to get you out of class?"

"Oh, Doctor," she said, leaning toward him, her eyes trained on his full, sensitive-looking lips. "I do want that from you. I do."

"You do?"

"More than life itself."

"Okay. No problem."

"No problem? That's it? That's all?"

"You got it. One note, coming up."

Savannah waited until she had the precious bit of paper in her hand before she ventured onto more dangerous ground.

"By the way," she said as she walked toward the door, remembering halfway across the floor that she should be limping.

"Yes?" He paused from scribbling on her chart and looked up at her expectantly. "You need a note to excuse you from drinking the green guck every morning, too?"

"Wow, could you do that?"

"No. The green guck is mandatory."

"Oh . . . then maybe you could just squelch a rumor that's going around the spa."

"Which one?"

"That Kat's death wasn't an accident. That she killed herself because she had breast cancer and didn't want to have surgery."

There.

A direct, unexpected jab to his solar plexus wouldn't have garnered more spectacular results. His breath left him in a gasp and his face went a deathly shade of pale.

She seldom used the "Hit 'Em Hard and Watch What Happens" technique. Mostly, because it ended a conversation so abruptly, and you couldn't get anything more out of your subject.

But she had seen Dirk use it numerous times, when all he needed was one good, solid, honest reaction. Observing the victim during the five seconds after the blow could often tell you what you wanted to know.

Slowly, the color began to return to his face, but she could see his hands tremble as he clutched his pen in a tight fist.

Finally, he found his breath and his voice. "I haven't heard that rumor, Ms. Reid," he said, each word clipped and deliberate. "But if I do hear it, I'll tell the gossipmonger that it's none of his ... or her ... damned business."

She gave him her cheeriest, most nonchalant smile. "You're absolutely right, Doctor. And the next time I hear it, I'll tell him ... or her ... the same thing. Thanks for the note."

She hurried out the door and closed it firmly behind her. One of the most important parts of the "Hit 'Em, Watch 'Em" game was to get the hell out of Dodge as quickly as possible before physical violence could erupt.

But her little doctor's visit had been a smashing success. She had a note to keep her out of that damned exercise class. And she had a new bit of information for her mental notebook:

Dr. Freeman Ross believed Kat Valentina had died at her own hand. Either that ... or he had helped her along.

There was no other reason for a man to turn *that* white.

CHAPTER TEN

Savannah had only gone a few yards along the trail when she heard, "Hey, Savannah, wait up!"

Turning around, she saw Tammy, running toward her from the pool area, waving her arms to get her attention. So much for a quiet, solitary walk among the daisies.

Tammy was wearing a tiny, hot pink bikini and beach sandals and had a Pocahontas towel draped around her shoulders. But, dressed for a nature hike or not, she seemed determined to tag along.

"How's your . . . ah . . . ankle?" Tammy asked when she caught up to her.

"My ankle? Oh, yeah, it's better."

"It must be, if you're going for a hike."

Savannah glanced around, but the only other living beings

in sight were some crows in a nearby oak, and a small, brown lizard, sunning itself on a rock.

Hopefully, she was still out of telescopic view from the nosy neighbor in the bell tower. "Actually," she said, "I was coming up here to make a private phone call."

"A phone call?"

Savannah pulled the cellular unit from her sweatpants pocket. "Thought I'd call Dirk and see if he's finished running those names for me."

"Oh. Do you want to be alone so you can talk dirty to dumb ol' Dirk?"

Savannah gave her a searching look to see if she was serious. But she couldn't tell for sure.

"I don't talk dirty to Dirk, dumb, old, or otherwise."

Tammy fell into step beside Savannah, her sandals slapping her feet as they walked along, kicking up twin puffs of dust.

"Are you telling me . . ." Tammy said with a mischievous grin, "that you and Dirk never . . . you know . . ."

Savannah laughed. "Why Tammy Hart, I'm shocked that you would even suggest such a thing."

"Is that a 'no'?"

"It's a 'it's none of your business what I've done with whom.'"

"That's a 'yes'! You've done it! You've done the nasty thing with Dirk! How revolting!"

Savannah gouged her in the ribs with her elbow. "Just think of Dirk and me as being like Marshal Dillon and Miss Kitty. Maybe they do; maybe they don't. It's sort of a mystery."

"Marshall who?"

Savannah groaned. "Oh, God. I feel so old."

"At least you aren't old and crippled, like you were this morning. Boy, talk about a cheap trick just to get out of some exercises."

"I needed to talk to Dr. Ross."

"You could have made an appointment *after* exercise class."

"Golly gee, I didn't think of that. Oh, well . . ."

They followed the trail that Dion had led Savannah on the day before. But it was much hotter today, and without Dion jogging along before her, Savannah didn't feel the need to run. A simple walk or even meander would do.

Tammy looked a bit out of place on the hike, wearing her bathing attire, but she didn't seem to care. She stared at the ground as they trudged along, seemingly lost in thought. "So, why did you need to talk to Dr. Ross?" she asked.

"I wanted to ask him about what we found in Kat's file last night."

"My God! You didn't tell him that we—"

"No, of course not. I told him there was a rumor going around that it was a suicide."

"You told him that outright?"

"Yeap. Sometimes that's the best way."

"And what did he say?"

"He believes it. Of course, he didn't actually admit it, but it was obvious."

"What do you mean, it was obvious?"

"He looked about like you did at the autopsy the other day."

Tammy flushed with humiliation at the recollection. "Oh . . . that bad?"

"Maybe a little worse. I think he really cared about Kat. I'm sure it wasn't easy for him to lose her that way."

Stopping in the middle of the path, Tammy lowered herself onto a rock. For a long time, she sat with her hands covering her face. Then she said, "I called the American Cancer Society today, Savannah. I talked to a nice lady on the phone for quite a while. You know, if they catch breast cancer in time, there's a really good chance of curing it. Kat probably didn't have to die."

Savannah sat on the rock next to her and wrapped her arm around her shoulders. "I know. I'm sorry, Tammy."

Tears flooded her eyes. "Why do you suppose she didn't take care of herself?"

"I don't know. The file said that her mother and sister both died of breast cancer. Maybe she thought there was no hope."

"There's always hope. *I* never would have given up like that."

She broke down and began to sob. Savannah pulled her closer and let her bury her face against her shoulder. Patting her glossy blond hair, she said, "I know you wouldn't have. But maybe you're a stronger person than Kat was."

"*Me?* Stronger than Kat?" Tammy pulled back and looked up at her with eyes filled with wonder at the very idea.

"Sure. I wouldn't be at all surprised. From what I've heard about Kat, she had more bravado than courage. And I know you well enough to say that you're a very strong woman."

Tammy wiped her eyes with the corner of her towel and sniffed. "Thanks for saying that. But sometimes I don't even feel like a woman. I feel like a kid."

"Well, join the club. We all feel that way once in a while.

Sometimes, when I'm getting ready to go out, putting on makeup, a nice dinner dress, and high heels, I half expect my granny Reid to barge through the door and scold me for playing dress-up with her stuff."

Tammy grinned and nodded. "I felt that way when I got my own apartment. I kept expecting my mom and dad to come home unexpectedly and bust me for pretending to be a grown-up."

They laughed, then shared a companionable moment of silence together. In the distance, a pair of doves cooed to each other, and a dragonfly floated by on lacy, iridescent wings. A slight breeze stirred the daisies and spread their wild scent.

"It's nice up here," Tammy said. "It's nice talking to you, Savannah. You're sorta like the big sister I never had."

"Big sister . . . yeah, that's me all right." She felt a pang of longing for her eight younger siblings in Georgia. But the sadness was short-lived, followed by a sense of relief that they were all adults now and on their own . . . at least in theory.

She pulled the phone out of her pocket again and punched some buttons. "Time to check in with Dirk and see what he's got for us, if anything."

It took five rings before the familiar, grumpy male voice mumbled, "Coulter here."

"Hi, Coulter here. Reid here. Whatcha doin'?"

"Staring at a green computer screen, going cross-eyed, getting the information that *you* asked for. You'd damned well better appreciate this."

"I know, I know . . . I'll owe you free apple fritters and ham sandwiches for the rest of your unnatural life." She made a face at Tammy, who giggled and held her ear close to the phone so that she could hear.

"I get ham *and cheese*," he said.

"That depends on what you've got for me."

"Oh, I think you're gonna like what you hear. Several interesting possibilities: Louis Hanks is in deep financial trouble. Seems Kat was practically throwing money away these past few months, got them into a helluva mess."

"Throwing it away . . . hmmm . . . like there was no tomorrow." She gave Tammy a sideways look, and she nodded solemnly.

"That's right," he continued. "Otherwise, Hanks is pretty clean. Dion Zeller—no record, no money, some hefty debts in the past, but he seems to be a good boy now. Bernadette Willis—your all-American cheerleader type, not even a traffic ticket."

"She's probably not old enough to drive," Savannah said dryly, still pissed about Bernadette's less-than-tactful body fat ratio references.

"Dr. Ross—no criminal record, but he's a bit controversial in the medical community. He's pretty outspoken about his belief in physician-assisted suicide."

"Really? Now that's interesting, because I'm beginning to think that might be what this was."

"Oh, yeah? Well, before you go too far down that road, here's something else you may want to think about. That massage guy, Josef Orlet . . ."

She waited anxiously, but Dirk held back, milking the moment for suspense, the way he always did when he had something good. She could feel Tammy's tension rising, too. Finally, she said, "All right, Coulter, spit it out."

"He's got a record."

"For what? Rubbing somebody the wrong way?"

"No. For harassing, and stalking, and attacking a young woman—an actress—about ten years ago."

"No way!"

She and Tammy traded knowing looks.

"He served seven years for it. I talked to one of his cellmates, and he says Orlet found a new sweetie while he was in the joint, someone new to focus his obsessions on."

"Let me guess . . . Kat Valentina?"

"That's right. Apparently he had her disco poster on his wall. Talked about her night and day. Told his cellmate that when he got out of the joint he was going to look her up, get close to her."

"Well, I'd say that her personal masseur is about as close as you can get."

"So . . ." She could hear the satisfaction in his voice. Dirk was pretty transparent; it was his greatest charm. You always knew what was going on inside his head. Not even a hint of mystery. "Did I earn my ham and cheese?" he asked.

"Oh, baby . . . you get ham, cheese, and a big ol' slap of dijon mustard."

He groaned. "Mmmm . . . I love it when you talk dirty."

"Shhhh, Tammy's listening in, and I told her that we don't do that sort of thing."

"Then she lied to you, Tammy," he said with a wicked laugh. "Me and Van . . . hell, we've done it *all*. She just won't admit—"

Savannah punched the red button once, effectively cutting him off. A few seconds later, the phone rang. Then again. And again.

"Aren't you going to answer that?" Tammy asked with a big grin plastered across her face.

"Nope." Savannah rose from the rock, dropped the phone into her pocket, and dusted off the seat of her pants.

Whistling a little tune, she strolled down the trail, heading back toward the spa with Tammy tripping along at her heels . . . and the phone still ringing in her pocket.

CHAPTER ELEVEN

As Savannah passed the recreation hall, the heavy bass beat of disco music reached out and pulled her backward twenty years. Instantly, she was in a world of slick, shining polyester, white suits, gold chains, poofed hair, and clichéd pickup lines.

Gee, those were the days. Thank goodness they're gone.

Deciding it would be a good night just to skip the tofu, bean-sprout dinner, she ventured into the hall to see if they were having some sort of disco cotillion. But the large room with its seating clusters, fireplace, Ping-Pong and air-hockey tables was unoccupied. Or so she thought, until she saw the big-screen television at the far end. One solitary figure sat on a worn leather sofa, watching *Disco Diva.*

It was Lou Hanks.

So involved was he with the dancing figures on the screen

that he didn't see her approach. While a younger—and Savannah had to admit, absolutely beautiful—Kat Valentina danced across a flashing, checkered floor with a stunning Dion Zeller, Lou watched with rapt attention. Tears flowed down his face. Occasionally, he dabbed at his nose with a wad of tissues.

Standing there, watching the famous dance sequence, Savannah could understand why the movie had become a cult classic. Although the plot was nonexistent and the acting dreadful, the choreography had been original and refreshing, and the moves blatantly sexual and provocatively executed by Kat and Dion.

They had been a magnetic couple, exuding sensuality with every graceful, seductive movement.

Around the world, women had watched and fallen hopelessly in love with Dion. And males from the ages of eight to eighty had lusted after Kat Valentina.

Obviously, the man sitting on the leather sofa had never gotten over her either. He seemed the total opposite of the callous jerk beside the pool with Bernadette the night before.

Long ago, Savannah had given up the notion of trying to figure people out. The human mind was simply too complex to be filed in a box labeled "Good" or "Bad."

Rather than intrude on his private moment, she turned to leave. But from the corner of his eye he saw her. He jumped, startled and more than a little embarrassed.

"I didn't mean to disturb you," she said. "I just heard the music and . . . well . . ."

He picked up the remote control and jabbed his thumb at one of the buttons, turning the volume down a few notches. "It's still pretty good, isn't it," he said, in between blowing his nose.

"Yes, it's wonderful. It brought back some memories."

"Good ones?"

"Some of them." She shrugged and laughed. "Sorry, but there were a lot of jerks on the scene at that time, with a lot of tired pickup lines."

"I know. I was one of them." He patted the sofa beside him. "Here, have a seat. I promise not to ask you about your sun sign."

She decided to join him, wondering again at the change in his demeanor. He seemed almost human. But then, looks could be deceiving. If nothing else, she had learned *that* during the disco era.

He pointed up to the screen, where Dion was twirling Kat around him, her full red skirt flying, showing her long, shapely legs to their best advantage.

"She was doing that the first time I saw her," Lou said as he reached into his pocket and pulled out pack of cigarettes. "It was in a disco on Forty-second Street in New York. I came in that night with another woman, but left with Kat."

Savannah recalled, years ago, having seen pictures of Kat Valentina in the tabloids with her manager/husband Lou Hanks. Lou had been the quintessential disco-scene hunk at that time—white suit and shoes, gaudy printed shirts unbuttoned nearly to his navel, and a zillion gold chains hanging low on his hairy chest.

Now, Lou the Disco King was an overweight, middle-aged nerd in a baggy golf shirt and plaid Bermuda shorts.

But on the front of those tabloids magazines, he had been gazing at his movie-star bride with adoration. And sitting on the old sofa, staring at her on a television screen, he wore the same love-besotted look.

"I fell hard for her," he said.

"I can imagine."

"She was the only thing I ever really cared about. This place ... everything ... it was all for her."

He took a deep pull on the cigarette, and Savannah wondered at the contradiction of the owner of a health spa smoking. "I had stopped," he said, as though reading her mind. "Drinking, too. Until, well, until this week. When ... it ... happened, I knew I was going to start one or the other. I figured smoking would get me in less trouble." He patted his ample belly. "And it has fewer calories."

Since Savannah wasn't sure what to say, she sat quietly and waited for him to continue. He seemed to want to unload; she was eager to listen and learn what she could.

"It wasn't all roses and light, you know," he said, hitting the fast-forward button on the remote. He advanced to the next dance number, then slowed it to normal speed and watched, still spellbound. "She was a spoiled brat. But I was the one who mostly spoiled her, so I guess it's my fault."

"It can be difficult when fame and fortune comes to someone so early in life," Savannah said.

"It didn't exactly 'come' to her," he said, his face flushing darkly as it had that day in Josef's massage room. "I worked my ass off for what we had—every bit of it—including that movie!"

The anger, the flip-switch change in his demeanor took her aback. This guy had a hair trigger.

"I'm sure you did. I understand you managed her career for years."

"I managed more than her career. I managed *Kat*. And it wasn't easy, either. She was the most immature, self-centered human being I've ever known. Thought she could do whatever she wanted to do, whenever she wanted, with anybody she wanted, and not pay any price."

Again, tabloid covers flashed through Savannah's mind. If even one-tenth of the press Kat had received over the years had been true, Lou would have had ample reason to be resentful.

"It must have been difficult," she said.

"It was hell. And when she got older and finally started to slow down when it came to the sexual stuff, she made up for it by spending money."

He took a long drag from his cigarette and released the smoke through his nose. "We were supposed to be partners in this spa. But she didn't do anything constructive around here, never even stuck her head in the office. Worse yet, she spent money right and left without consulting me, or even letting me know until I received the bills. Thanks to her, it was all I could do just to keep this ship afloat."

They sat, silently watching the movie for several long, tense minutes. Lou seemed embarrassed by his outburst. Savannah's mental cogs were spinning, processing the new information.

As the woman in the movie glided across the screen, a sensual vision wrapped in red, the hard, hostile expression on Lou's face began to soften. His eyes filled with tears again. He mashed his cigarette into the overloaded tray.

"But you loved her anyway," Savannah said. "Through it all, you never stopped."

The tears slipped from his eyes and dribbled down his cheeks. His double chin trembled like a little boy's.

"Of course I loved her," he said. He waved a hand toward the screen and the younger, softer version of the woman who had been his partner—for better, and apparently, a lot worse, for more than two decades.

"Just look at her," he said. "I couldn't help myself. We were all in love with Kat. And when the damned coroner finally releases her body, there's going to be a lot of hearts buried in that casket along with her . . . including mine."

Tammy grabbed Savannah the minute she walked through the door into their shared room.

"You aren't going to believe what I did!" she exclaimed, hopping up and down.

Savannah watched in amazement. Every molecule in Tammy's body seemed to zing with energy.

Oh, to be so young again, she thought. Then she reminded herself that she hadn't been that animated even at the age of eight.

"You're making me tired, just watching you," she said. "Stop bouncing around and tell me. . . . What did you do?"

"I broke into his room! I did it! I did a B&E. All by myself, too!"

"Good grief. I've created a monster—Tammy the Cat Burglar." She pulled her over to her bed and sat her down. "Now . . . whose room are we talking about?"

"Josef Orlet's!"

"You broke into Josef Orlet's room, after finding out that he has a prison record for stalking and assault?"

"Well, yeah! That's why I picked his room. He seemed the most likely to be a murderer."

Savannah stared at her, wondering at this convoluted "logic." Tammy was brilliant when it came to computers, modems, information highways ... things that totally confounded Savannah. But when it came to simple common sense, Savannah sometimes thought the young lady was two cream puffs short of a baker's dozen.

"Don't you *ever* do that again! Promise me, right now," Savannah said, using her bossiest oldest-sibling voice. "You could have gotten yourself hurt, or worse. Why, if he'd come back while you were there ..."

"Well, he *didn't* come back, because I was smart enough to wait until he had started giving a massage before I raided his room. Geez, Savannah, give me a little credit."

"All right, so you didn't get caught. But I still want you to promise that you won't try anything like that again without talking it over with me first."

"I'm not going to promise you any such thing. Do you want an assistant who thinks on her feet and takes initiative? Or do you want a mindless robot, who'll follow your every order without question and—"

"The robot! No doubt about it; I'll take the brain-dead robot. At least it won't take stupid chances and get its transistors shot out."

That did it. Tammy's lower lip protruded, and she began to huff and puff like an asthmatic Pekingese. "Okay," she said. "If what I did was so stupid, then I'm not going to tell you what cool, awful things I saw in his room."

"How cool?"

"Extremely cool."

"How awful?"

"*Awful* awful." She shuddered. "I was *totally* grossed out. Let's just say, the first thing I did when I left his room was find a sink and wash my hands."

"Tammy, you get grossed out over earthworms and fly droppings. I don't know if you're the most reliable judge of grossness."

"Okay, so I don't like creepy or crawly things. But, believe me, what I saw in there was a whole other category of gross."

"And you aren't going to tell me what it was?"

"Nope. Not until you take back the 'stupid' comment."

"Would you settle for 'less than wise'?"

Tammy considered that for a moment, grinned, and nodded. "I guess."

"So, what did you see? Was it really that good?"

"Yeah. Even better." She literally shivered with excitement, looking like a kid who was hoping for a new red bicycle on Christmas Eve. "Wanna be 'less than wise' and go check it out with me?"

"You're absolutely sure Lou Hanks gets a massage *every* evening at seven?" Savannah said as they stood outside the back window of Josef Orlet's apartment.

"Every evening for as long as I've worked here."

"Which has been . . . ?"

"About three months."

Three months wasn't long enough to put Savannah's mind completely at ease. Without the benefits of gun, badge, and backup, she found she was a lot less feisty about entering the residences of known violent criminals.

But then, if she'd had a badge, she would have had to get a search warrant, and she certainly didn't have enough legal cause for that. So, being a civilian wasn't without its advantages.

"How did you do this earlier?" she asked as she toyed with the window, trying to ease it upward.

"It was stiff at first, but I just gave it a good push . . . like this . . ."

Tammy grabbed the sill along with Savannah, they both shoved, and the window shot to the top with a resounding whack that sounded like a firecracker going off.

"Great!" Savannah whispered. "Now that we've alerted the whole complex—"

They waited to see if there would be any negative repercussions, but, if anyone had heard, thankfully, they weren't concerned enough to check it out.

"What's directly beneath the window?" Savannah asked as she tested her footing on top of a water meter near the ground.

"His bed."

With one hike, she raised herself to the sill and swung her leg inside.

"Hey, pretty good," Tammy remarked. "It took me three tries."

"You don't have to be a size zero to be light on your feet, you know," Savannah told her as she swung the other leg inside and stepped on Josef Orlet's unmade daybed.

She offered Tammy a hand up, then waited for her eyes to adjust to the semi-darkness of the room. It didn't take long for her to see that the small studio apartment was filthy.

"Not exactly Johnny Homemaker, is he?" she said as she

took in the piles of dirty, smelly dishes and empty food containers on the kitchen counter and the heaps of soiled laundry on the floor.

The television and VCR were practically buried in stacks of videotapes—obviously Orlet's favorite pastime. Most appeared to be the X-rated variety.

"Did I tell you it was gross, or what?" Tammy said.

Savannah had the unpleasant thought that Tammy might have persuaded her to break into Josef Orlet's apartment just to see what a lousy housekeeper he was.

"Yes, you did," she said. "But, I'm sorry to say it isn't that much worse than your all-American frat house apartment. Surely, that wasn't what you had in mind when you said—"

"No, of course not. I wanted you to have a look in that drawer." She pointed to a small chest in the far corner of the room.

"Which drawer?"

"The bottom one. The only one that's closed."

"Mmmm. It *is* the only one closed. Do you think that has significance?"

"Oh, I think so. If I were him, I wouldn't want anyone seeing what's inside."

Savannah walked over to the chest and knelt in front of it. With her fingers around the handles, she looked back over her shoulder at Tammy.

"I'm not going to find decomposing body parts in here, am I?"

"No. It isn't *that* gross, or I would have run out of here screaming." Tammy thought for a moment. "You haven't really opened drawers and found . . . that . . . have you?"

"I used to walk a beat in the tough part of Hollywood. You don't even want to know what I found in drawers, Dumpsters, alleys."

She pulled the drawer open, but the dim, evening light coming through the open window wasn't enough to see inside.

"Did you remember to bring the flashlight this time?" she asked Tammy.

Instantly, she produced it from the waistband of her shorts. "Don't ever say *I'm* beyond rehabilitation," she said, handing it to her with grand aplomb.

Savannah took it from her, switched it on, and shined the beam into the drawer.

"Ah, ha ... Kat Valentina memorabilia," she said as she studied the magazine clippings, newspaper articles, and hundreds of candid shots of Kat doing everything from sitting in a sauna, to taking a bath, to having sex with several individuals at once in a hot tub.

"It doesn't look like Kat posed for most of those," Tammy remarked, kneeling beside Savannah.

"No, I'm sure she didn't know they were being taken, or she would have smiled that famous, toothy grin of hers."

Tammy's silence told Savannah she didn't fully appreciate the joke.

Savannah pulled the drawer out farther and saw something that looked like a Barbie doll. But, pulling it out, she saw that it was larger, about fourteen inches tall, blond, and wore a shimmering red disco dress.

"They made Kat Valentina dolls?" Savannah asked.

"Yes, a few. Kat showed me hers. It was like that one ... well, without the ... alterations."

Savannah had just noticed what Tammy meant. Beneath

the full, red skirt, someone had made some rather vulgar changes to the doll's anatomy. Black pubic hair had been drawn with ink on the otherwise generic area, and some kind of sharp instrument had been used to gouge a ragged, pseudo-vagina.

"Cute. Josef should stick to playing with cars and trucks, like good little boys." She rummaged deeper into the drawer. "What have we here? Does Josef like to dress up in ladies' undies?"

She pulled out one of several satin-and-lace thongs that were buried beneath the photos.

"That's what I was referring to, when I said I washed my hands right away," Tammy told her. "I don't think he just *wears* them . . . if you know what I mean."

"How nice," Savannah said, dropping the panties as though they were crawling with vermin. "They're . . . um . . . crusty."

"Gross, huh?"

"Yes, my dear. That's definitely gross. They're also too small for Josef's rear end. I'd venture a guess that they were Kat's."

"You think he stole them from her?"

"Or she left them behind, here or elsewhere. I understand Kat wasn't averse to shedding her clothes wherever she got the urge."

Satisfied that she had uncovered enough of Josef's kinky habits to suit her purposes, Savannah slid the drawer closed.

"Ready to go wash your hands?" Tammy asked as Savannah handed her back the flashlight.

"Maybe a long, hot shower with some antibacterial soap

would be nice," Savannah replied, heading back toward the daybed and the open window.

But a second later, they heard a sound that made them freeze—a key in the door lock.

"Oh, great, he's back!" Savannah whispered. "The shit's gonna hit the fan now!"

CHAPTER TWELVE

Savannah knew she would have just enough time to vault through the window, but Orlet would have the door open before Tammy could make it. "Quick, under the bed!" she whispered as she yanked the window down.

They had just disappeared into the nest of dust bunnies beneath the daybed when the door swung open. Quarters were a bit tight, but both women were well hidden beneath the chenille bedspread that spilled onto the floor.

Tammy's face was to the wall, her back pressed tightly against Savannah's. Through a gap between the bedspread and a stack of dirty laundry, Savannah watched a pair of men's sneakers walk by on the way to the bathroom in the rear of the apartment.

He disappeared inside, and they heard the distinctive tinkling in the toilet.

"What are we going to do?" Tammy whispered.

With their backs pressed together, Savannah could feel Tammy's heart pounding and hear her breath coming hard and fast. "Sh-h-h . . ." she said. "Just be quiet and try to calm down, before you hyperventilate."

A moment later, the toilet flushed and Orlet returned to the main living area. They heard the refrigerator open, some bottles clink, then the door slam closed. The bottle cap rattled when it hit the countertop.

Savannah didn't know whether to be relieved or worried when he turned on the television and flipped to a baseball game. With the sound of the TV filling the room, they were less likely to be heard—just in case Tammy started to gasp for air or one of them inhaled a dust ball and sneezed. On the other hand, the sportscaster had just announced that it was only the third inning. So, she was afraid they might have to lie under the daybed until the Yankees won the pennant.

He walked over to the bed and plopped down on it so hard that a couple of the springs gouged into Savannah's hip. She stifled a yell but decided to get even with him as soon as possible. No two-bit pervert, whose idea of a good time was sexually mutilating fashion dolls, poked her and got away with it.

As two more innings played and Orlet guzzled more beer, Tammy lay so perfectly still that Savannah was afraid maybe she had passed out. Reaching for Tammy's hand, she found it and gave her what she hoped was a reassuring squeeze. The fingers that wrapped around hers were pretty clammy, but at least they squeezed back.

Savannah was just about to think they would be stuck through extra innings, when Orlet tossed his empty bottle onto the floor a few inches from her nose, walked over to the television, and switched it off.

She listened closely as he punched in some numbers on the telephone.

Please God, let him be making a date. Please, let him leave before our tailbones fuse and we become Siamese twins! Please, let—

"Yeah, it's me again," he said. "So, I gave you time to think about it. What's it gonna be?"

He fidgeted a while, listening, then said, "I'm glad you decided to be smart. You're buying yourself some good insurance."

Savannah felt her ears perk up like a cocker spaniel's. The coarseness of his voice, the nasty smile in his tone sounded as if he was doing business as Orlet, the ex-con, rather than the respected masseur. Somehow, she didn't believe he was a part-time representative for Mutual of Omaha.

"No, I haven't told anybody, and I won't," he said, "as long as you show up in ... say ... ten minutes in the rear parking lot. Yeah, that's right. Have it in an envelope. All of it."

Savannah had to resist doing a jig beneath the bed and giving away their position.

He was leaving! Better yet, *they* could leave! In less than ten minutes!

And, maybe best of all, he was pulling some sort of extortion scam on somebody. She didn't have to exercise much imagination to hope it might have something to do with Kat Valentina's death.

He paid another visit to the bathroom to get rid of some

recycled beer, then . . . finally . . . left, locking the door behind him.

"Did you hear that!" Tammy whispered as they crawled out from under the bed and flexed their cramped limbs. "Did you? He's blackmailing somebody!"

Savannah scrambled up onto the bed and raised the window. "That's what it sounded like." She sat on the sill and threw one leg over. "Get a move on, kid. Let's boogey out to the parking lot and see who it is."

"Are you starting to feel like you've lived most of your life in bushes?" Savannah asked, as she and Tammy crouched behind some azaleas at the edge of the rear parking lot.

"It's better than hiding under a bed with some ex-con swigging beer on top of you." Tammy sat down on the dew-damp ground, obviously too tired to squat.

From this dubious vantage point, they had a clear view of the area, which was lit with one halfhearted streetlamp. By its puny light they could see the comings and goings of anyone who decided to conduct a meeting in the middle of the asphalt.

So far, neither Josef Orlet nor his telephone companion had shown. And the appointed ten minutes had come and gone.

"Are you sure this is the only rear parking lot on the property?" Savannah asked, afraid they were cooling their heels in the azaleas for nothing.

"Sure I'm sure. I know my parking lots. This is it." She hesitated, thinking. "Unless it's that other one down there by the—"

"Oh, no. I knew it."

"Hey, shhhh. We've got company."

Tammy pointed to the opposite side of the lot, where Josef Orlet had just appeared, casually strolling around the perimeter as though he were simply taking the evening breeze.

He walked over beneath the streetlamp, looked at his watch, then glanced around. For a while, he stood there, tapping his foot, exuding impatience. Then he continued his border patrol.

He had made the circuit twice, when a second figure appeared, coming from the direction of the main complex.

Tammy tapped Savannah's shoulder and pointed. Savannah nodded that she, too, had seen the newcomer.

The two men met beside some parked cars, too far away for Savannah to hear what they were saying. But, by the light of the streetlamp, Savannah could clearly see the patrician features of the Royal Palms's resident physician.

"Dr. Ross?" Tammy whispered.

"Seems so. I was sorta hoping it would be somebody else," Savannah replied, recalling the doctor's gentle touch and kind bedside manner.

"Can you hear them?"

"Not a word. But he's handing Josef the envelope. He must have been the one we overheard him talking to on the phone."

As quickly as the doctor had appeared, he left. Soon, Josef followed, both men heading back toward the main complex.

"Well, that didn't take long," Tammy remarked as they left their screen of bushes.

"Doesn't take long to pay off a blackmailer," Savannah said. "At least not the first time."

"Do you think he'll come after him again and ask for more?"

"They often do."

"Poor Dr. Ross."

Savannah brushed the dirt off her knees, picked some leaves out of Tammy's hair, and decided it was time to go back to the room and have that nice, hot shower.

"Eh . . . don't feel too sorry for Dr. Ross," she told Tammy as they carefully chose their footing along the dark pathway of uneven stones that led back to their dormitory.

"Most people don't do business with extortionists unless they've got something to hide . . . usually a crime of their own."

"I wonder what crime Dr. Ross committed."

"That makes two of us."

Savannah waited until she was absolutely certain that Tammy was asleep before she slipped the cell phone out from under her pillow and punched in Dirk's number.

He sounded groggy when he answered and, therefore, even more grumpy than usual.

"Hi, it's me," she whispered, keeping an eye on Sleeping Beauty in the next bed.

"Whoopee," he replied without an ounce of enthusiasm.

"I'm gonna break out of this joint tonight. I've got a serious craving for a piece of cherry pie with a big scoop of ice cream."

She heard him yawn. "Go ahead. You have my blessing. I can't believe you've been there . . . what has it been . . . forty-eight hours now?"

"Don't get smart with me, buddy. Just meet me at the coffee shop on Agoura Road near the highway in half an hour."

"Only if I can put my finger in your pie."

She punched the off button.

Years ago, she had learned, it was the best way to handle Dirk when he was feeling feisty.

"Cute outfit," Dirk said as Savannah and her gray sweatsuit slid into the booth across from him.

"Up yours." She took a swig of the coffee he had thoughtfully already ordered for her. "It's the Royal Palms uniform. I think the idea is that we're supposed to be ready and eager to sweat out impurities at a moment's notice. They're very big on purification there."

"It would take them a lot longer than a week or two to get all the chocolate, pralines, and cream out of *your* arteries."

She toasted him with her coffee. "Here, here."

A sleepy, bored-looking waitress in a pink-and-white-striped uniform with ketchup stains strolled over to their table and took their orders: Savannah—cherry pie with a double scoop of vanilla, Dirk—a couple of donuts.

"Aren't you afraid of perpetuating a stereotype with the donut routine," Savannah asked.

"Nope. I'm not in uniform. The stereotype thing only counts if you're wearin' the blues."

Glancing around, Savannah decided they weren't likely to be pegged as cops by either of the other two customers, a biker dude in leather and chains, sitting at the snack bar, or the bag lady in the corner, who was sipping her token cup of coffee and having an animated conversation with her invisible companions.

The joint had passed its prime, which might have been in the mid-sixties. As with the spa, the Mediterranean look must have been "in" when the restaurant had last been decorated with heavy, wrought-iron light fixtures, black velvet paintings of matadors on the walls, and avocado green leatherette seats.

But the coffee was rich and fresh. And with the prospect of a real live dessert—sans the tofu—on the horizon, Savannah decided that life was temporarily worth living.

"So, did you just want somebody to pig out with tonight?" Dirk asked. "Or is there a real reason for you hauling me out of bed?"

"Gluttony loves company," she said. "But I also needed someone to talk to. Someone with a keen sense of the criminal mind, someone with years of experience under his belt, someone I respect and trust."

With every word, Dirk swelled like a toad sitting on the only lily in the pond. *How typically male*, she thought. He was just too easy.

The waitress set their sweets in front of them, and Savannah wasted no time digging in. "But since I didn't know anybody like that," she added around a mouthful of ice cream, "I called you."

"Gee, thanks. What have you got?"

"Don't know yet. It's been a busy twenty-four hours. So far, I've found out the following—Get out your little black book, Babycakes. You're gonna need to take notes."

Half an hour later, Dirk sat there, staring at his notebook, chewing on the end of his pen. The donuts and two more of their siblings had disappeared, along with Savannah's pie.

"So, which do you think it was, suicide or murder?" he said.

"Don't know yet. It may have even been an accident for

all I know, just like Dr. Jennifer said. But you have to admit, the other possibilities are intriguing."

"Who do you think ransacked your room?"

"I don't know who. I don't even know why."

"Then, why do you think Dr. Ross is paying off Orlet?"

Savannah shrugged. "I didn't say I had any answers for you. At the moment, I'm just collecting questions."

"I think you've got enough for the moment." He continued to scribble on the book, but Savannah took a peek and saw that he was doodling. He was up to no good.

"What's next?" she said.

"I think I'll bring Orlet into the station and put some pressure on him. I'll squeeze him like a ripe zit and see what pops."

Savannah gave him a deadpan stare. "Tammy's right. You *are* gross."

He was less than devastated at the insult. "I'll bring Orlet in about noon. You wanna watch from behind the one-way mirror?"

"But that's lunchtime. I'll miss the spa's alfalfa-sprout, shredded-carrot, and goat-cheese soufflé."

"We'll go out for a cheeseburger and fries afterward. Your treat."

"A chance to buy you food! I'll be there."

CHAPTER THIRTEEN

"Come on, Chicken Little, rise and shine," Tammy demanded, standing beside Savannah's bed, hands on her hips. "You're going to be late for early-morning exercises."

Savannah covered her head with a pillow and groaned. "Leave me alone. I didn't get to sleep until an hour ago."

She didn't dare tell Tammy she had sneaked out to meet Dirk. That would have eventually led to a discussion about cherry pie à la mode. Some things were better left unsaid.

"But you have to get your juices flowing."

"My juices are happy right where they are, thank you."

Tammy's lower lip protruded in a self-righteous pout. "Now, Savannah, how are you going to lose any weight while you're here if you don't go with the program?"

"What makes you think I want to lose weight?" She uncovered her head and glared, bleary-eyed at her assistant.

"Some of us actually like ourselves, whatever weight we are. And it isn't easy in a society that loves to make us feel as though our value as human beings in inversely proportional to our numbers on the scale."

"Well, I . . . I . . ." Tammy sputtered. "I didn't mean to imply that . . ."

"And you'd better not, either." She sighed and shook her head sadly. "Really, Tammy, I thought better of you. I truly believed you were more open-minded, more liberal with your thinking than that. I mean . . . to judge another human being on such a trivial, shallow, prejudicial—"

"No, please! I'm so, so sorry," Tammy exclaimed, nearly in tears. "I'll never . . . never . . . I . . ." She backed out of the room, her hands held high in surrender. Even after she closed the door behind her, Savannah could hear her apologizing on her way down the hall.

Savannah giggled and snuggled deeper between the sheets. *Ah, I'm good*, she thought. If there was anything Tammy was more proud of than her slender, fit body, it was her reputation as a bleeding-heart humanitarian.

The kid didn't have a prejudiced bone in her body. But, if making her think she did, bought Savannah some extra time in bed, it was all worthwhile.

Yes . . . she could luxuriate between the sheets for another hour, *and* she had made a morning person feel bad about crawling out of bed to exercise!

A *skinny* morning person . . . and that was the worst kind.

Yes, she *was* good. Very good, indeed.

An hour and a half later, a rare pang of conscience propelled Savannah out of bed and onto the hiking trails in the hills above the spa. It was still early morning, and she had plenty of time before her noon appointment to watch Dirk roast Josef Orlet's tri-tips on the station grill.

She figured if she took a little jaunt around the property, she could kill two birds with one jog: First, she could proudly announce to Tammy that she *had* gotten her exercise for the day. So there! And second, she might get another look at the neighboring estate. Anybody as nosy as Phoebe Chesterfield might have a few stories to tell.

As she neared the crest of the hill, Savannah saw a figure in a brightly colored, flowered dress moving along the wisteria-covered arbor. Although a large straw bonnet concealed the wearer's face, Savannah had a feeling she had found Miss Phoebe the Snoop.

Rather than alerting the old lady to her presence, Savannah waited until she was only a few yards away to hail her. No point in giving her getaway time.

"Hello, neighbor," she called, jogging across the lawn to the arbor. "I just dropped in to get acquainted."

Phoebe Chesterfield turned and stared at her, the look of shock as clear as the lines on her face. Apparently, she wasn't accustomed to being greeted in such an open, friendly manner.

"My name is Savannah Reid," she told her. "I'm a guest at the spa for a week or so. I suppose that makes us neighbors. I was just admiring your lovely garden. Do you do much of it yourself?"

There. She had delivered that with just the right amount of casual flippancy. At least, she hoped so.

But Phoebe just continued to stare at her with pale blue eyes the color of the bachelor's buttons that bloomed in profusion on the hill nearby. She had a delicate beauty about her, suggesting that she had been a handsome woman in her day. Clouds of silver hair cascaded freely down her back and around her shoulders. Her straw bonnet was tied with blue ribbons, the same shade as her eyes, and she had stuck a fresh daisy in its band. Like a lady from the Victorian era, she wore white gloves, and a wicker basket hung from one arm.

But the moment she opened her mouth, the fragile picture of gentility and charm disappeared. Her voice was as harsh as her appearance was refined.

"What are you doing on our property?" she demanded. "Didn't you see the No Trespassing signs?"

"Well, yes . . . I saw a couple. But I thought the spa had posted them. I thought I was still on Royal Palms property."

"You aren't! You're on Chesterfield land, and I'll thank you to leave right away, before I have my servants shoot you."

"That would be a bit drastic, don't you think? Isn't it enough that we've had one mysterious, violent death in the neighborhood this week?"

The pale blue eyes sparkled and her peaches-and-cream coloring heightened. One finely plucked eyebrow lifted a notch.

"Mysterious? Violent?"

Savannah laughed inwardly, congratulating herself on knowing how to bait a busybody.

"You mean you haven't heard what happened?"

Phoebe sniffed and tossed her head. "I heard that that good-for-nothing harlot, Kat Valentina, drowned herself in a tub of mud. A fitting end for the likes of her, I'd say, considering the filthy life she's led. But I didn't know there was anything mysterious about it . . . or violent. . . ."

She paused, and Savannah knew she was expected to fill

in the blank. She didn't. Let the old biddy stew in her own curiosity for a while.

"Oh, well . . ." Savannah said, turning as though to leave. "I don't want to bother you. I can see that you're busy and—"

"I'm not all that busy. I was just going to pick some roses for this evening's dinner table." She hesitated, then added, "You can hold this for me, if you like."

She held out her wicker basket, which was half-filled with cut flowers.

"I *would* like. Thank you."

Phoebe Chesterfield led her through the backyard, past the flowing fountains, a bronze sundial, garden gargoyles, and colorful beds of pansies, impatiens, lobelia, and marigolds.

"Do you do all the gardening yourself?" Savannah asked.

"I have a fellow who weeds and waters for me. But I do the rest. It keeps me off the streets and out of pool halls."

Savannah chuckled, but Phoebe kept a completely straight face. She had assumed the old lady was kidding.

What she wondered, but couldn't ask, was how Phoebe had time to tend the garden and still keep tabs on everyone from her telescope in the bell tower.

They passed an herb garden that scented the air with spearmint, lavender, and sage. "This reminds me of my granny Reid's yard," Savannah told her, allowing the sweet memories to flood over her. "She had a spearmint bush, too. Told me it was a chewing gum tree. When I was about four, I found sticks of spearmint gum 'growing ' from it."

"Humph."

From Phoebe's monosyllabic reply, Savannah didn't know

if she appreciated the childhood tale or not. "Do you have grandchildren of your own?"

"No. Neither my brother nor I has ever married," was the curt reply.

They entered the rose garden and Savannah was astonished at the beauty and variety of her collection. Against a backdrop of emerald rhododendron foliage Phoebe had a breathtaking display of deep scarlet blossoms mixed with equally elegant whites.

"Are those Mr. Lincolns and John F. Kennedys?" she asked, breathing in the honey-sweet fragrance of one full, snowy rose and its accompanying apple green buds.

"Yes, they are."

"What a wonderful idea, displaying them together like that. The effect is quite dramatic."

Phoebe smiled just enough for Savannah to know she had touched a chord with the woman through her garden.

"And is that a Fortune Teller?" she asked, pointing to a bush with unusual magenta flowers.

"Yes, it is."

"I thought so. I love that distinctive, lemony fragrance. And your Roselina is lovely. I don't think I've ever seen one so full." She waved a hand in the direction of a copper arbor laden with deep pink wild roses. "Do you use Epsom salts to balance the soil?"

"Yes, I do. And I feed each bush at least two banana peels, to enhance the mineral content."

"With excellent results, if I do say so myself."

Phoebe studied her quietly for a moment, and Savannah thought she saw a light of something that might be grudging respect in those pale blue eyes. "How do you know so much

about roses?" she said, snipping a perfect Moon Shadow bud
and laying the velvety lavender blossom carefully in the basket
Savannah was holding.

"My granny Reid taught me. She says you can always tell
a true lady by her love affair with roses."

"Humph." Phoebe gave Savannah a knowing sideways
glance and lowered her voice to a whisper. "And you can tell
a woman who *isn't* a lady by the other affairs she has . . . if
you know what I mean."

"I don't know for sure," Savannah said, adopting Phoebe's
conspiratorial tone. "But I have heard rumors."

"I've done more than heard. I've seen." She pointed to
the mission tower and its belfry.

"I'll bet you've seen a lot of things from up there," Savannah said, winking at her. "In fact, you could probably write a
book about what you've witnessed."

Assuming a pained expression, Phoebe nodded emphatically. "It hasn't been easy, living next door to all that debauch-
ery over the years. All the nakedness. The fornication. The
various and sundry iniquities."

"I can imagine." Savannah shook her head and clucked
her tongue.

"There have been times when I wondered why the earth
didn't just open and swallow them whole, like with Sodom
and Gomorrah."

Harking back to her Sunday school days, Savannah was
fairly certain that *hadn't* been the fate of Sodom or Gomorrah.
But she didn't think it conducive to argue theology with Miss
Chesterfield here in her rose garden. Instead, she decided to
lead the conversation gently to a more specific topic: Kat
Valentina.

"Well, it looks as though Justice had her way, after all," Savannah said, keeping her voice low and secretive . . . though from whom, she wasn't sure. They had only rosebushes for company. "Ms. Valentina *did* meet a pretty dreadful end."

"Oh, I don't think it was all that bad. Got drunk and passed out in a mud bath . . . that's what the paper said." Phoebe carefully chose and snipped another bud. "It was probably quick and painless."

"But she was so young. And then, there are all the rumors."

Again, the carefully plucked eyebrow twitched, registering the woman's interest, though Phoebe never took her eyes off her roses. "Oh, yes, you mentioned that before," she said offhandedly. "Exactly which rumors do you mean?"

"That she might have committed suicide . . . or that it might have even been murder."

This time both of Phoebe's eyebrows flew up. She didn't even pretend to be nonchalant. "Really? They're saying that? Who's saying that?"

Savannah shrugged. "Oh, they . . . a few people . . . here and there."

"What makes them think so?"

"I'm not sure. But they certainly have their suspicions. What do you think?"

"I think either suicide . . . or worse, is entirely possible. Kat Valentina was, pardon my language, an absolute strumpet, a woman of the very worst character. She even came after my brother Ford, you know, and him old enough to be her grandfather."

Savannah heard a sound, a rustling, behind her, and turned to see a dignified gentleman with the same thick, silver hair and pale blue eyes as Phoebe standing there. He wore a scowl on his handsome face as he walked closer to them. He was dressed in a gray sport shirt and charcoal slacks and looked remarkably fit for his sixty-plus or so years.

"Now Phoebe," he said. "If you're going to gossip about me behind my back, at least be sure of your facts. I might have been old enough to be Miss Valentina's father, but certainly not her grandfather."

Phoebe sniffed her disdain. "Grandfather, father . . . you still made a fool of yourself over that girl."

He gave his sister a sad, indulgent smile. "Maybe so, but I was in good company. I've been reading the articles about her in the paper since her death. It seems mine wasn't the only heart she snared."

Holding out his hand to Savannah, he said, "By the way, I'm Ford Chesterfield, the fool in question. And you are?"

She shook it and was surprised at the firmness and vitality of his touch. "I'm Savannah Reid," she replied. "A guest at the spa. I was out for a hike and saw your sister's beautiful garden."

"Yes, Phoebe has many talents . . . and far too many interests for her own good."

He gave his sister a pointed look, but she chose to ignore him, concentrating on her rose cutting.

Savannah weighed the advantages of hanging around and trying to get anything else out of Phoebe Chesterfield. It wasn't too likely, with her brother standing there. Obviously, he didn't approve of her "many interests." Their little gossip tête-à-tête seemed to have come to an abrupt ending.

"Well, I guess I'll continue with my hike," Savannah said, setting the basket filled with flowers on the ground at Phoebe's feet. "Thank you for sharing your gardening tips with me. I'll pass the banana peel suggestion on to my granny Reid."

Unexpectedly, Phoebe handed Savannah the Moon Shadow bud she had just cut. "Here," she said. "These dry nicely. Do that and then send it along to your very ladylike grandmother."

Savannah took the rose and for a moment her eyes met Phoebe's, and the two women connected. In that split second, Savannah decided that maybe Phoebe wasn't such a bad sort, after all. Nosy, yes. Judgmental, definitely.

But as Savannah wished Phoebe and her brother good day and headed down the hill, she decided that anybody who could grow a perfect Moon Shadow rose couldn't be all bad.

CHAPTER FOURTEEN

"Are you saying you want me to *lie* for you? Is that what you're telling me?" Tammy stood in the middle of their room, wearing a look of indignation.

Savannah wore only a towel. "That's exactly what I'm asking you to do."

She pulled some clean clothes from her suitcase and spread them on the bed. "I have to go into town and see Dirk, and you have to cover for me here. Tell them I have a migraine, that I'm sleeping it off."

"But you don't, and you aren't."

"So? What does that have to do with the price of Arkansas cotton?"

Tammy looked confused. "What does cotton have to do with this?"

Savannah sighed, feeling a depth of fatigue that had nothing to do with her morning hike through the daisies. "Tammy Lou ..." Tammy hated it when she called her that, which was precisely why she did. "Are you telling me that you never, never, ever tell a lie. Not even a little white fib?"

Tammy lifted her chin a couple of notches. "I live my life in such a way that I don't *do* things that I'm ashamed of, things that I would have to lie about to my fellow human beings."

Savannah stared at her for a long time, wondering whether to pin a gold medal to her chest or barf on her pink tennis shoes.

"Well, that's most commendable," she said. "And I agree with you, at least in principle. But this is business, and in the course of earning a living, we sometimes have to blacken our souls by uttering a falsehood. So, if you won't do it because I ask you to as a friend, then as your boss, I'm telling you to. Got it?"

"Oh, okay." She seemed enormously relieved. "No problem."

Savannah filed that one away for future consideration. Tammy's sliding scale of moral values was a never-ending source of amazement and amusement for her.

Tammy headed for the doorway, then turned around abruptly and fixed her with a suspicious eye. "Wait just a minute. This trip into town really *is* business, isn't it?" she said. "I mean ... you wouldn't just be sneaking off to get a big, gorpy dessert, or something disgusting like that, are you?"

"Tammy! I'm shocked."

"Bull pucky. You're going to do it. You're going to break your diet and forfeit all the good the spa has done for you. That's so sad, Savannah."

"Oh, Tammy, Tammy ... Ta-m-m-my. Don't worry. I promise not to consume a single calorie while I'm away from the Royal Palms Spa."

"Cross your heart?"

"And swear to swallow my bubble gum."

Tammy appeared mollified. "Good. See you later this afternoon."

After she had left the room and Savannah was getting dressed to go, she didn't feel the slightest twinge of guilt. The cheap burger place where Dirk would want to eat always microwaved their beef patties. And microwaving food removed every single smidgen of a calorie.

Hell, everybody knew that!

Whenever possible, Savannah avoided the San Carmelita Police Station, like some people avoided the old house where they had once lived with a much-beloved, much-despised ex-spouse. The place brought such bittersweet memories the moment she walked through the door.

Officer Kenny Bates, the day-shift desk clerk definitely fell into the "bitter" category. The term "greasy" referred to more than his thinning hair and bad skin. There were eight females on the S.C.P.D., and Bates had made it his life's ambition to do the Grizzly Bear Hump with every one of them. So far, his score was zero, but that didn't seem to dampen his enthusiasm.

"Hey, hey, hey, Sa-van-ahhh!" he exclaimed as she walked up to the desk. His eyes slid over her with the sexual appeal of a slimy slug. "Are we looking good today, or what?"

"Not we, Master Bates," she said coolly. "I look pretty

good. You, on the other hand, are as ugly as a warthog's backside."

He laughed, far too loudly, reminding her of a Georgia mule she had once known. "Wanna come over to my place tonight?" he said. "We can toss back some brewskies and watch TV. I get X-rated channels now . . . three of 'em."

"I'd rather have a mammogram . . ."

"I could order a pizza with lotsa meat."

". . . a barium enema, and a pap smear."

"Hey, kinky stuff! We could play doctor, too, if that's what you're into."

She glowered at him. "Hand me the damned clipboard, Bates, before I yank your tonsils out through your asshole."

He pushed the board across the desk to her. She jotted down her name and the time and shoved it back at him.

"So, is that a 'yes' or a 'no'?" he called after her as she hurried down the hall to the detectives' squad room.

Five minutes later, she was standing in a tiny room, hardly larger than a closet, watching through a one-way mirror as Dirk questioned Josef Orlet.

Sitting at a table in a straight-backed chair, with Dirk pacing the floor behind him, Orlet looked a lot less happy than Savannah had ever seen him. But then, she couldn't really blame him for his rotten mood. Being interrogated by Dirk Coulter wasn't exactly the bright spot in anyone's day.

"You keep giving me answers like that," Dirk was saying, "and you'll be renewing old acquaintances back in the joint. I understand some of your 'husbands' there in San Quentin are really missin' you."

"I told you, I don't know nothin' about Dr. Ross. I've

only talked to him a time or two . . . about one of the guests at the spa. That's all, man."

"And what if I told you that a couple of very credible witnesses overheard you blackmailing him?"

"They're lyin'."

"And they *saw* you accept the envelope full of dough from him. Does that make them blind, too?"

"Yeah . . . well, who are these witnesses?"

Standing behind Orlet, Dirk leaned over him, literally breathing down his neck. "Unlike you, they're responsible, law-abiding citizens. They're the sort of people that a jury believes. And that's all that's important to you right now, buddy. 'Cause this is going to be your third felony offense, which means you'll be goin' in forever."

Even from twelve feet away, behind the glass, Savannah could see Orlet sweating. He was furiously picking and biting at a hangnail on his thumb that was starting to bleed. Savannah made a mental note not to schedule any more massages with him.

She knew that Dirk was bluffing. No jury would convict the man of blackmail, even if she and Tammy testified to everything they had seen and heard. The fact that they had broken into his apartment and were hiding under the bed when they overheard the phone call might mar their credibility a tad.

But Dirk wasn't one to let a little thing like the absence of evidence slow him down.

"Or . . ." he said, walking around to the front of the table where Orlet could see him, "you could tell me what it was that you had on Dr. Ross. Then maybe *he* would be the one sharing the honeymoon with your cellmates in San Quentin. And you could remain a free, productive member of society."

Orlet gnawed his thumb and spit. Dirk leaned forward on the table, his hands far apart and fingers splayed. He looked like he was about to crawl into Orlet's shirt with him.

"Listen, Joe . . . I'm a very determined sort of guy," he said. "I'll get one of you, believe me. Who's it gonna be? You or him?"

Savannah watched Orlet as he bent under the pressure . . . and broke.

"All right, all right." He swiped a shaking hand across his wet forehead. "I think the doctor helped Kat kill herself, 'cause she was sick and wanted to die. You know, like one of those physician-assisted suicides."

"You *think?* I'm not interested in what you think, pal. Pardon me, but you ain't exactly no Einstein. I only want to hear what you *know.*"

"I don't know anything for sure. But I heard Dr. Ross and Kat talking one night about how she had this lump in her breast that needed to be cut out. She said she'd rather just die and get it over with, and she asked him to help her."

"Where were you when you heard all this?"

Josef wriggled on his chair. "I was . . . um . . . walking by her window and—"

"Oh, okay. You were outside her window, doin' the Peepin' Tom routine."

"No, I wasn't! I was just—"

"Yeah, yeah, so she asked the good doctor to help her croak herself. What did he say?"

"He told her she was nuts. That he cared too much about her to do something like that."

Dirk pulled out an empty chair, turned it around, and sat down, straddling the back. "Well, excuse me, but that don't sound like somebody who was interested in helping somebody off herself."

"I know. But that was only a couple of weeks before she died. And I saw something weird."

"Well, I don't know that you'd be the best judge of what's weird and what ain't, but what did you see?"

"After Kat was found dead . . . later that night, I was out walking around the grounds, and I saw the doctor putting some strange-looking equipment into his trunk."

"What kind of equipment?"

"I don't know. But it had a tank and a plastic bag, and the tank and the bag were hooked together with a hose. I remembered seeing something like that before on television. It looked like the kind of gizmo that Dr. Death guy uses to help people kill themselves."

"And Ross was putting this stuff into his car?"

"Yeah, real sneaky and nervous like, late that night. And then he drove away and didn't come back for over an hour. I figured he used it on Kat and then dumped it somewhere."

"And that's when you decided you'd make him pay you to keep this little secret, right?"

"No way. I'm not saying I did that. I'm just telling you what I saw and heard, because I'm a good citizen, doing my duty and all."

"Uh-huh. And you probably pleaded with the good doctor to turn himself in."

"That's true. I did."

"Yeah, yeah. You're so full of shit, your eyes are turnin'

brown. Get outta here before I change my mind and bust you anyway."

Josef shot up off his chair. "You mean . . . I can go?"

"Yeah, this time. But if I get wind of you trying to squeeze Dr. Ross, or anybody else, for more money, I'll have your ass in a sling before you know what's hit you. Got that?"

"No problem, man. I was just trying to do the right thing here. That's all."

"Sure, sure. You're a real fuckin' Eagle Scout. Get lost."

Savannah waited for Dirk to join her in the tiny observation "closet."

"Well, well," she said, "it appears that Dr. Kevorkian has competition."

"No kidding! Cool, huh?"

Dirk was jazzed; the excitement was glowing all over his street-worn, experience-weary face. As far as Savannah was concerned, it was his most endearing quality, this tendency practically to jump out of his hide at the prospect of catching one of the "bad guys."

"What now?"

"One of us has to talk to Dr. Liu, to get her to reconsider her 'accidental death' ruling. Maybe convince her to run some more tests."

Savannah gave him a poke in the ribs. "What's this 'one of us' bullshit? You're the investigating officer; you do it."

"I would. I mean, it's not like I'm trying to get out of it or anything like that. But she really likes you, you both being girls and all, and—"

"And nothing. You're scared of sweet little Dr. Jenny. You're a lily-livered, yellow-backed chicken!"

"I'm not either. And she's not all that sweet. Not when

you question one of her rulings. Hell, she's bitten my head off for less—like asking her if she'd done certain tests. She may look little and cute and feminine, but it's deceiving. You get her on a bad day and she can be a real bitch!"

Savannah tucked her hands into her armpits, began to flap her arms and cackle. "Ba-a-awwk! Ba-a-awwk!"

"Stop it! I am not!" he said, giving her a push. "All right, I'll make a deal with you. You talk to her; I'll buy you chocolate."

"Okay—a one-pound box of Godiva assorted cremes."

"Deal."

She snickered, knowing that Dirk would die when he saw the price of Godiva chocolate.

Linking her arm through his, she left the room with him. As they strolled companionably out the back door of the station, he said, "What's with the chocolate? I thought you were on some sort of diet at that spa."

"They aren't for me. They're for Jennifer. You don't think I'm going to go in there unarmed, do you?"

CHAPTER FIFTEEN

"Godiva chocolates! Oh, Savannah, you shouldn't have!" Jennifer clapped her hands with delight and reached for the gold-foil box with an eagerness that could only have been born of a serious PMS craving.

Savannah could have admitted that she hadn't—Dirk had—but she wasn't that magnanimous. After all, it had been *her* idea, and in the end, he had nagged her into paying half. So . . .

"You're welcome. You do such a good job around here, I thought you deserved a little treat." *Oh, boy*, she thought, *too much, too sweet*. She had definitely tipped her hand.

Jennifer eyed her suspiciously across her desk, then waved toward the chair beside it. "Have a seat," she said, guardedly. "And a chocolate."

Savannah chose one of her favorites with a silky lemon

center. But the moment she bit into it, Jennifer said, "Why are you buttering me up, Savannah? Spit it out."

Savannah nearly did as the chocolate caught in her throat and choked her. Finally, she found her voice. "What do you mean? Like I said, I thought you deserve—"

"Of course I deserve. But your idea of a little treat is a simple candy bar, not Godiva cremes. You're here to weasel something out of me. What is it?"

"Well, if you really want to know—"

"I do. But I think *you* should know—whether I'm going to give it to you or not—I'm still going to eat your chocolates."

"As you should. I wouldn't have it any other way."

"Without guilt."

"I understand."

Jennifer took a nibble of a raspberry creme, chewed, and closed her eyes in ecstasy. "Heaven," she said. "Pure heaven. What do you want?"

"To bounce a theory off you."

"Bounce away."

"Could Kat Valentina's death have been a physician-assisted suicide?"

Rather than reply immediately, Jennifer pushed away from her desk and rolled her chair over to some gray metal file cabinets nearby. There she retrieved a file from the drawer, then rolled back to the desk.

Savannah saw it was Kat's folder as the doctor thumbed through it, glancing over each form while she chewed thoughtfully.

"Nope," she said, slamming it closed.

"No . . . just like that?" Savannah wanted more bang for her chocolate buck.

"That's right. No. At least, there's no indication of anything like that. Maybe you should tell me why you think it's a possibility."

"First of all, Kat Valentina had breast cancer, and—"

"I know. Left breast, upper/outer quadrant."

"That's right. How did you know?"

Jennifer gave her a withering look and another piece of candy. "I did an autopsy on her body. And I'm thorough. You said so yourself, remember? That's why I get chocolate from my adoring fans."

Savannah felt a bit deflated. She had intended to trump Jennifer with that one. So much for the old "I Know Something You Don't Know" routine. You had to get up pretty early in the morning to put one over on Dr. Liu, and Savannah had never claimed to be an early riser.

"I believe she may have wanted to commit suicide because of the cancer," Savannah offered.

"I doubt it. The disease could probably have been arrested at that point. None of the surrounding lymph glands were involved. There was no reason for her to take her own life."

"If she was afraid of the surgery, of possible mutilation?"

Jennifer scowled. "Was she that vain?"

"Maybe."

Sitting back in her chair, the doctor crossed her arms over her chest. "No. I can't see it. Without more corroborating evidence it's too great a stretch."

"Her physician was in love with her, would probably do anything she asked. He was seen sneaking some strange-looking equipment into his trunk and driving away with it."

"What sort of equipment?"

"A metal rack with bottles and tubes hanging from it."

"Like an IV drip to administer lethal drugs?"

"Exactly." Savannah tried to hide her enthusiasm; Dr. Jenny seemed to be getting the picture.

"Nope."

"No? Again? Why not?"

"No punctures of any kind, from an IV or anything else."

"Oh." *Yes,* Savannah decided, *deflated* was the word for the way she was feeling.

"Besides, anything like that, given in a deadly dose, would have probably shown up on my toxicology screen."

"Probably?" Savannah was grasping for a straw and she knew it. But she was far past caring, too hard-up for pride.

"Yes, probably. And with no more than you have to go on, Savannah, that's close enough."

Savannah could hear the metaphorical book slam closed. And she knew Dr. Jenny well enough not to waste time trying to pry it open again . . . at least, not right now.

"Have another," Jennifer said, holding out the gold box to her. "You'll feel better."

"I doubt it. This case is like walking on a treadmill— you're going through the motions, but you're getting nowhere."

She chose a mocha and bit into it. The bittersweet flavor filled her mouth and soothed her soul.

"See there," Dr. Liu said, giving her a companionable smile. "There's no situation on earth that can't be improved by chocolate."

Savannah's strategy had been: get from the parking area to the dormitory without Princess Eagle Eye spying her. And at the time, it had seemed like a good plan.

So far, she had managed to avoid Tammy's aerobics class and had hoped to leave Royal Palms with her record intact.

But Tammy was beginning to take the rejection personally, so she supposed she would have to make the obligatory appearance soon, in the interest of preserving domestic tranquility.

Not today. Ple-e-ase, not today, she thought as she skirted the group's perimeter.

Like a welcome answer to the less-than-noble prayer, Tammy spotted her, but rather than trying to recruit her, dismissed the group.

"That's it for this afternoon, ladies . . . gentleman," she told the four red-faced women and one fellow who had actually worked up a sweat in their infamous Royal Palms sweat suits. "I'm so proud of you all. You did *faaaan-tastic!* See you tomorrow afternoon. Savannah! Savannah! Yoo-hoo, wait up!"

She scurried across the lawn to intercept her at the edge of the tennis court.

Savannah clapped her hand over Tammy's mouth. "Shhhh. I'm trying to keep a low profile, remember?"

"Oh, just give it up," Tammy mumbled through her fingers. "Nobody bought the migraine baloney anyway."

"So I'm busted?"

"They figure you were lying low somewhere to get out of aerobics and hiking . . . or maybe you snuck away so that you could eat some garbage."

Savannah reminded herself not to burp in Tammy's presence for the next few hours. Miss Marple-etta would be sure to smell the chocolate.

"They have dirty, suspicious minds," Savannah said. "Let them think whatever they want."

Tammy fell into step beside her and wiped her forehead with a white hand towel that bore the spa's emblem, two intertwining palm trees, embroidered in blue. Savannah didn't know why Tammy bothered—she never broke a sweat, even when exercising vigorously.

Sometimes she seemed so much more like a life-size doll than a human being, that Savannah wondered if she had "Made in Japan" stamped on her cute little rear.

"So, guess what happened about an hour ago . . ." Tammy said, lowering her voice and glancing around.

"Dumb ol' Dirk stopped by and grilled Dr. Ross about Kat?"

Tammy stopped in the middle of the path and propped her hands on her waist. "That's a pretty good guess."

"So, what happened?"

"Dumb ol' Dirk stopped by and grilled Dr. Ross about Kat. How did you know?"

"I've been working all morning . . . detecting . . . just like I told you. What did you think I was doing, sitting in some restaurant, pigging out on cheese blintzes?"

Tammy looked satisfactorily abashed. "Well . . . yeah, kind of."

Savannah shook her head. "Oh, ye of little faith." She took her by the arm. "Let's go back to the room, and you can tell me all about Dirk and Dr. Ross."

"But that's all I know."

"That's it? Geez, you'll never make it as a gossip columnist. Now my granny Reid . . . *she* was an ever-flowing fount of knowledge when it came to the goings-on in our little town. Her motto was if you can't say something good about somebody . . . come sit down here by me in the porch swing and . . ."

* * *

Having weaseled absolutely nothing of any value out of Tammy, Savannah had to wait until after sundown to sneak away and meet Dirk. Her curiosity was killing her, wondering how Dirk's questioning of the doctor had gone. And she was able to convince herself that her interest had nothing to do with the fact that Dr. Freeman Ross was a hunk. Nothing at all.

She found Dirk sitting in his old Skylark about a quarter mile down the road from the spa's main entrance. The car was parked in a fairly secluded area, between an orange grove and a lemon grove.

As Savannah climbed into the Buick, it occurred to her that the first time she had sat in a car in an area like that, she had lost her virginity. Of course, that had been around the turn of the millennium, so the memory was a bit hazy. But she was pretty sure it had been either a peach or pecan orchard.

She breathed in the sweet perfume of the dew-damp orange blossoms. "I'll bet half of this county was spawned in these citrus groves," she told Dirk, who was sipping coffee from a Styrofoam cup and looking bored.

"Is that a proposition?" he asked, shoving a similar cup into her hand.

"You wish."

"We could always climb into the backseat and see if we still know how it's done."

"How romantic. We could wallow around back there with your fast-food wrappers, mildewed laundry, and oily car parts."

"Mmmm . . . you get me hot when you talk dirty."

She grunted. "Tammy says you questioned Ross this afternoon."

"That's right. I questioned; he didn't have many answers."

"Not even about the suicide equipment he was getting rid of?"

"He says it was a carpet shampooer that he'd rented from a local grocery store."

"The doctor cleans his own carpets?"

"Says he's very domestic, likes to do it himself and make sure it's done right."

"Cute, domestic, and a clean freak ... not a bad set of qualities in a man. Unless, of course, he's some sort of Angel of Death in his spare time." Savannah took a sip of the coffee from the Styrofoam cup and made a wry face. "Good grief! That's awful! I've tasted Mississippi mud that was more flavorful than this."

"So, don't bitch; it was free."

"And worth every penny you spent for it." She set the cup on the dash. "Are you going to check with the grocery store about his 'rental'?"

"Already did."

"And?"

"They never heard of the good Dr. Ross, let alone rented him any carpet shampooer."

"Why ... that liar!"

"Yeah." Dirk drained his own coffee and started on hers. "Lyin' is probably the *least* of what he's done."

Savannah shook her head in disgust. "And to think, I let him palpate my ankle!"

* * *

They should either get rid of some of this shrubbery, install brighter lights, or hire some security guards, Savannah thought as she paused in the middle of the stone walkway and peered into the shadows to her left. A second ago, she had heard the distinct sound of something—smaller than a Cadillac, but definitely larger than the proverbial bread box—moving in the bushes.

"I'm getting tired of this," she said, keeping her voice calm and even, in spite of the fact that her pulse was pounding in her ears. "I don't cotton to being spied on. When I find out who you are, I'm going to jerk a knothole in your ass, mark my words."

No reply. No sound of any kind. No movement.

But she could feel him, her, or them . . . watching. She could almost hear their breathing and smell their nervous sweat.

"If watching me walk from one place to another is your idea of entertainment," she said, "it's a sad commentary on your social life."

Still nothing.

Most people she knew might have chalked her original misgivings up to an overactive imagination. But long ago, Savannah had learned to trust her instincts about such things. As a cop, her life had depended on it. Occasionally, as a private investigator, it still did.

Once again, she walked away, keeping an eye on her back. As before, her voyeur didn't attempt to contact her— a frustration and relief in one.

She felt eyes watching her until she entered the dormitory and closed the door behind her.

Weird, she thought. *Very weird.*

But it was pretty much in keeping with everything else connected to this case. On the surface, everything appeared straightforward, cut-and-dried. But beneath there was an unsettling feeling that nothing was as it seemed.

She passed through the empty hallway and opened the door to her and Tammy's room. Flipping on the light switch, she glanced down and saw a white envelope lying on the floor. Apparently, someone had shoved it under her door.

The spy in the bushes? Maybe.

At least their room didn't look as though it had been caught up in Dorothy's cyclone and dumped in the Land of Oz.

Maybe it's more money, she thought excitedly as she ripped open the envelope. But this one was thin, containing only one folded piece of paper.

Oh, well, it wasn't money . . . but it *was* an intriguing invitation.

CHAPTER SIXTEEN

"Oh, my God . . . Savannah, you aren't going to go, are you?" Tammy said as she stood over Savannah's shoulder, staring down at the note she had spread on the bed before her.

"Of course, I'm going to go. How often do I get asked out by a doctor? Granny Reid would be ecstatic."

"I don't think this counts. He isn't exactly inviting you to dinner and a play." Tammy sat down on the bed beside Savannah and crossed her legs, yoga-style. Savannah had always secretly hated anyone agile enough to do that. But at the moment she had other, more pressing concerns than flexibility envy.

She read the note for the fifth time. The words had been scribbled with the stereotypical physician's scrawl across a piece of the spa's stationery. It read:

Dear Savannah,

Would you please meet me in Cottage #4 around nine this evening? I have some important matters to discuss with you and would be grateful if you could find time for me.

Remember, I wrote you that note for your bogus ankle sprain. So, you owe me one.

Sincerely,
Freeman Ross

"Hmmm . . . I wonder how I should dress," she mused. "The simple black dress with pearls and heels, or maybe—"

"I think a swimsuit would be more in order. Cottage #4 has an herbal hot tub. Ooo-la-la." Tammy flopped on her tummy on the bed and began to pluck nervously at the velvet pile of the bedspread. "Unless, of course, romance isn't what's on his mind," she added. "Maybe he wants to drown you, the way he did Kat."

"We don't know that he killed Kat."

"We don't know that he didn't. Besides, you can't even be sure that Dr. Ross was the one who wrote that letter and shoved it under our door."

"It's his handwriting. I already compared it to the excuse he wrote for me."

Both women sighed. Savannah picked up the note, folded it twice, and tucked it inside her bra.

"Which swimsuit are you going to wear?" Tammy asked, ever on fashion patrol. "The Victoria's Secret one-piece or your new bikini."

"Whichever one I can best hide my Beretta in."

Tammy mulled that one over for a few seconds. "The

one-piece," she decided. "Plus, it shows off your boobs good, and your butt doesn't look too big."

"Yeah, that's what I figure, too."

Normally, the heady floral fragrance that filled the bathhouse would have put Savannah in a romantic mood. But the smell reminded her of the mud bath where Kat Valentina's body had been found. That not only spoiled the ambience, but the memory prompted her to be careful this evening.

There was more than a chance that Kat Valentina had *not* died an accidental death. And if there was, at least, a possibility that Dr. Freeman Ross had something to do with it, Savannah had to stay alert and resist any temptation to succumb to fanciful distractions.

"Yoo-hoo," she called out, looking around the small room. "Anybody around?"

Her voice echoed off the blue-and-white-tiled walls and bounced back at her. But no one else replied.

Maybe she had been stood up.

Or worse yet, maybe she had been *set* up.

She could feel the comforting weight of the Baretta in the right pocket of her terry-cloth cover-up. For extra reassurance, she slipped her hand inside and curled her fingers around the grip.

Hearing a noise behind her, she spun around and saw Freeman Ross standing there in a deliciously small and tight swimsuit with a fluffy white towel slung over one shoulder. He tossed the towel onto a redwood bench and gave her a welcoming smile that was warmer—and more appealing—than she had expected.

If he were concealing a weapon, it would have to be a

tiny one, she figured, like maybe one of those plastic cocktail toothpicks, shaped like a sword. His all-too-brief briefs scarcely even hid the bare necessities. And, from what she could tell from one quick, ladylike glance, his necessities were more than minimal. Quite a bit more.

He walked toward her, moving more like a professional athlete than a physician. Since when did they make doctors who were all muscle and could pass for Olympic divers in their swimsuits?

A flood of some erotic, exotic hormone hit her system and quivered through her body. It was the closest thing to sex she had experienced in a long time.

Too long, she decided.

"Savannah, I'm glad you could come," he told her, holding out his hand.

Come? Well, I didn't actually . . . I just . . .

"Oh! Yes, well, I couldn't turn down a mysterious invitation slipped under the door like that. Nice dramatic touch."

He smiled. "I thought it would appeal to the sleuth in you." She noticed he wasn't wearing his tortoiseshell glasses. With his muscular physique, the transformation from Clark Kent into the Man of Steel was pretty convincing. "I was hoping to find a location more appropriate, like a hidden staircase, a secret room, or even a cloak closet," he said, "but Royal Palms has pretty mundane floor plans for most of its buildings."

"And the Chesterfields' bell tower is probably occupied . . . by Phoebe."

"Exactly."

"Then this will have to do." She pointed to the spa, a small, intimate, round tub of white tiles, trimmed with royal blue. The center of its bottom glowed with an aqua light, and the water bubbled gently, sending herbal-scented steam into the air.

As Freeman Ross lowered his gorgeous self into the water, Savannah allowed her terry-cloth cover-up to slide off her shoulders. Carefully—while trying to look nonchalant—she placed it on the tiles at the edge of the tub, making sure it would be readily accessible while she was in the water.

She felt his eyes on her, but she couldn't interpret the expression to tell whether the one-piece had been the best choice after all. And when she sat down across from him, she saw he was wearing a strange little smile that she couldn't quite decipher.

"Is that where it is?" he asked, nodding toward her strategically discarded cover-up.

He couldn't know, she thought. *Or he's guessing.*

"Where *what* is?" She batted her blue eyes.

"Your gun."

Mmmm . . . good guesser.

"Gun? I came out here to have an herbal bubble and a conversation with you. Do I need a gun to do that?"

"Do you answer most questions with another question?"

Bat, bat. "Doesn't everyone?"

He laughed. She couldn't tell if it was nervous laughter or if he was genuinely amused. Although she prided herself on being an astute judge of character, motivation, and intentions, she decided that Dr. Ross wasn't an easy man to read.

"Are you going to shoot me, Savannah?" he asked, still wearing that enigmatic grin.

"Are you going to misbehave?"

"With a woman who's packing a pistol, a lady who has a black belt in karate? Not likely."

She raised one eyebrow. "How do you know I'm a black belt?"

"I read the papers. You were quite the celebrity around here some time back. A detective lady who—"

She blushed. "I think *infamous* is more like it. Getting myself canned from the police department wasn't exactly my greatest career achievement."

"You were treated unfairly."

"I think so, too. But my life is better now, so I'm not complaining. In the long run, they did me a favor."

"You enjoy being a private detective?"

She didn't like where this was headed. The topic was getting too personal, and she wasn't going to learn anything about him if they sat here and rehashed her ancient history.

"Yeah, I like it. Usually. How about you? Do you like being a doctor?"

"I did . . . back when I had a real practice and actually healed people. Now I'm a baby-sitter for the guests at Royal Palms. The most important thing I do around here is examine a twisted ankle from time to time. And most of those are phony." He sighed and slipped lower into the water. "A fake doctor, doctoring fakes."

She felt guilty for a moment, as though her own duplicity had added to his sense of futility. "What happened to your practice?" she asked.

"I was brought up on charges and lost my position at the hospital."

"What charges?"

"One of my patients died under mysterious circumstances," he said in a straightforward manner that she both respected and mistrusted. What could he possibly gain by being so candid with her?

"They suspected you of murder?"

"That's what they called it."

"And what did you call it?"

"Physician-assisted suicide. Or, at least, that's what I would have called it, if I had done it. I was cleared, of course, or I wouldn't be practicing medicine."

"Of course." She waited for him to continue. When he didn't she said, "Well . . . did you do it?"

"She was an elderly woman in her mid-eighties, a cancer patient, in horrible pain. Every day I visited her, and every day she begged me to end the suffering for her."

"And you did?"

He studied her thoughtfully for a while before answering, as though deciding whether to tell her the truth or not. Finally, he said, "She died, peacefully in her sleep. If she hadn't, I might have helped her."

"But 'might have' doesn't count . . . legally, that is."

"Thankfully, no. If they jailed you for 'might-haves,' 90 percent of us would be behind bars."

For a long time, they sat there with the bubbles and fragrant warmth rising around them, while Savannah tried to determine whether or not he had just lied to her. Damn, where was a polygraph expert when you needed one?

"If I hadn't intended to tell you the truth, Savannah," he said, "I wouldn't have brought up the subject in the first place."

"That's sorta what I was thinking. And I was wondering why you asked me here this evening."

He grinned and glanced quickly down at her chest, which was floating nicely on top of the scented water. "Can't a man ask a beautiful woman to join him in a spa without him having an ulterior motive?"

"No. Men always have ulterior motives ... especially when they're wearing skimpy swimsuits."

He threw back his head and laughed heartily. "So, you noticed."

"I'm a sighted female between the ages of eight and eighty. Of course I noticed." She mentally checked the position of her cover-up and the Beretta. "So, does that mean you invited me here to seduce me?"

"Not entirely."

"I didn't think so."

"Although if you tried to seduce me, I certainly wouldn't object."

"I don't think so."

"Hmmm." He frowned. "Then the swimsuit didn't work as well as I'd hoped."

"It works very well. If you didn't wear it to seduce me, I'd say you wore it to distract me while you pump me for information. And, if that's true, you made an excellent choice. I'm definitely distracted."

Again, he laughed, but this time he looked a bit embarrassed, which told her that her instincts had been right. "How did you know?" he asked.

"Because that's why I chose this particular suit." She pointed to her abundant cleavage. "Is it working?"

"So well that I'm going to have to wait a while before I can climb out of this tub without embarrassing myself."

In the interest of keeping a clear head, she didn't dare

think about the brevity of his swimsuit or the consequences of any male reactions to her charms.

"Enough pleasantries," she said. "You invited me here to find out something. What is it?"

"I'd like to know why you're here."

"You already asked me that."

"Yes, you said it was to drop some pounds and get into shape."

"Is that so hard to believe?"

"For you? Yes. You're already in great shape, and I have a feeling you're one of those rare, lucky people who actually likes themselves . . . every single pound. Am I right?"

She laughed. "Yes and no. I do like myself . . . all of me. But luck had nothing to do with it. Believe me, in a society that insists a grown woman have the body of a prepubescent girl, you have to work hard to achieve any degree of self-acceptance. Appreciation of your own flesh isn't something you attain by 'lucking out.'"

Finished with her soliloquy, she drew a deep breath and waited for his reply. He smiled at her, thoughtfully, then said, "I stand corrected. But you haven't changed my opinion of why you're here."

"Which is?"

"I think you're visiting the Royal Palms in an official capacity. It's just a bit too coincidental that within forty-eight hours of Kat's death, a former police detective and current private investigator shows up."

Her mind ran through a list of several untruths to tell him. They varied from little white fibs to downright dirty black lies. But she knew he wouldn't believe any of them, so what was the point?

"The only question is . . . " he continued, ". . . who hired you? Are you working for some individual, the insurance company, or your ex-partner—the guy who questioned me all afternoon?"

He even knew that Dirk was her ex-partner. Savannah found this a bit unsettling. She much preferred to know other people's business to having them know hers. Dr. Ross was a tad too informed for comfort where she was concerned.

"That isn't the only question," she said. "There's another: Why do *you* want to know?"

"If you'll answer mine, I'll answer yours," he replied with a sly grin.

I'd rather play, You Show Me Yours, I'll Show You Mine, she thought. But she resolved to stick to business. At least for the moment.

"Okay," she said, "but you won't believe me when I tell you."

"Try me."

She donned her most innocent, convincing look, meant to instill confidence and trust. "I don't know who hired me."

His smile evaporated. "You're right. I don't believe you."

"You don't have to. But it's true. They hired me anonymously, and they haven't bothered to identify themselves yet."

He mulled that over for several moments, then said, "Who do you think it is?"

"I haven't a clue. In fact, I sorta hoped it might be you."

"Sorry. I'm innocent."

"Are you?"

His grin returned. "Absolutely. Can't you tell?"

"No. I have a hard time reading you. I'll bet you're good at poker."

"Good? I'm excellent."

"And modest." She chuckled with him, then fixed him with a blue laser stare. "Now it's your turn. Why do you care who I am or why I'm here?"

"Because, in spite of what I told you the other day, I don't think Kat's death was an accident. I think she might have been murdered. And if she was, the cops are going to figure that out sooner or later. When they do, I think they're going to come after me."

"You? Why you?"

"Because I had an excellent motive."

Savannah could feel her pulse rate crank up a notch. "And that was . . . ?"

"I loved her. And I couldn't have her," he said with a sigh. "Isn't that the best motive of all?"

Savannah shrugged. "I don't know if it's the best one. But I'd say it's in the top ten."

CHAPTER SEVENTEEN

"When did you finally get in last night?" Tammy demanded, as she and Savannah sat in the dining hall, eating their nutritious, cleansing breakfast of miso soup. "I tried my best to stay awake, but I eventually nodded off."

"When did you go to sleep?" Savannah took a bite of the bland concoction and grimaced.

"Just after eleven, I think."

"Hmm . . . I came in about eleven-thirty."

Tammy looked across the table at an elderly gentleman who was devouring his soup with a gusto that must have been born of acute starvation. She fixed Savannah with a suspicious eye, and whispered, "You weren't *eating*, were you?"

"You say that like it was a crime."

"Around here, it is."

"Well, I wasn't eating. I was indulging other appetites by developing a long, deeply satisfying, intimate relationship."

Tammy's eyes widened. "With Dr. Ross?"

"No. To be perfectly honest . . . it was with one of the spa jets. But Dr. Ross and his teeny-tiny bathing suit were my inspiration."

Tammy gasped and looked around, obviously mortified that someone else might have overheard this vulgarity. But the old fellow was miso-absorbed, and the other five guests were too far away to eavesdrop.

"That's disgusting," she said, taking a quick sip of her protein drink, followed by a green-gunk chaser.

"Yeah, well . . . you spend half an hour in the close proximity of a spa with a man as gorgeous as Freeman Ross and then tell me that you don't feel like sitting on an air jet."

"Savannah, for heaven's sake! I don't want to hear what you . . . sat on!"

The fellow across the table looked up from his bowl, his eyes aglow with sudden interest. "I do!"

"Oh, hush and eat your gruel," Savannah told him before turning back to Tammy. "You know, kiddo. You used to remind me of my younger brothers and sisters. But lately, you've been coming across more like my mother."

"Well, somebody needs to. I swear, you're out of control."

"You don't know what out of control is. You ought to see me at a Ben & Jerry's ice-cream parlor. Mrs. Fields and See's candies are good places to lose it, too."

Tammy shuddered. "Oh, yuck. All that sugar, the chocolate, the cream and butter."

"Mmmmm . . . exactly." She took another spoonful of

her soup and nearly gagged. "Oops. Here comes trouble," she said, nodding toward the door.

Louis Hanks had just entered the room. And judging from the stormy look on his face and the way he was striding straight for their table, he had direct confrontation on his mind.

"Looks like I'm in the doghouse again," Savannah whispered.

"If you ask me," Tammy replied smugly, "I think you might as well fill out a change-of-address card."

"This had better be important," Savannah said as she faced off with Lou Hanks across a massage table. "I was right in the middle of a bowl of scrumptious miso soup."

He had practically dragged her from the dining room, down the hall, and into this eight-by-eight-foot cubicle, which contained nothing but a padded table, a tray of oils, and a stack of towels, and now . . . the angry owner of Royal Palms Spa and the apparent recipient of that rage.

"To hell with you and your miso," he said, his face scarlet and eyes bugged. "The cops are accusing me and my employees of murdering my wife!"

"Murdering her? Really . . . ?"

"Don't 'Really' me, as if you don't know anything about it."

Savannah mentally rehearsed a few karate moves, just in case he decided to vault over the table and go for her throat. He certainly looked mad enough to try it.

Though she doubted that the chubby Lou was accustomed to vaulting from place to place. He seemed more of a plodder, but you couldn't always tell. Some plodders became athletes when they were furious.

"I probably don't know as much as you think I do," she said. "Which cops and which employees?"

"Your old partner and Dr. Ross."

"That's only *one* cop and *one* employee. Besides, Dirk isn't all that old, he's just a lousy dresser who's going prematurely bald."

Lou's scowl deepened. "Do you think my wife's death is a joke, Miss Reid?"

"Not at all. But when I feel threatened, I tend to resort to sarcasm. And I don't like your aggressive tone."

"And I don't like you coming to my spa, pretending to be a guest, and snooping around."

"Snooping? Is that what you think I'm doing?"

"That's exactly what I think you're doing. Are you going to deny it?"

Savannah thought for a moment, then shook her head. "No. I'd say 'snooping' about covers it."

"Then you lied to me. You told me you weren't here to investigate my wife's death."

"I told you I wasn't here on behalf of your life-insurance company. And that's still true."

"Then you're working for the cops."

Savannah laughed. "No danger of that, I'm afraid. The San Carmelita Police Department and I parted ways long ago."

"But you've been reporting back to that Detective Coulter guy."

"I don't report to Dirk or anybody else anymore. That's the nice thing about being self-employed."

"But you've been telling him what's going on around here."

"Dirk is a friend of mine. We talk about a lot of things.

Besides, I wasn't aware there was anything 'going on around here.' Have I missed something?"

Lou gave her a searching, hostile look. "I don't think you miss anything, Miss Reid."

"Thank you, Mr. Hanks. I'll take that as a compliment."

"I didn't mean it to be. My wife's death was a sad and unfortunate accident. Your poking around here only makes the tragedy that much worse."

"I can understand why you feel that way. But what if your wife *didn't* have an accident?"

"She didn't kill herself! I told you that before! Kat didn't commit suicide!"

"What if it wasn't an accident *or* suicide? What if she was murdered?"

His face went a sick shade of white that reminded her of some kind of chalky antidiarrhea medicine.

"Murdered? You think somebody actually killed her. Deliberately?"

"I don't know yet. But I think Kat deserves to have it checked out. If there's any possibility it might be homicide, you would want that person caught and punished. Wouldn't you?"

He sputtered and stuttered for a moment, then said, "Well, I . . . I guess so. I mean, yeah, sure I would."

"Then it's a good thing that I'm a guest here at this particular time," she said smoothly, giving him her most conciliatory smile. "I'll keep my eyes open to possibilities. And that way, if anything does 'pop up,' I'd be the first to know. Probably even before the police, right?"

"And would you tell me if anything 'popped up,' that is?"

"You're Kat's ex-husband, her closest living relative, the owner of the spa."

"Is that a 'yes'?"

She shrugged and gave him a grin. "It's a 'maybe.'"

Looking only a little mollified, he turned to leave the room. At the door she stopped him.

"By the way, Lou," she said as he waited, hand on the doorknob. "Kat's life-insurance policy . . . you said it wouldn't pay off if she committed suicide. Let me guess . . . an accident or homicide would fly, right?"

He left. And slammed the door so hard behind him that Savannah could swear her teeth rattled.

"Bingo," she said.

"You asked to see me?" Savannah said as she stuck her head into the spa's office, where Bernadette sat at her desk, phone in hand.

"Oh, yes. Please come in, Ms. Reid," she said, slamming the receiver down without saying good-bye to the person on the other end.

Savannah steeled herself, figuring she had been called on the carpet to receive her walking papers. Lou Hanks probably didn't have the gonads to do it himself, so she was expecting the edict to be handed down by his secretary/pool buddy.

The skinny young redhead jumped up from her desk and ushered Savannah to a comfortable chair. "May I get you some sparkling water or a protein drink?" she offered.

"No thanks. I suppose a double-malted chocolate and peanut butter milk shake would be out of the question."

Bernadette gave her a nervous chuckle, as though she

had just overheard some blatant blasphemy while standing in a church and wasn't sure how to react.

"So, why did you ask me to come to the office?" Savannah said, wanting to get her eviction over with as soon as possible. There was no point in prolonging the humiliation.

"I realized that when you registered with us the other day, I forgot to have you sign one of the release forms. It's a very important one. I hope you don't mind."

Savannah studied the form that the redhead thrust at her. "I signed one of these already. I'm sure of it."

"I'm sorry, but I don't have it in my files. So, if you would sign another . . . "

As Bernadette returned to her own chair behind her desk, Savannah studied her face. The young woman was lying through her nicely capped teeth. Unlike Dr. Freeman Ross, Bernadette was easy to read.

"You know very well that I've already signed one of these forms," Savannah told her. "Why don't you just tell me the real reason why you asked me to come by?"

Bernadette blushed so brilliantly that Savannah decided maybe she *was* a real redhead after all. Her freckles practically stood out on stems. She picked up a pencil and began to fidget with it.

"Well . . . I . . . "

Savannah gave her one of her best, comforting, "big-sister" looks. "It's all right. You can tell me. Just spit it out."

"Ah . . . okay . . . mmmm . . . I . . . " Nervously, she began to doodle on a notepad in front of her. Savannah glanced down to see what she was sketching. It was a simple cartoon cat—a couple of circles with ears, eyes, a tail, and whiskers.

Whether this was some sort of cryptic clue or great Freudian symbolism, Savannah didn't know. But either way, she was losing her patience.

"Bernadette, unless you're going to draw some sort of treasure map there, put that pencil down, look me straight in the eye, and tell me what's on your mind."

"Okay." She drew a deep breath. "Dion killed Kat."

Savannah had to do a quick facial adjustment to keep her jaw from dropping onto her chest. Talk about candor!

"Dion murdered Kat? Are you sure?"

Bernadette nodded, red curls bobbing. "Yeah, I'm pretty sure."

"When we're talking homicide, you've got to do better than pretty sure. Is this something you know for a fact, or not?"

"Yeah, kinda."

Savannah sighed. "Let me rephrase my question: Why do you think Dion killed Kat?"

"I heard them arguing right before she died."

"They had an argument in front of you?"

"Not exactly in front of me. They were in Dion's cottage, and I was standing outside the window. I wasn't, like, peeking in or anything. I was just walking by on my way to the pool when I heard them. So, I stopped and, you know, listened a little."

"It's a good thing you only listened a little, otherwise someone might have accused you of eavesdropping."

Bernadette nodded vigorously. "That's right. But I wasn't. It's just that, when he told her he was going to kill her, my ears perked up."

Savannah could feel her own ears standing to attention. "He said he was going to kill her?"

"Yeah. He told her that if she told what he had told her, he was gonna kill her."

Experiencing a bit of mental vertigo, Savannah said, "Would you mind explaining that? No, wait a minute. Can you just tell me, as best you recall, exactly what he said?"

Bernadette concentrated, brow furrowed from the effort. "Okay, I've got it. He said, 'You don't have to tell anyone anything, Kat. You're just threatening to expose me out of spite.' And then she said, 'Can you blame me, considering how you've treated me?' And he said, 'If you tell anyone— anybody at all—I swear, I'll kill you'"

"And what did Kat say to that?"

"She laughed at him."

Savannah experienced a nice adrenaline jolt that was better than a hit of double Dutch chocolate. "A man tells her he's going to kill her, and she laughs at him?"

"Yeah, Kat could be really irritating when she wanted to be. I'm not surprised she was killed. Kat was that way to everybody. It was just a matter of time until *somebody* knocked her off."

CHAPTER EIGHTEEN

Savannah couldn't locate Dion until late afternoon. On a hunch, she decided to take a run along the foothills. Sure enough, there he was, jogging through the marguerite daisies and wild sage.

As always, he was gorgeous, tanned, and glistening with just a misting of perspiration. Not enough to run in rivulets down his forehead ... the way it was streaming down hers. No, Dion was and always had been a "star." And apparently, "stars" didn't sweat. At least, not as much as your run-of-the-mill private detective.

She wiped her forehead on her Royal Palms sweatshirt sleeve and picked up her pace so that she could catch him where their paths intersected.

"Hi, Savannah," he called, seemingly pleased to see her, as she approached. "Running off a little excess energy?"

"Excess energy?" She fell into step beside him. "I've been getting out of bed at dawn, eating salad, and exercising like a hyperactive Tasmanian devil. Who has any energy at all, let alone *excess?*"

Dion laughed and shot her a breathtaking smile. "All that clean eating and activity is supposed to invigorate you."

"Yeah, I've heard the theory," she said. "Do you mind if we stop and catch our breath under those avocado trees over there?"

As soon as she uttered the words, Savannah realized that *he* didn't need to catch *his* breath. No, she was the only one huffing and puffing enough to blow down a little pig's brick house.

"Sure, no problem," he said, heading for the copse of trees she had indicated. "But don't be tempted to smuggle any back for guacamole."

"Real food, high fat content, heaven forbid. Would I be shot at sunrise? Or would they be extra cruel and have me do morning exercises first?"

"I wouldn't tattle on you. But these trees belong to the Chesterfields, and Phoebe is probably spying on us this very minute. Rumor has it she keeps a rifle with buckshot and a scope in that bell tower with her to shoot anybody who touches the forbidden fruit."

Rifle, buckshot, a scope . . . Mr. Movie Star didn't know diddly about firearms, she decided. Obviously, he hadn't played in many Westerns.

But, since the plan was to get him to open up to her, she figured that insulting him wasn't the best way to gain his confidence.

When they reached the shade of the avocado trees, he

pulled a sipper full of water from his fanny pack and offered it to her. She drank gratefully, then returned it, and he did the same.

"If Phoebe Chesterfield sees all and knows all about what goes on around here, I should try to talk to her again," Savannah said, thinking aloud. "She must have an opinion or two about Kat's death."

"What about Kat's death?" Dion's turquoise eyes searched Savannah's with a degree of intensity that interested her. "She died of an accident, right? I mean, that's what the medical examiner said."

"Then, for the moment, that's what we go on."

"What do you mean? Don't you think it *was* accidental?"

Did he look scared, angry, shocked, worried, or a bit of all of the above? Savannah watched him carefully, trying to evaluate. But the man was an actor, after all. That complicated things a little.

For right now, she decided on "worried"—which could mean anything.

"I don't know," she said. "I've heard rumors that Kat might have been done in by somebody ... maybe somebody she had a fight with just before she died."

There. Her verbal arrow had found and pierced its bull's-eye. Actor or not, the look on his face was pure shock, quickly followed by fear.

"Who said that? Who?"

"Oh, I can't say for sure. You know how gossip is; it just splatters like a wet cow pie through a fan and lands on everybody. It's hard to tell where it got started."

He took a long swig from the sipper, and she noticed he was gripping the container a lot harder than necessary.

"Did any of these gossips have any idea who might have done it?"

"Oh, I heard a theory or two, but none I'd get too excited about. Not unless there was some sort of physical evidence to back it up, that is."

Was he looking a little pale beneath his perfect movie-star tan? she wondered. Or was it wishful thinking on her part?

Not that she wanted Dion Zeller to be a murderer, per se. But right now, she would take any lead she could get. High-and-dry private detectives couldn't be choosy.

"Don't believe everything you hear, Savannah," he said as he poured some of his water into his palm and splashed it over his face. "Just because someone disagreed with Kat doesn't mean they killed her. Kat was a controversial, difficult woman; a lot of us had differences with her. We couldn't all have murdered her."

"Sounds like you're speaking from experience. Did *you* have problems with her?"

He didn't answer right away. She could practically hear his mental hard drive whirring.

Finally, he said, "I loved Kat; she was one of the dearest friends I ever had. Sure we had problems, some nasty arguments, all that. But I never, never would have hurt her."

"Did you ever threaten her?"

Yes, his tan was definitely fading.

"I might have. In the heat of an argument people say a lot of things they don't mean."

Savannah weighed the risk of asking her next question. She was alone on a hillside with man who outweighed her by at least fifty pounds, a man in excellent shape, who might be a killer. On the other hand, this was the perfect opportunity, the only one she might have.

Besides, she figured the Beretta tucked into her waistband gave her an edge. So, she decided to go for it.

"Do you think Kat meant it when she threatened to tell on you?" she asked him, quietly, smoothly delivering the verbal punch to his diaphragm.

The real thing couldn't have had a more dramatic effect. He gasped, and, for a moment, she actually thought he might pass out on her.

She saw a wild, desperate look in his eyes as he stared at her, trying to look through her, to see how much she knew. But Savannah was an excellent poker player, and she knew she wasn't giving anything away.

When he recovered his breath and some of his composure, he said, "Kat was a kid at heart. That was both her charm and her downfall. She made a lot of threats she never intended to carry out. I knew that about her, so I just ignored anything she said that I didn't like."

"Then the rumors I've heard ... they must be a lot of hogwash, huh?"

"I don't know what you've heard and how much of this you're making up, Savannah. You strike me as a person who might spin a yarn or two if it suited your purpose."

She laughed. "That's true. I've been known to embroider the truth from time to time. It's my Southern heritage." Her smile melted. "But rumors about murder are serious stuff. They don't need embellishing to get my attention."

He shoved the water bottle back into his fanny pack and zipped it closed with a flourish. "Well, before you pay too much attention to any rumors you hear, you might consider the source. Whoever is spreading this crap ... I'll bet you could trace it directly back to Lou."

"Why would he spread gossip about you?"

"He wouldn't. He'd get somebody else to do it for him. God knows, he's got enough lame brains at his beck and call. And he's the one who wants Kat's death to be an accident or murder. Anything but a suicide."

So, Dion knew about the insurance policy, too. Was it public knowledge?

"Lou hasn't paid any of us our salaries for the past month," he continued, "because he's flat broke. If that insurance money doesn't come through, this place is going to be closing ... soon, too."

"It's that bad? He told you that himself?"

"You're damned right. So take those rumors you've heard with a grain of salt, Savannah. Like I said, consider the source."

Without another word, he took off down the trail, heading back toward the spa and leaving her alone with the avocado trees.

But the last thing on her mind was guacamole. As he had requested, she *was* considering the source.

Bernadette.

If there was anyone at the spa who was firmly ensconced in Lou's back pocket, it was Bernadette. In fact, it was safe to say, she was right there in the front ... of his Jockeys.

A sudden yearning for the perfume of roses and the company of an older woman led Savannah to Phoebe Chesterfield's garden again. As she had hoped, she found the lady there, tending her botanical paradise.

This time, Miss Chesterfield had abandoned the flouncy

skirt in favor of slacks. But her blouse bore the same splash of bright color in the form of scarlet tulips and yellow daffodils. Her flowing waves of silver hair were, once again, covered with the straw bonnet decorated with a sprig of freshly picked lavender.

Instead of cutting roses, she was in a less delicate position—on her hands and knees digging in a flower bed.

"Ah, you caught me in my dungarees," she said, as she dusted the dirt from her leather gloves, squinting up at Savannah. The late-afternoon sun shone in her eyes and gave her fair skin a rosy glow.

For a moment, Savannah felt a pang of nostalgia, remembering her granny Reid and the wonderful bonding moments the two of them had shared while planting seeds, separating bulbs, or even spreading manure.

Gran had glowed with the same health and vitality that radiated from Phoebe Chesterfield. Long ago, Savannah had formulated the theory that gardening kept a woman young—not to mention beautiful—if she only used enough sunscreen and wore a wide-brimmed bonnet.

"I had intended to get my landscaper to do this job for me," Phoebe said, pointing to the hole she had just dug and the bareroot bush beside it. "But he won't be by until Tuesday, and that azalea was going downhill fast over there. Too much sun, I expect."

"Yes. That would be my guess, too." Savannah nodded thoughtfully. "It should do much better here in the partial shade. I believe you rescued it just in time."

"Well, the job isn't done yet."

Was that a slight hint Savannah heard in Phoebe's tone? It almost sounded as though the Royal Palms's Official Pain-

in-the-Backside Neighbor was asking another person for help . . .
maybe even a moment or two of female companionship.

"I could give you a hand with it, if you like," Savannah
said, eager to feel the cool richness of the soil running through
her fingers again. It had been too long since she had been in
touch with Nature.

"You're probably busy," Phoebe replied curtly.

"Not at all. I'd love to help."

A moment later, both women were on their knees, and
Phoebe was mixing a bit of bonemeal into the hole she had
just dug. Savannah fetched a bucket of water which she poured
in, once Phoebe had finished.

"Now . . . there you go," Savannah said as she eased the
azalea into the ground and began to gather the dirt around its
roots. Phoebe helped her, and in a couple of minutes, the bush
was transplanted.

"There, that didn't take long," Savannah said, looking
down at her manicure, which was now ruined, but she didn't
care. Some experiences were worth the price of vanity.

Savannah took a look around, but they appeared to be
alone in the garden. "The last time I was here," she ventured,
"you mentioned something about Kat Valentina actually making a play for your brother. Is that really true?"

She had delivered the question with just the right front-
porch-gossip tone, and Phoebe responded predictably.

"A play? Heavens no," she replied. "She wasn't playing
at all. She was *working* at it. I tell you, it was absolutely
disgusting. An old codger like him. . . . "

Savannah thought it best not to mention that Brother
Ford Chesterfield appeared to be several years younger than
his sister, Phoebe. And having seen the gentleman, Savannah

could understand Kat's attraction to him. In spite of his advancing years, he was a physically fit, handsome man with sharp, intelligent eyes.

And, of course, he appeared to be very wealthy. For a woman like Kat, that had to mean more than his thick silver hair or youthful physique.

"How serious were they? I mean, did they actually . . . ?" *Oops,* she thought. *That wasn't exactly the most graceful verbal soft-shoe shuffle you've ever accomplished, old girl.*

But Phoebe didn't seem insulted. She pursed her thin lips and nodded vigorously. "Oh, yes, they did. Kat would do 'it' with anyone, and of course, my brother couldn't help himself."

"He couldn't? Why not?"

"Well, he's a man. They're weak, you know. All of them. Ever since Adam took a bite of that apple, they've been more animal than human . . . helpless to control their lust."

"Well, I don't know if I'd go so far as to say that they're all helpless—"

"But it's true. They're weak, and they're foolish. Without their mothers, sisters, and wives to keep them in line, they'd never survive."

Savannah cleared her throat, trying to put aside all of Granny Reid's admonitions about respecting one's elders. Gran had also taught her to confront bigotry wherever she encountered it. Those instructions seemed to contradict each other, given the present company.

"I don't think a person has to be male to be foolish," she said as gently as she could.

Phoebe slipped off one of her gloves and began to fan herself with it. "Of course not. Women are stupid, too. They marry men, don't they? That's why I never married. I practically reared my younger brother, and one man is enough responsibility for any woman."

"I understand."

"You do not. I don't see any ring on that finger of yours."

"No, but I'm the oldest of nine siblings. Some of them were boys. All of them—boys *and* girls—were a peck of trouble. From time to time, they still are."

"It's true; we're never too old to get into trouble." Phoebe looked away, over the hills to the setting sun, and assumed a philosophical expression. "We get too soon old and too late smart," she said.

"Truer words were never spoken."

The two women shared a moment of companionable silence before Savannah decided to turn the conversation back to more fertile ground.

"How did you feel about your brother's affair with Kat?" she asked.

"I thought he was an idiot, and I told him so. Of course, it didn't carry much weight with him. I tell him that at least twice a week."

"How long did it last?"

Phoebe shot her a look of indignation and shock. "Well, that's a pretty personal question. But, considering my brother's age, I doubt he lasted very long at all. A man of his years has to think of his heart, especially with a younger little tart like Kat Valentina. I—"

"No, I'm sorry. I meant, the affair in general."

"Oh. Three weeks . . . more or less. I'm not exactly certain."

Savannah bet that Phoebe *was* certain. With the aid of her telescope and acute curiosity, she probably knew when *everyone's* affairs began and ended. She would have kept a close account of her brother's activities.

"Who terminated it?"

"My brother, of course. But not before she asked him to marry her. *She* proposed to *him!* Can you believe such a thing? What is this world coming to, anyway, when women are on bended knees, offering engagement rings? These times we live in are perverse, I tell you. Perverse."

"She offered him an engagement ring . . . " Savannah just couldn't picture that. ". . . on her *knees?*"

Phoebe waved her glove at her. "Oh, pooh, of course not. Don't take me literally, girl. A flaming strumpet like that? She was probably lying flat on her back at the time."

"And he refused?"

"Her proposal of marriage? Most certainly. He may be foolish, but he isn't dim-witted."

"I see."

Savannah didn't see, but she was afraid to ask for clarification, which she was fairly sure would only confuse her further.

"How did Kat feel about him turning her down?" Savannah asked, still trying to picture Kat Valentina proposing to Ford Chesterfield, while lying on her back.

"Oh, I suppose she had a bit of a snit fit about it. But there wasn't anything she could do. His mind was made up. And anyone who knows my brother is all too aware of how stubborn he can be."

"How long ago did all this happen?"

"Recently."

"*Very* recently?"

Phoebe gave her a wary look, as though realizing for the

first time that she was speaking to a stranger about private, family matters.

"Yes, but I'm sure it had nothing to do with what happened to her," Phoebe said. "Nothing at all. As charming as he may be, my brother isn't the sort of man women kill themselves over."

Savannah watched Phoebe carefully, noting every expression that crossed her still-handsome face. Age might have traced a crease here and there in the porcelain skin, but her blue eyes still glowed with an enthusiasm for life that gave Savannah hope for her own later years.

But, as closely as she studied her, Savannah wasn't sure if Phoebe Chesterfield was telling her the truth or not. She wouldn't put it past her to embroider the facts to suit her fancy, or even fabricate them altogether.

In her experience, Savannah had come to believe that most people did one or the other to some degree and from time to time. The trick was figuring out how much and when.

But the sun was rapidly disappearing behind hills that had changed from a tawny suede to purple velvet, and she needed to return to the spa while she could still see the trail.

"I'd like to drop by again sometime and talk to your brother about Ms. Valentina," she said. "I'm sure you've told me the most important facts, but he might have something to add."

"No, he wouldn't," was Phoebe's brusque reply. "He won't even talk to me about her . . . and me his own sister. He's a private man, Ford is. I'm sure he wouldn't give you the time of day."

"All the same, I'd like to try."

Phoebe shrugged. "It's your time. Waste it if you want."

Savannah bent over to pluck one of the dainty coral blossoms from the azalea bush they had just planted. "May I?" she asked.

"Of course," Phoebe replied, seemingly relieved to change the subject. "But why do you want one little flower? If you like, go ahead and cut yourself a bouquet." She waved her arm, indicating that the entire garden was Savannah's.

"Thank you, but this is all I need. It's for my potpourri . . . a very special one."

At the mere mention of flowers, Phoebe's face shone. "Special? Is it a secret blend?"

"There's no secret, but it is very personal. It contains flowers from special occasions throughout my life: a petal from my gardenia prom corsage, a pinch from each Christmas tree, a rose from my sister's bridal bouquet, spices from my grandmother's herb garden . . . and a carnation from my grandpa's casket spray."

"That's nice," Phoebe said, looking away. But Savannah thought she saw a misting of tears in her eyes. "But why are you going to put *my* azaleas in your special potpourri?"

"Because I want to remember this moment, planting your flowers with you and watching the sun set over the mountains. It's a lovely memory."

Phoebe cleared her throat, bent over, and picked another blossom. With a shy, childlike smile, she dropped it into Savannah's hand with the other flower. "Here then," she said. "You might as well remember me twice as often."

Briskly, she gathered her tools, then took off down the cobblestone path toward the house, leaving Savannah with the distinct impression that she wouldn't need two tiny coral blossoms to remember Phoebe Chesterfield.

CHAPTER NINETEEN

"Boy, when the sun goes down around here, it drops like a lead balloon," Savannah whispered to the daisy-studded bushes as she maneuvered along the now-dark trail. The tiny white flowers glowed faintly in the remaining twilight, marking the edges of the path that wound down the hill toward the spa.

Only moments before, her way had seemed clear enough. Now, she had the uneasy feeling that one bad step could send her skidding through thorny brush, past the occasional rattlesnake den.

Okay, so there probably weren't a lot of snakes slithering around at this time of night. Weren't they supposed to conduct their reptilian business out on the rocks when the sun was hottest?

Either way, she didn't relish the idea of tumbling into

Mr. and Mrs. Rattler's living room while they were watching the evening news and eating their TV dinners.

"Bring a flashlight next time, nitwit," she told herself, "or be sure to get home before dark."

Of course, she had the Beretta tucked into her waistband. But right then, she would have traded it for a three-dollar penlight or even a candle.

Once she thought she saw a slender beam of light cut through the darkness, farther down the hill and off to her right. But the next instant it was gone, and she finally decided she had imagined the whole thing.

About halfway down, she lost even those last few rays that had illuminated the daisies for her. Without their guidance, she was fairly stuck. Although she could see the lights of the spa, glowing at the bottom of the hill, the trail leading to it was a switchback.

For half a second she considered heading straight down—the shortest distance between two points and all that high-school-geometry stuff. But she quickly discarded the idea as foolhardy. Wading through thistles and nettles as high as her armpits, not to mention close encounters with various species of nocturnal California wildlife didn't appeal to her.

"Okay, so call me a city girl," she said to the crickets she could hear, chirping in the distance. Or were they frogs? "Point proven," she added.

Maybe a cane might help. If she could get her hands on some kind of sturdy stick, she could wave it around in front of her. As a kid she had played a pretty mean game of blind-man's bluff. Hopefully, it was sort of like riding a bicycle, and she hadn't forgotten.

A little farther ahead, she could just make out the dark

silhouettes of the avocado trees that marked the edge of the Chesterfields' property. Perhaps a branch from one of those might do the trick.

Only tripping once and stumbling twice, she made it to the tree and began to feel around among the limbs for a suitable candidate. The thought occurred to her that it might be nice to have a handsaw or a pair of tree nippers for the job. But she had split more than her share of wood with karate chops over the years. What was one more?

She had just selected her branch of choice, when she heard a soft thud directly behind her . . . like something dropping to the ground.

An avocado?

But even as the thought shot through her head, and she whirled around to face the source of the sound, Savannah knew it hadn't been an avocado dropping. She recognized wishful thinking for what it was . . . even if when she heard it inside her own brain.

In the darkness, she caught the stealthy crunch of feet on leaves, two steps, directly in front of her. A swoosh of movement as an arm swung toward her head.

She ducked and felt the blow graze the top of her hair.

A figure, slightly blacker than the blackness around her, came into focus before her. Her startled mind went on hold as her karate training took over. Sure, she still had the Beretta tucked in her waistband, but there was no point in using it . . . unless it was necessary.

Taking a half step back, she braced herself, and delivered a side kick to the figure's midsection.

She heard a sick, gagging gasp as her assailant fought for breath.

Good luck, she thought. That had been an effective one. She had felt the shock reverberate through every muscle and nerve in her body.

To make certain she had completed the job, she gave another kick slightly higher. Again, contact was made . . . nice and solid, just as she had intended.

Her attacker groaned, fell backward, and crashed on the dried leaves beneath the tree, sounding as though they were thrashing about in a bowl of crispy breakfast cereal.

"Mess with me, will ya?" she said. "I'll tie your tally-whacker in a Windsor knot and see how you like it."

Her assailant didn't reply; she didn't think they were capable, which was fine with her. But she heard him—or her—struggle to their feet and stagger away, taking that shortest-between-two-points, thistle-infested trail which she had deliberately avoided earlier.

"Hmmm . . . decided not to stick around for seconds," she replied, feeling the adrenaline hit her knees and turn them to mush, now that the immediate danger had passed.

She took one step forward, stepped on something round and cylindrical, and her right foot shot out from under her. Landing in the crispy leaves—where her attacker had just been floundering—she sat there on her aching butt, feeling stupid and clumsy.

So much for agility. So much for grace. So much for being a martial-arts expert.

Beneath her calf, she could feel the round, hard object that had caused her downfall. As her fingers closed around it, doing a tactile examination, she began to laugh.

"Why, thanks," she said. "How very accommodating of you."

Her fingertip found the switch on the side of the object and flipped it. A cone of light appeared in the darkness, illuminating the path before her. She pointed the beam down the hill, but her opponent appeared to be long gone.

"Much better than a fallen avocado or a dish of guacamole any day," she said, giving the light a twirl like a cheerleader's baton.

Of course, there *was* that bag of chips she had smuggled into her room after her foray into the "real world" to see Dirk. They really could use some sort of dip.

Shining her newly acquired flashlight up into the tree, she checked the fruit until she found a couple that were nice and ripe.

As she headed down the trail—which she could now see clearly, thanks to her unknown combatant—she decided that she *could* have her flashlight, her chips, and guacamole—and eat them, too.

"Where have you been?" Tammy grabbed Savannah by the forearm and dragged her into their room. "I've been worried sick about you! First, you don't show up for lunch, then you miss dinner, too! I've never known you to skip a meal, let alone two in a row."

"Thanks a lot," Savannah replied dryly as she walked over to the bed, sat down, and began to slip out of her sneakers and socks. "I skip a lot of meals. Now between-meal snacks . . . that's a different story."

"Anyway, I'm glad you're finally back. I have something extremely cool to show you."

" 'Extremely cool'? Oh, Tammy, you've been in California

too long. What would your New York family think of your vocabulary . . . or lack of one?"

Tammy gave her a dirty look. "Okay, Georgia girl . . . I have something to show you that's hotter than a Waynesboro cotton field at high noon. Is that better?"

Savannah returned the look. "Just show me what you've got, kid, before I clean your clock. I've done it once tonight, and I'm up to another round."

"What?"

"Never mind. What is it?"

"This." Proudly, Tammy thrust a beige envelope into her face. "Somebody slid it under our door while we were out. It's addressed to you, so I didn't open it."

Savannah studied the envelope, which bore a striking resemblance to the one in her mailbox that had contained all the cash. She also examined the somewhat puckered, ever-so-slightly damp seal. "What does it say?" she asked.

Tammy's mouth opened and closed a few times and her eyes bugged a little, making her look a bit like a guppy.

"Say?" she sputtered. "How would I know what it says? Like I told you, it has your name on it. I wouldn't dream of—"

"Oh, can it. You steamed it open. I *know* you steamed it open. And now you know that I know . . . so, stop lying before your tongue turns black and falls out of your head."

"But how did you . . . "

"I had eight younger brothers and sisters, Tammy. I know when somebody's jerking my chain, and it pisses me off. So, don't do it." She took a nail file from the nightstand and carefully slit the top of the envelope. "Besides, if it had been addressed to you, *I* would have steamed it open."

"You would have?"

"Certainly. I'm just as nosy as you. But I'm a detective; I get paid for it."

Tammy snorted and plopped down on the bed beside her. "I do, too, at least in theory. You haven't written me a check yet this week."

"Stop bitching, or I won't tell you what's in my letter that you've already read."

She unfolded the sheet of matching beige stationery and read the typed words.

Dear Ms. Reid,

From what I can see, you've been doing a good job, pursuing this matter for me as I requested. It appears my money was well spent. But I'm anxious to know if you've formulated any theories as to Kat Valentina's death.

I understand it is customary for private detectives to provide reports, detailing their findings to their clients. Would you please write me such a report as soon as possible?

Leave your report in the mailbox at the entrance to the spa on La Palma Drive at nine o'clock this evening. Immediately after putting your report into the box, go directly to the public phone in the spa's main lobby near the rest rooms. I'll call you then to reveal my identity to you and give you further instructions. Please have your

*assistant, Tammy Hart, with you at the phone, as I
would like to speak with her, too. Thank you.*

"Whoever our client may be, they don't seem to have
any problem with assertiveness," Savannah said, mulling over
the letter's message and general tone.

"But at least we'll be able to find out who it is when they
call the public phone tonight."

Savannah chuckled. Ah . . . the naïveté of youth. "They
aren't going to call and tell us anything, kiddo," she told her.

"But they said . . . "

"I know. They want me at the lobby phone so they can
pick up the report without being seen. And they're smart
enough to demand that you be there, too. That way, I can't
have you posted as a lookout near the mailbox."

"Oh." Tammy looked perturbed that she had been duped.
"You'd better hurry. It's almost nine o'clock, and you have to
write your report."

"Yes, and it's too late to call Dirk. He couldn't make it
up here that quickly."

"What are you going to do? How are we going to be at
the phone booth and keep an eye on the mailbox at the same
time?"

Savannah tapped her fingernails on the envelope and
chewed her bottom lip. "I'll think of something," she said. "In
fact, it's coming to me right now."

CHAPTER TWENTY

"The stars are out," Tammy said as they hurried along the gravel driveway that led from the Royal Palms entrance to La Palma Drive.

"More importantly, the moon is up," Savannah replied. "I just hope half a moon is enough."

She held her report in her hand, a hastily scribbled account of what she had uncovered so far. Which wasn't much, once she left out a few pertinent facts that she didn't feel like sharing with some anonymous somebody—paying client or not.

"Maybe they'll call us and tell us who they are." Tammy's voice sounded so hopeful that Savannah didn't want to discourage her, but . . .

"Not meaning to sneeze on your ice cream," she said,

"but if our client calls and tells us who they are, I'll eat a cockroach dipped in Tabasco sauce."

"That's hardly a fair bet. You'll eat almost anything."

Savannah gave her a warning grunt, which seemed to work, because the younger woman stayed quiet for an entire thirty seconds or so.

They reached the end of the driveway and exited the wrought-iron gates. By the light of one streetlamp overhanging the gate, they found a large white mailbox with the spa's address painted on the side, along with the omnipresent symbol of the twin palms.

Savannah shoved her folded report inside and slammed the small door closed. Looking around, she couldn't see or hear any life-forms other than the usual crickets and occasional coyote howl.

She supposed her client was crouching behind a sage bush somewhere. But since she could see at least five hundred bushes from the spot where she stood, she decided not to waste too much time examining each one.

"There we go," she told Tammy. "Sorta like leaving a letter for Santa. And like the old fellow with the white beard, our person probably won't show as long as we're on the scene. So let's boogie."

"Do you think they're watching us right now?"

"Yeah, most likely."

"Oooo . . . creepy."

They headed back through the gates and up the driveway, their sneakers crunching loudly on the gravel.

"How do you learn all that stuff?" Tammy asked thoughtfully.

"What stuff?"

"You know, what people are going to do and all that."

Savannah chuckled. "You get burned a lot. And if you're smart, you learn from it. If you don't, you spend a lot of time waiting for phones to ring, waiting for crooks to turn themselves in, waiting for lots of frogs to turn into princes. Eventually you learn. It's a matter of self-preservation."

"Sounds like you learned the hard way."

"The hard way is the only way, kiddo. None of life's greatest lessons are learned when we're having a good time. Sadly, it just doesn't work that way."

"I wonder why that is."

Tammy sighed, sounding battle-weary. Savannah suppressed a chuckle. She knew quite a bit about Tammy's past life, and her sheltered existence hadn't been all that challenging. As a cop, Savannah had seen truly traumatized lives. And most of the people she knew—herself included—were pretty spoiled to think their own lives difficult.

"I guess life has to slap us upside the noggin to get our attention," she said.

"What's a noggin?"

"Your head."

"Oh."

"What's the matter? Don't you speak Georgian?"

"I'm learning the language. But sometimes I still need a translation."

They arrived back at the spa's gilded front doors and stepped into the lobby, which was nearly deserted at this relatively late hour. A toga-garbed Bernadette sat at the desk in the shadows of the giant plaster-cast Adam and Eve monstrosities. She gave them a nod and a curious look as they passed on their way to the rest room/public phone alcove in the rear.

"Now what?" Tammy asked as they took their positions on each side of the black, wall-mounted phone.

"We wait. It isn't hard; we're women. And if there's anything we women are good at, it's hanging out, waiting for the damned phone to ring."

"*Now* what?" Tammy shifted from one foot to the other, staring at the silent telephone.

Savannah gave her an "oh, please" look and a dismissive wave of her hand. "You need to get somebody to write you some new material; the old reruns are starting to bore me."

"But it's been over fifteen minutes! When are they going to call?"

"I already told you. There isn't going to be any call. This is just a ruse to get us out away from the mailbox so that they can pick up my report."

"Shoot." Tammy's lower lip protruded a couple of notches. "I was really hoping they'd call just so that I could tell you 'Nanny, nanny, boo, boo.'"

"That's so immature and childish of you."

"So, why are we waiting here?"

"Just on the far-flung, outside chance that I might be wrong and you might be right. But, as we can see, you blew it . . . again." She glanced at her watch. "Nine-twenty. That's long enough."

She took a step out of the alcove and looked around the lobby. Bernadette and her toga were still sitting at the desk. She was hard at work, nose deep in some sort of romance novel. No one and nothing else stirred.

Turning back to Tammy, Savannah said, "Keep an eye

opened while I'm in the ladies' room, and let me know if anybody's coming."

"Sure!" Tammy looked excited, relieved to have the wait over. "What are you going to do? Make the phone call?"

"That's exactly what I'm going to do." She lowered her voice and whispered, "If anybody comes this way, knock on the door . . . use the secret knock."

Tammy's eyes widened. "But I don't know the secret knock. What is it?"

"Do you mean to tell me that you don't know the secret detectives' knock?"

Tammy shook her head.

"It's three hard, two soft, three hard and a soft. Got that?"

"Three hard, two soft, another hard . . . and . . . oh shoot, what was the rest?"

Savannah stifled a snicker. "That's okay, Tam. Don't sweat it. If anybody's coming, just open the door a crack and tell me so."

"You got it."

The ladies' room had three stalls, a couple of sinks, and, standing in each corner, miniature statuettes resembling those in the lobby. The mirrors over the sinks were surrounded by a ring of bright, Hollywood dressing table-type lightbulbs that did nothing to flatter a woman's face. Savannah was surprised that Kat Valentina would have allowed such things in her establishment.

But then, these mirrors were for lobby visitors, more than spa guests, and maybe they were intended to instill self-doubt and loathing, like Adam and Eve with their unrealistically perfect bodies.

Savannah ducked into the third stall and bolted the door behind her. After listening and hearing nothing but the overhead fan spinning, she pulled her cellular phone from her waistband, where she had tucked it next to her Beretta.

Punching "redial" she listened to the phone play its non-melodic tune at lightning speed. After ten rings, the party on the other end answered.

"Halloo," said Phoebe Chesterfield with a voice that was strong, but sounded a bit breathless.

"It's Savannah Reid, Miss Chesterfield."

"Yes, Savannah. I'm sorry it took me so long to answer, but I had to run down from the bell tower."

"Then you were watching for me with your telescope?"

"You asked me to, didn't you?"

"Yes, but—"

"Well, unlike these younger people today, I keep my word. When I say I'm going to do something, you can bet your life on me doing it."

"That's wonderful to hear." Savannah was impatient to get off the morality lesson and on to the latest news bulletin. "So . . . did you keep an eye on the mailbox area for me?"

"Yes, I watched it. I watched it like a hawk from the minute you called me, until just now when I heard the phone ring."

"And did you see someone take anything from the mailbox?"

"I certainly did."

"That's fantastic!" Savannah could feel her heart rate rise appreciatively. "Who was it?"

"I'm not going to tell you."

"Wh—what?"

"I said, 'I'm not going to tell you.' I think I'll just keep it to myself," Phoebe Chesterfield replied as cool as a sprig of mint floating on top of a julep.

"But you can't do that! I'm the one who told you somebody was going to be there in the first place. . . ." *You nosy old biddy body*, she added silently, biting the words off on her tongue.

"Well, *you* didn't tell *me* why they were there and what they were doing. And you didn't mention why you wanted me to spy on them. Why should I share my information with you, if you're holding back on me?"

Savannah had to give her that round. She had a point, but—

"Phoebe, I can't tell you. I'm a professional private detective, and as a professional, there are certain things I'm not at liberty to discuss with other people."

"Then I'm not at liberty either. But I will tell you one thing. The person you were asking about—"

"Yes?"

"They didn't just take something out of the box. They put something in, too. Good night, Savannah. Sleep tight."

Click.

Dial tone.

"She hung up on me." Savannah stared at the phone until the operator's recorded voice came on the line, telling her to hang up the phone and try her call again later. "First she holds out on me, and then she hangs up on me! Why the gall of some people!"

A series of frantic, erratic knocks sounded on the restroom door. Savannah jumped. "What the hell?"

Suddenly, it occurred to her that this was Tammy's version of the secret detectives' knock.

She tucked the phone into her waistband, lowered her blouse, and walked out of the stall, just in time to see Tammy's head poke inside the door.

"She's coming. I think Bernadette's taking a potty break."

"Thanks."

"Did I do the knock right?"

Savannah gave her a deep-dimpled grin. "You did it perfectly."

"Gee, thanks."

Chuckling to herself, Savannah walked over to the blue-and-white-tiled sinks and washed her hands. As she was drying them on a small white hand towel, Bernadette entered, gave her a brief nod, and headed for the first stall.

"Nice evening," Savannah told her.

"Yeah. But you guys had better get in bed. Lights-out in half an hour, and exercises begin at dawn."

She disappeared inside the cubicle, and Savannah stuck her tongue out at the closed door. "No shit," she whispered, as she looked around for a receptacle for the used towel.

For one brief, perverse moment, she considered hanging it on Eve's perky boob or Adam's ridiculously large dick. But in the end, she decided to be a lady and tossed it into the white wicker hamper beneath the sink.

Granny Reid would have been proud.

"I can't believe she held out on you like that!" Tammy trudged along beside Savannah as they retraced their steps back down the driveway they had walked less than thirty minutes before. "If it hadn't been for you, she wouldn't have even known anything was going down."

"I reminded her of that," Savannah said, "but—although she was adamant about fulfilling her promise to me to spy on said party—she didn't feel morally obligated to spill her guts about what she saw."

"She probably didn't see anything at all and just doesn't want to admit it."

Savannah nodded. The kid was getting better. "I thought of that, too. But if she didn't see the person, how would she know they put something into the box."

"Maybe she made it up."

"No. I don't think so. She may be a self-righteous pain in the ass, but I don't think Phoebe Chesterfield lies. It's a feeling I get about her. Besides, we'll know soon."

Again, they exited the iron gates and walked over to the mailbox. Around them, the night seemed even quieter and darker than before. This time, Savannah didn't feel as though they were being watched. Whoever their nocturnal visitor had been, she was pretty sure they had come and gone.

Before reaching into the mailbox, she shined her flashlight—the one Fate had provided on the hillside—inside . . . just in case her contact hadn't liked her report and had left something, like a rattler, behind.

Inside, she saw a single piece of the beige stationery, folded in half. She took it out and opened it.

"What does it say?" Tammy asked, straining to read over her shoulder.

"It seems my client isn't particularly pleased with my theories," she said, studying the typed words.

Dear Savannah,

   By the way, I have heard that you think Kat may have committed suicide. That simply isn't true. She was murdered. I'm sure of it. Your job is to find out who killed her. I don't want you to waste your time and my money pursuing a dead end, so to speak.

"Well, I'd like to know why they're so sure it was a homicide," Savannah said. "They want results, but they're tying my hands here by not telling me at least everything they know."

"I'll bet you're frustrated, not being able to tell them that."

"Right now I'd just settle for a name or a face. Hell, I'd be content just to know who hired me."

CHAPTER TWENTY-ONE

Savannah lay in bed, listening to Tammy's soft snoring, cradling the cell phone next to her side, waiting, waiting. The phosphorous green numbers on the digital clock on her nightstand said it was ten-thirty.

Any minute now. Any minute.

There. The telltale buzz against her ribs signaled the call she had been waiting for ... dying for. Finally, help was on the way.

"Hello," she breathed into the phone, hardly daring to even whisper. "Yes ... yes ... oh, yes, yes, yes.... I'll meet you there in ten minutes. Thank you. Thank you so-o-o-o much."

Turning off the phone, she buried it beneath her pillow, then slipped out of bed. Already fully dressed in her simple, basic black dress, she tiptoed over to the vanity, scooped up some accessories, tugged on a pair of sneakers . . . and sneaked out of the room.

Tammy snored on, oblivious to her roommate's escape. It was all Savannah could do not to cackle with glee.

A few minutes later, she stood at the end of the gravel driveway, outside the wrought-iron gates for the third time that evening. Balancing herself with one hand on the mailbox, she slipped off the sneakers and replaced them with her black suede pumps.

She had fastened a string of pearls around her neck and was adjusting a pearl drop earring when the classic Bentley rounded the corner. Its graceful curves glistened like liquid silver in the light of the half-moon.

The elegant machine pulled to a stop beside her. The front door opened and John Gibson exited, dressed in formal chauffeur's livery. His thick, wavy hair glowed as silver as the car when he opened the back door for her and graciously ushered her inside.

"Good evening, *mademoiselle*," he said, flashing her a debonair smile.

"And good evening to you, too, Gibson," she replied in her best aristocratic voice—which sounded a bit like Julie Andrews, south of the Mason-Dixon line.

Once inside, she found herself seated on sumptuous leather next to Ryan Stone. He was dressed in a black tuxedo and was holding a flute of champagne and a lavender rose, both of which he gave to her, along with a kiss on her cheek.

"Bless you," she said, breathing in the rose's delicate fragrance. John Gibson got into the driver's seat and the Bentley glided down the dark road like a silver cloud. "Bless you both. How ever did you know that I needed to get away from this place for a few hours? How did you know I had reached the point of desperation?"

Ryan chuckled, reached for her hand and folded it between his. "Maybe it was the message on our answering service . . . the one you left this evening."

Savannah nodded thoughtfully. "You mean the one saying, 'Come and break me out of this place, before I cut my strings and go straight up'?"

"That is precisely the one that got our attention," John said from the front seat. "Since we aren't intimately familiar with your Georgian vernacular, we weren't sure what 'cutting one's strings' entailed. But it did sound a bit desperate."

"Or maybe it was all the crying," Ryan said. "The sniffling, the hysterical wailing there at the end. That was when we knew you were in a bad way."

She took a sip of her champagne, sighed, and laid her head on his broad shoulder. "That's what I love about you gay guys . . . you're so sensitive."

Ryan laughed. "That's just a silly stereotype, Savannah. I'm surprised at you. The next thing you'll be accusing us of is dressing snazzy and being good decorators."

"Have I ever told you how good you look in a tux and how much I *love* what you did with your apartment? I mean, the mahogany wainscoting, the dark green leather sofa, the diamond-tucked winged-back chair . . . that whole Tudor look is just so—"

Ryan placed two fingers on her lips. "Savannah . . ."

"Uh-huh?"

"Be quiet, enjoy your freedom, and drink your champagne so that I can refill your glass."

"Okay."

Savannah couldn't believe her good fortune. John and Ryan had actually convinced Antoine to reopen the restaurant and cook dinner for them at eleven o'clock at night. The twosome had an uncanny knack for talking anyone into anything. And Savannah had been the happy recipient of their talent on many occasions.

"For you, *mademoiselle*, I would never sleep again," Antoine gushed as he placed a lingering kiss on the back of her hand. "It is a pleasure, as always, to serve you and your friends."

Moments later, the dishes began to arrive, and Savannah was sure she had died and gone to a culinary paradise.

"So, tell me, Savannah, have you been having a wonderful time at your spa?" John Gibson asked, toasting her with a glass of Chardonnay. "Have they been properly pampering you, as you deserve?"

"Pampered? Not that I've noticed," she said. "Mostly they feed us this green gruel and make us jump up and down and run through the hills like wild rabbits. I've been there nearly a week and I've only received one massage."

"Green gruel, how revo-o-olting!" John shook his head. "And only one massage. What kind of spa is this?"

"I thought all spas were like that."

Ryan handed her a tiny croissant, stuffed with succulent crabmeat. "I'm sorry your experience has been so unpleasant. John and I have visited some marvelous spas. Salt rubs, hot-oil massages, herbal wraps . . . ah . . . the pleasures never end. And the food is healthy and wholesome, but delectable."

"Yeah, well, the Royal Palms is a no-frills sort of club. I don't know if it ever was legitimate, but it certainly isn't now. They're obviously operating on very limited resources. I think they're in serious financial trouble."

"Yes, they are," John said, scooping some pâté onto a bit of bread. "We've checked for you. The Internal Revenue Service has a lien on the property, and the bank is about to foreclose on their mortgage. Several of their creditors are bringing lawsuits against them. I'd say bankruptcy is on the near horizon."

"Lou Hanks needs Kat's life insurance money," Savannah said. "No doubt about it. But that's hardly proof of murder."

"To be honest, Savannah, there's no evidence of homicide at all, is there?" Ryan asked.

She could see the doubt in his eyes, hear it in his voice. It seemed nearly everyone thought Kat's death had been accidental. Was she stupid for believing otherwise when there wasn't a shred of physical evidence to support her suspicions? She supposed time would tell.

"No," she said, "none. The only reason why I've even questioned the circumstances is because of the notes and money I've received from my anonymous client."

"But they won't even tell you who they are, let alone who murdered her . . . or how the killer supposedly did it."

"I know. I've been feeling my way around in the dark with this case, figuratively . . . and literally," she added, remembering the night before in the avocado grove.

"Were there any signs of injury at all on the body?" John asked her. "Anything to indicate a struggle?"

"None. Not a scratch or a bruise."

Ryan took a sip of his wine. "Ms. Valentina was relatively young. As a professional dancer, she must have been fairly strong. Besides, she was known for her fiery personality. I can't imagine her going down without a struggle."

"Me either," Savannah admitted.

John toyed with his bread and scowled, thinking. "Unless she was already unconscious when she slipped beneath the mud."

"That's what Dr. Liu decided," Savannah said. "Jennifer believes the heat from the mud bath, combined with the alcohol from the margaritas, caused her to faint. She passed out, slid deeper into the bath, and drowned."

"Did the doctor find mud in her lungs?" Ryan asked.

"Yes. So she was alive and still breathing when she went down."

"Such a sad business." John shook his head. "And I'm sure Dr. Liu ran the standard toxicology tests. . . ."

"She did," Savannah said. "And the only thing amiss was Kat's extraordinarily high blood alcohol level. Although, from what I understand, a high alcohol content wasn't unusual for Kat Valentina."

Ryan replenished her wineglass, then gave her a sympathetic smile. "I know you're working hard on this, Savannah, and I understand that you have a gut-level feeling about it. But, if she *was* murdered, how do you suppose they did it without leaving any signs of violence on the body?"

"I don't know. Maybe somebody slipped her a mickey in the margarita pitcher."

John brightened. "Now, there's a thought. Did the doctor test the residue on the pitcher and glass?"

"Not to my knowledge. I don't think she would, unless something showed up in the toxicology screen. Why test the glassware if there's nothing in the body?"

"True."

Both men looked as confused and discouraged as Savannah felt.

As though on cue, Antoine appeared, bearing another tray of canapés. Savannah's spirits immediately lifted.

"Enough shop talk about gruesome and ghoulish topics," she said. "Why work when we can eat? *Bon appetit.*"

An hour later, Savannah felt like Cinderella being driven home in her carriage after the ball. But she couldn't get her mind off the case. Settled in the backseat with Ryan, she recounted her misadventures, the frustrations she and Tammy had experienced, trying to be everywhere and watch everyone at once.

When she finished telling them about the avocado-grove attack and the mailbox fiasco, Ryan said, "That's it. I know you're an independent woman, Savannah, who likes to do everything herself. But I think it's time to pool our resources."

Leaning forward, he tapped John on the shoulder. "What do you think, old chap?" he said. "Would you like to spend a little time with me at a wonderful spa? It comes highly recommended."

"So I've heard," John replied dryly. "It sounds perfectly splendid. I can scarcely control my enthusiasm."

Ryan laughed, and said to Savannah, "That's what I've always loved about the British . . . their unbridled apathy."

Like Cinderella shedding her finery, Savannah propped herself against the mailbox, slipped off her suede pumps, and replaced them with her sneakers. Tucking the heels under her arm, she walked as quietly as possible along the gravel driveway. The last thing she needed was to get busted, creeping back into the Royal Palms with the smell of wine and French cuisine on her breath and a sated look on her face.

Avoiding the front entrance, she took a circuitous path around the main building to the dormitory. The night air was cool and sea-damp, chilling her through the light silk dress. As she hugged her arms across her chest for warmth, she wished she had accepted Ryan's offer of his evening jacket.

She had almost taken the coat, eager for the opportunity to feel his body warmth and breathe his cologne for a few minutes. But then she had realized it might be a bit difficult to explain the presence of a man's tuxedo jacket in her closet the next morning to the nosy, ever-vigilant Tammy.

Just when she thought she was home free, her hand on the doorknob, her foot poised to step across the threshold . . . a door to one of the private cottages farther down the path opened. Out stepped Bernadette, moving with the same degree of stealth and guilt as she.

Savannah didn't have to do much high-level detecting to determine why Bernadette was slinking around at this late hour; she had just exited Louis Hanks's bungalow.

Most people wouldn't have broadcast the fact that they were sleeping with the boss, although Savannah surmised that the secret was being kept only in Bernadette's delusional fantasies. From the rumors and gossip flying around the place, everyone and their dog appeared to know the score.

For a moment, both women pretended not to see the other. Savannah had decided it would be easier, less complicated this way.

But Bernadette seemed to reconsider.

"Savannah, yoo-hoo," she called softly, beckoning her. In the silent, still night, the half whisper seemed to boom along the dark passageway. Even the crickets hushed their chirping to listen.

"I was looking for you earlier," the young redhead said, as Savannah reluctantly approached, "but I couldn't find you anywhere. Did you leave the grounds?"

"Leave? Why would I want to do a thing like that?"

"Everyone wants to leave. That's why it's so depressing to work here."

"So, why do you . . . ?" Savannah gave a slight nod toward Hanks's bungalow. "Work here, that is?"

"Lou's going to help me get into the movies. Just like he did for Kat. He made her everything she was, you know, and he never really got enough credit for it. But, when I get to the top, I won't forget who put me there. No, sirree. I'll owe it all to Lou."

"Um . . . I see." Savannah shook her head, watching the stars sparkle in Bernadette's eyes. The girl was really out there if she thought she was going to be the next Kat Valentina. Even if Lou *had* been responsible for Kat's success, Bernadette wasn't a likely candidate to fill Kat's dancing slippers. That was painfully obvious to Savannah, just by looking at the young woman. Bernadette was one of those sad people with far more blind, misguided ambition than talent or wisdom.

"Did you get a chance to talk to Dion?" Bernadette asked, a tad too eagerly.

"About what?"

"About the fight he had with Kat right before she died. You know, when he said he would kill her."

"Yes, actually, we did discuss that briefly and—"

"And?"

Yes, Savannah decided, Bernadette was much too eager. The urgency on her face was more than just a mere appetite for gossip.

"And he said he would never hurt Kat, that she was one of his dearest friends."

"Yeah, yeah, everybody says that. So what? It doesn't mean he didn't do it."

"That's true. But all we had was a short conversation on the topic. I didn't expect him to break down and confess murder to me, then and there."

"But I'm sure he did it."

"*You* may be sure. I might suspect. But the authorities are going to need a lot more . . . like some physical evidence, for instance."

Bernadette glanced up and down the empty passageway and lowered her voice. "I know where you could find some."

"Really? Where?"

"In his room."

"What do you think I would find in his room?"

"Maybe some love letters or something like that."

"From him to Kat?"

"More like, from Kat to him. Everybody knew she had the hots for him . . . ever since they made that movie together."

"Did they have an affair?"

"I don't know. Don't think so. But if they didn't, it's more because Kat wasn't Dion's type."

"I thought Kat was everybody's type."

Bernadette donned an unattractive, contemptuous sneer. It occurred to Savannah that it was easy to have contempt for the "other woman." At least, it made things easier to rationalize.

"She wasn't *everybody's* type," Bernadette said. "She just thought she was. There were lots of guys who resisted her charms. Dion was one of them. He's too classy for the likes of Kat Valentina."

"You think so?"

"I *know* so. It was ridiculous how she used to chase him, when everybody knew he wasn't the least bit interested in her."

"That must have been pretty humiliating for her."

"No kidding. I'm surprised it wasn't *her* who killed *him*."

"You're that sure he did it?"

"I think she probably had an accident. But if anybody murdered her, I think it was Dion. Why don't you check out his room tomorrow? He's going into town to do some errands for Lou about nine o'clock. And he'll be gone for at least two hours."

She fished around in her sweater pocket and pulled out a key. Dropping it into Savannah's hand, she said, "Nobody would bother you . . . if you wanted to take a look around, that is."

Savannah curled her fingers around the key and felt it, like small, cold, metal teeth against her palm.

"How accommodating of you," she said with a sarcastic edge to her voice.

Bernadette didn't seem to notice. "No problem," she returned with a toss of coppery curls. "Just trying to help."

As the redhead turned and walked away, Savannah wondered at the ease and convenience of this new tip. Too easy. Too convenient. Information or evidence that was dumped into her lap was usually worthless.

She tossed the key up, watched it flip and turn, reflecting the moonlight, then snatched it out of the air and held it tightly.

But a tip was a tip. And she intended to follow through on this one. At nine o'clock—or a few minutes after, just to make sure he wasn't coming back—she would be inside Dion Zeller's bedroom.

Oh, how she would have been the envy of thousands of females. Except, of course, they would never know, because she was a good girl. She didn't break and enter . . . and tell.

CHAPTER TWENTY-TWO

"I don't wanna play lookout; it's bo-o-oring," Tammy whined, as they stood near the door of Dion's cottage.

The bungalow occupied the most prestigious location of any of the others, at the end—offering more privacy—and conveniently situated between the pool and tennis courts. Apparently, Kat had provided her co-star with her best guesthouse. Savannah thought that fact particularly poignant, considering that she was about to search that cottage for evidence that Dion might have murdered his benefactor.

She glanced around, but the couple playing tennis nearby seemed totally absorbed, and the lone swimmer in the pool was intent on doing laps.

"Stop your complaining," she told Tammy. "Monopoly takes too long to set up, and I don't play doctor with other girls. So, 'lookout' it is."

"Okay, but don't ask me to do that stupid detective knock thing. I mentioned it to Dirk yesterday on the phone, and he laughed himself stupid over it."

"With Dirk, that shouldn't have taken very long."

Savannah hurried to the door, slipped the key into the lock, and turned it, thinking how much easier her job was when she had the appropriate provisions.

"Be out in a few," she said, then disappeared inside, leaving a pouting Tammy to keep watch.

The first thing she noticed about the room was the strong smell of glue. The odor was all too familiar to her, as she had smelled it too often in the bedrooms of wigged-out teenagers and the living rooms of assorted "adults" who were old enough to know better.

Dion Zeller is a sniffer? she thought, wondering how anyone as robust-looking as he could have a substance-abuse problem. But one glance around told her the reason for the smell, and it had nothing to do with addiction . . . except maybe to detail.

Everywhere she looked, she saw models, miniatures of every mode of transportation imaginable, meticulously crafted and displayed. From the ceiling hung a strange mixture of vintage WWI and WWII aircraft, the Starship *Enterprise*, and a flock of pterodactyls. The walnut bookshelves along one wall held no books, but tiny classic automobiles and trucks, including her own 1968 SS/RS Camaro.

Around the ceiling, making a complete circuit, was a railroad track with three trains, switching stations, and a matching same-scale Dickensian village.

In the corner of the main living area sat a large table, racks of tiny paint jars, a can of brushes, a lighted magnifying glass on a swiveling arm, and an array of delicate knives, drills, saws, and tweezers.

Apparently, Dion Zeller had more patience than she, maybe more than anyone she knew. And he was truly an artist, a master at creating this Lilliputian world of his.

Savannah recalled the tanned, golden-haired demigod who had run beside her through the foothills, and tried to imagine him sitting at that table, painting details so tiny, so ornate.

The two images simply wouldn't merge in her mind. But she had learned long ago that human beings had many facets: hidden talents, secrets dreams, vices, and virtues. It took so long to truly get to know someone, and even then, there were always surprises.

Once she got over her initial amazement at the models, she began to assess the rest of the room. Although, the only extraordinary feature was the miniature collection. Everything else was neat but bachelor generic.

An oversize entertainment center held a large television, stereo system, and accompanying videos and CDs. The furniture was leather, chrome, and glass and recently dusted.

The kitchenette was predictably austere for a guy who probably ate most of his meals in the spa dining room. She found the bedroom equally utilitarian—hardly a sex symbol's den of iniquity, as Dion's female following would have liked to imagine.

The one thing Savannah had been expecting to see was conspicuously absent in the cottage—any signs, posters, or memorabilia of the star's "glory days." There was no indication Dion had ever been one of the leading icons of the sexual revolution, the object of so many women's fantasies and adoration.

Somehow, the fact made Savannah like and respect him even more. Unlike Kat, he hadn't lived in the past, feeding off old exploits and memories of bygone fame.

But she couldn't imagine that he hadn't kept some tangible reminder of that pinnacle of his career. He must have stashed something, somewhere.

But where?

As she glanced around the apartment, she noticed one thing that seemed out of place with the rest of the modern decor—an old sea chest at the foot of his bed. The strongbox was a charming antique, made of teak with brass fittings with a faded painting of a clipper ship in full sail across the front.

Savannah knelt in front of the chest and slid the bolt aside to open it. The hinges protested with a spine-shivering little groan as she lifted the lid and looked inside.

"Oh, Georgia girl, your brilliance never fails to dazzle me," she whispered to herself. "But then, I'm pretty easy to impress, so . . ."

Yes, this was Dion Zeller's sentimental stash, no doubt about it. She saw photo albums and loose snapshots, stacks of letters bundled with rubber bands, a lady's lace handkerchief which looked at least fifty years old, a tassel from a graduation cap, a small, well-worn, well-loved teddy bear, a pair of champagne flutes, a New Year's Eve party hat, and dozens of other items that symbolized the special moments of a man's life.

As always when searching the private things of someone she knew, especially someone she liked, Savannah felt a wave of guilt. At times like these, she sometimes asked herself if the business of detection was blackening her soul. As always, she told herself the end justified the means, the highest objective was to secure justice for injured parties.

And, as always, it worked. Kind of.

Rationalization aside, she still felt like a heel.

But her pangs of conscience evaporated as her interest was piqued. She had picked up one of the bundles of letters. They had all been written on a distinctive, rose-tinted stationery with the same, sweeping, feminine hand.

They were love letters. From Kat Valentina to her former co-star.

Savannah scanned several of them and felt her cheeks flush a pleasant shade of peach at the florid, torrid phraseology. Kat had a real way with words, and she didn't seem shy about using them . . . or shy about anything, for that matter.

While Savannah liked to think she had been around the romance block a few times herself, she had to admit that Kat had her beat. Ms. Valentina seemed to have paved the very road, poured the sidewalk, and planted the decorative shrubbery.

Whatever Kat might have been, she hadn't been a prude. She had been madly, desperately in love with her longtime friend. And—as Savannah read the letters and marked the nonprogression of their relationship—she realized that Kat's amorous feelings had not been returned. At all.

If the tide had run the other way, Savannah might have suspected Dion of killing a woman who wouldn't return his affection, but how could the contents of these letters have led to Kat's own demise? Something seemed askew, and Savannah couldn't quite figure out what.

Savannah took more time than she had intended to read all the letters. But other than an ever-heightening level of agitation, the theme seemed consistent, month after month. Kat wanted Dion; Dion didn't want Kat.

When Savannah checked the dates in the upper right hand corner, she realized that Kat had been pursuing him for the past four years, at least. That was a long time for a woman to be scorned.

So, why hadn't Dion been the one lying, lifeless, in the mud bath, staring into eternity?

Still looking for answers, Savannah began to flip through one of the photograph albums. The pictures were pretty standard fare: vacation shots, assorted pets, a few cars, and family holiday get-togethers.

Then she came to a series of other photos, taken on a tropical island somewhere, on what must have been a romantic getaway with a lover.

A much younger Dion looked happy, relaxed and completely infatuated by the sweetheart at his side. Apparently, those had been happy times for the two of them, and Savannah found herself wondering what had happened to end the relationship.

She wondered if Dion still grieved for his lost love. Did his mate on the tropical island know that he still had these photos, that he obviously treasured them and kept them with those few items that were dearest to his heart?

Savannah couldn't help wondering.

Because she knew that smiling face, the one next to Dion's in the pictures. She knew it all too well. And she never ceased to be amazed that, no matter how completely you thought you knew a person, they always, always had more secrets. You never knew it all.

* * *

"I'm so glad you got my message," Savannah said as Ryan stepped into the gazebo and sat beside her on the cushioned bench. "And thanks for coming alone."

"No problem." He gave her an affectionate peck on her cheek. "Your note made it clear you wanted it that way. I always aim to please a pretty lady."

Briefly, Savannah wondered if she would ever get over this silly, futile crush she had on Ryan Stone. His very nearness set her pantaloons aquiver, and the effect didn't appear to be lessening over time.

"Did John see my note?" she asked.

"Yes, the young redhaired receptionist gave it to us right after we registered."

"Was he upset that I didn't invite him, too?"

"Upset?" Ryan thought for a moment. "No, I wouldn't say he was upset. Maybe a bit curious. For that matter, so am I."

Savannah turned and looked across the landscape, drawing from the tranquility the view offered. Golden, late-afternoon sunlight gilded the tawny foothills, causing even the ragged scrub brush to look like royal velvet, gracefully draped to display its luxurious pile to the greatest advantage.

In the distance, she could see a sparkling, blue strip of ocean that disappeared into sea haze and the purple islands at the farthest edge of the horizon.

"I'm sorry to be so mysterious," she said. "I just thought it would be better if you and I talked privately first." She turned to him and gave him a searching look. "You see, it's about Dion Zeller."

He nodded knowingly. "I had a feeling you'd be asking

me about Dion, sooner or later. You're a good detective, Savannah. I knew it was just a matter of time before you and I were going to be strolling down memory lane together. My memories, that is, and *my* lane."

"Do you mind talking about him?"

"Not at all. Dion was an important part of my life, a very nice part. But that was a long time ago."

"Then you knew him . . . before John?"

"Yes. Right before. I met John a few months after Dion and I parted ways."

Savannah was relieved, though she chided herself for worrying in the first place. From what she knew of Ryan, he was an honorable man, a gentleman whose word was sacred. She would have been surprised if he had been unfaithful to his partner.

"I searched Dion's room today, and I found some pictures of the two of you, vacationing, I think."

A shy smile crossed Ryan's face, and he said, "Hmmm . . . so, he kept them. That's sort of nice to know, I guess."

"Were you together for long?"

"A little over a year."

"He seems like a nice man. Did you care a lot for him?"

It was Ryan's turn to stare off into the distant ocean haze, remembering. "Yes. A lot. Dion is . . . well, at least he was . . . a very kind, intelligent, funny, caring person. Quite the opposite of the mindless hunk in his movies. Although, I don't know what he's like now. It's been a long time since we saw each other or even spoke."

"What happened?" she asked. "Why did you go your separate ways?"

Ryan sighed, and she could see in his eyes how the memories still caused him pain. "Dion lived his life in secrecy, hiding who he was from those he loved most: immediate family, close friends, business associates. I couldn't do that. I came out young, in my early twenties. And I hated the lying, the sneaking around, the facade that he insisted we wear. I couldn't. I cared for him, but I couldn't, wouldn't live the lie."

"I understand. Do you think he stayed in the closet because of his career?"

Ryan shook his head. "No, definitely not. Dion's fame and momentary fortune never meant that much to him. It was his family's and friends' disapproval that he couldn't risk. He couldn't bear the thought of being rejected by them if they found out."

Flashing back on her conversation with Bernadette, Savannah said, "I heard via the grapevine that Kat had the hots for him."

Ryan chuckled. "So? Are you surprised? In case you hadn't noticed, he's gorgeous."

"Oh, I noticed." She rolled her eyes. "Believe me, I noticed big time. But Kat was his co-star, one of his best friends. She must have known he was gay."

"Like I said, Dion's life was a secret, and guarding that secret consumed most of his time and energy. I'm not surprised that Kat didn't know. Very few people did."

"Maybe she found out later. I hear she threatened to expose him for something, just before she died. Do you think that could be what it was?"

"To my knowledge, Dion conducted his affairs—no pun intended—with integrity. I don't know any other clandestine activities that he would have wanted to keep hidden. But, remember, I haven't been in contact with him for years. People change."

Savannah thought of what Bernadette had said about Dion threatening Kat's life.

"Would the Dion you knew and cared for have committed murder?"

Ryan laughed, but there was no humor in the sound. "Long ago, I gave up trying to figure out what a person would or wouldn't do. Who knows what any of us are capable of doing under the right or wrong circumstances?" He took a deep breath. "But to answer your question: No, I don't believe the Dion I knew would kill anyone."

"Not even if they threatened to expose him, to tell the world—and more importantly, his friends and family—he was gay?"

Ryan thought long and hard before he answered. "Once again, I can't imagine him murdering someone. But I can tell you one thing . . . if Dion Zeller ever *would* kill another human being, that would be the reason why."

By the time Savannah and Ryan had left the gazebo and strolled back to the guests' dormitory, the sun had set and the spa's daily activities were winding down. Several swimmers splashed in the pool, and one elderly man was enjoying a tennis lesson from Bernadette on the court. Other than those individuals, they saw no one as they entered the dorm and headed for their appointed rooms.

"Early to bed and early to rise," she said as they walked down the hallway and arrived at her door, "makes me cranky and puffy 'round the eyes."

Ryan leaned over and placed a kiss on the top of her

head. "My dear, it would take more than a few early risings to ruin your sweet disposition."

"You think far too highly of me," she said, flashing him a dimpled grin. "But please don't stop. I need at least one friend who thinks I'm adorable ... deluded though he may be."

He tweaked the end of her nose. "Good night, Savannah."

"You, too. Sleep tight, and don't let the bedbugs bite."

He grimaced. "That's revolting."

"Not at all. It's a quaint Southern phrase. Actually, in my childhood circles it was considered a ritualistic nightly blessing ... sort of. But then I was also told, 'Don't let the bogeyman catch you with your bloomers down when you're contemplatin' philosophy in the outhouse.' So much for quaint Southern phraseology."

She gave him a kiss on the cheek, then a wave good-bye as he continued on down the hall to the room he now shared with John Gibson.

Mercy, that man is a hunk and a half, she thought, while watching him walk away. Ryan was as dark and handsome as Dion was gold and gorgeous; they must have made a stunning couple.

Oh, well. . . .

She unlocked her door—or at least, she *started* to unlock the door—but found someone had beaten her to it.

It's probably Tammy, she told herself as she turned the knob and eased the door open a crack. *Even though I told her to be sure it was locked all the time, she must have forgotten.*

But she knew it wasn't Tammy. She could hear someone rummaging around in the room, and if it were Tammy, the hair on the back of her neck wouldn't be standing at attention. And she wouldn't have gooseflesh on her arms.

She reached into her sweater pocket and pulled out the Beretta, feeling its reassuring cold metal weight in her palm. Never, in all her years of carrying the weapon, had she actually been forced to shoot anyone with it. And for that, she was infinitely grateful.

But she had scared the crap out of more than a few, and that had been just fine and dandy with her. One of the advantages of carrying a big gun was its fright quotient. Looking down that cavernous barrel tended to make even a hardened criminal reconsider his position on a number of society's most controversial issues.

Bracing herself, holding the gun with both hands, she kicked the door the rest of the way open and found herself face-to-face with the intruder.

"What the hell are you doing in my room?" she asked the person who stood only about six feet in front of her, face frozen in shock.

When no reply was forthcoming, she added, "Never mind what you're doing here. What I want to know is: Were you the asshole who tried to knock me over the head in the avocado grove? 'Cause if you were, I'm gonna plug you one, right between your beady little eyes."

CHAPTER TWENTY-THREE

Savannah had found her former assailant; no doubt about it. She could tell by the way he refused to meet her eyes as she stared him down over the Beretta's barrel.

"Okay, Josef, cough it up. Why were you stalking me in the oleanders and trying to bash my brains in under the avocados? What did I ever do to you?"

"You went through my room, messed with my stuff without my permission."

His eyes were coldly angry, and Savannah made a mental note to herself to watch this one. He was more than pissed; he was big, he was ugly, and he was dangerous. She wondered if Kat Valentina had looked into those eyes the night she had died.

"You went through my room first," she said, taking a verbal stab in the dark. Of course, she had no way of knowing if Josef had been the one to rearrange and redecorate their room when she had first arrived, but it was worth a try. "And you left mine a mess. At least I was neat when I searched yours."

Score one for the girls' team, she thought when his eyes widened with surprise and maybe a touch of guilt. Gee, maybe Josef the Terrible had a wee bit of a conscience, after all. Or, perhaps, his reaction had been mere discomfort at having been caught.

"What were you looking for when you tore our room to shreds?" she asked, deciding to press her advantage. After all, since she had him at gunpoint, she would probably never have a better time to grill him.

When he didn't answer, she waved the gun a bit for emphasis. "Well?"

"Information," was his curt, tight-lipped reply.

"About what?"

"About why you were here. It was pretty obvious you didn't come to the Royal Palms to get into shape."

The way he gave her a quick, sarcastic, visual scan up and down her body made her want to nick one of his overly developed biceps with a bullet . . . just for effect . . . one little grazing wound. It probably wouldn't bleed much, and the shag carpet was pretty ratty anyway.

"You're here to get something on Kat, aren't you?" he said bitterly.

"On Kat? She's the one who's dead, remember?"

"Yeah, but you're trying to say she killed herself. You're going to ruin her reputation."

"Her reputation?" Savannah almost chuckled but reconsidered. Josef didn't look like a guy who was particularly skilled in impulse control, and there was nothing to be gained by pushing him beyond his limits. If he charged her, she'd have to shoot him—and that would sully her pristine record.

"Kat may have done some things that you and other self-righteous bitches didn't approve of," he said, "but she didn't kill herself. She wouldn't do that. She *wouldn't*. It must have been an accident, just like that doctor lady said it was."

"So, maybe somebody else killed her." She watched him closely and saw his pupils dilate. "If that happened, if someone murdered her, do you want them to get away with it?"

His face twisted with an emotion she couldn't quite read. "Is that . . . is that what you think happened?" he asked. A muscle twitched in his cheek.

"May have."

Her arm was developing a cramp from holding the heavy pistol, but it seemed a small price to pay. She thought of the woman he had been convicted of stalking. She remembered the whistle of the wooden club over her head in the avocado grove.

No, she was going to keep Josef Orlet at attention, paying attention, as long as possible.

"I already told the cops," he said, "if Kat was murdered, that hoity-toity doctor did it. She was sick, and afraid she was going to suffer and all that. She asked him to put her away, nice and gentle, and he agreed to."

"How do you know all this?"

"She told me so herself."

Savannah eyed him skeptically. Somehow, Josef Orlet didn't seem the sort of individual to whom Kat Valentina would confide her heart's deepest secrets.

"*She* told *you* all of this?"

"Yeah." The word caught in his throat. He gave a little cough, and added, "Or I might of heard them talking about it together. I don't remember for sure."

"You heard him tell her that he would assist her suicide?"

"Yeah, but she changed her mind. I talked her out of it later."

"You did, huh?" He didn't seem the type who could talk people back from the cliff edge of Death's Big Jump either.

"That's right. I told her how I felt about her. And, since she felt the same way about me, she decided she had too much to live for. So she canceled their little appointment."

"She admitted she was in love with you?"

"She sure did."

"I see."

"What's the matter, don't you believe me?"

"Nope."

She saw the flash of bad temper cross his face before he looked down the barrel of the gun and got control of it. "Well, that's what she said, the day before she died. If you ask *me* what happened, it was an accident, like they said. She drank too much and got too hot. But if it wasn't accidental, if somebody did kill her, then I figure it was the doc. Maybe he decided to keep their appointment, whether she wanted to or not."

"Why would he do a thing like that?"

" 'Cause maybe when she told him that she had changed her mind, she also said she was in love with me. And maybe he couldn't handle it."

"That's sorta stretching it a bit, don't you think?"

"Stretching what? That a beautiful woman like Kat would have a thing for a guy like me? What's so unbelievable about that?"

Hearing a sound behind her, Savannah took a quick glance and saw Tammy entering the room.

"Hey, what's . . . !" she exclaimed when she saw Savannah's drawn gun.

"It's okay," Savannah told her. "Mr. Orlet was paying us a visit. But, darn it, we weren't home at the time, so we couldn't show him much hospitality. And now we've got a zillion things to do, so he's going to have to leave."

She turned to Orlet. "Sorry you have to rush away like this. Maybe next time you can take off your coat, throw it in the corner, and stay a spell."

With the barrel of the gun, she waved him toward the door. Tammy quickly moved aside to let him pass and to stay out of Savannah's line of fire.

Orlet wasted no time disappearing.

"Was he breaking into our room?" Tammy asked, her mouth gaping.

"Seems so. Must be one of those nosy jerks who needs to buy a life of their own."

"You think he was the one who did it before?"

"I know so; he admitted it."

"And you let him go?"

Savannah shrugged and tucked her pistol back into her pocket. "There wasn't really much point in holding him. I'm investigating a suspicious death, not busting burglars. Besides, to the best of my knowledge, he didn't steal anything from us."

"But he wasn't supposed to be in our room."

"I know. But we can't exactly lock him up in San Quentin for trespassing."

Tammy shuddered. "Maybe not, but he gives me the creeps."

"And you aren't the one he tried to brain in the avocado grove."

"Brain? Someone tried to hurt you?"

"Yeah, lock the door and sit yourself down on the bed, kiddo. We've got some catching up to do."

Savannah had barely filled Tammy in on the latest pertinent details when she received a summons, via Bernadette, from Dion.

"He wanted me to give you this," the redhead had said, standing at Savannah's and Tammy's door with the small, folded note in her hand.

"What does it say?" Savannah asked her.

Bernadette's eyes widened in a poor imitation of surprise and righteous indignation. "How would I know? He told me it was for *you.*"

"Yeah, right," Savannah had said before closing the door in her face. The Pope himself wouldn't have been able to resist sneaking one little peek, and Savannah had a strong notion that Bernadette wasn't even Catholic.

After assuring Tammy that she would be fine, answering the summons in the note, Savannah had taken off for Dion's cottage, flashlight in one pocket, Beretta in the other. All she needed, she decided, was a couple of sticks to rub together and she would rival the Girl Scouts for readiness.

When Dion answered the door, she was shocked at his appearance. His eyes were red and swollen, as though he had been crying, and he radiated none of the vibrancy she had found so attractive before.

"Come in," he told her, ushering her inside and over to a black-and-white leather chair beneath a model of the *Spirit of St. Louis*. "I'd offer you a drink, but I'm out of cola, and I don't drink booze."

"That's all right," she said. "Why did you want to see me?"

He collapsed onto a matching chair beside hers and ran his fingers through his mussed blond hair. He looked tired, anxious, and more than a little afraid.

"You've been asking me a lot of questions," he said. "In fact, you've been questioning *everybody*. So, I thought you shouldn't mind if I asked *you* a few."

She searched his eyes for hostility, but she saw none. "Go ahead," she said.

"I had a long talk with Ryan Stone," he began, "and he says you know about us."

"That's right. Ryan is a close friend of mine; we share a lot of things."

"Did Ryan tell you first, or did you find out on your own?"

She considered a couple of lies, then discarded them. She liked Dion and figured he deserved an honest answer . . . though not too detailed. "I uncovered your relationship with Ryan in the course of my investigation here," she said. "And when I asked him, he confirmed it."

Dion took a deep breath and she could see the pain etched deeply in his face. For the first time, he looked his age; he looked like a has-been disco star.

"What do you intend to do with this newfound information of yours, Savannah?" he asked.

"At the moment, nothing."

He looked only slightly mollified. "And later?"

"That remains to be seen. I have no desire to betray my friend's confidence, or to hurt someone he cares for."

"I see."

He stood and walked over to his table, where his latest model, a clipper ship, was spread out in hundreds of tiny pieces. Picking up one of the yardarms, he turned the piece over and over in his fingers, like a miniature band major's baton.

"If Kat *was* murdered," he said, "and you think she was . . . there will be an in-depth investigation. Isn't that true?"

She could see where this was leading, but she couldn't think of any way to head him off at the verbal pass. Besides, she had already decided to be honest with him.

"Yes," she said. "I suspect there will be."

"And whatever information you've uncovered . . . you'll be forced to reveal it?"

"If it's pertinent to the case, I suppose I will."

He swallowed hard. "Do you think my relationship with Ryan will be of interest to the authorities?"

"Probably not."

"How about my lack of interest in returning Kat's affection . . . and the reasons for that?"

Savannah shrugged. "Maybe."

"I can't go through that, Savannah. I *can't*. Please believe me."

"Please, don't worry about it, Dion," she said, trying to sound as convincing as possible. "Really, there's no reason to fear the worst . . . not yet."

He turned to her with more anguish on his handsome face than she could recall seeing in a long time. Her heart went out to him . . . for all the good it did.

"And are you going to tell me when it's time to worry?"

he asked. "Are you going to tell me when my life, as I've lived it so far, will be over, when it's going to come crashing around my head?"

"Dion . . . I . . ."

She stood, walked over to him and put her hand on his arm. She thought of what Ryan had said about Dion's unforgiving, unsupportive friends and family.

Words of advice sprang to her mind, lectures about having the courage to live with honesty and openness, despite society's judgments and criticisms. But Savannah quickly reminded herself that only a fool offered advice that they, themselves, had never been in a position to take. It was always so easy, when you were on the outside, looking in. Or so it seemed.

No, she would do them both a favor and keep her pious platitudes to herself.

She couldn't think of anything else to say. And she had always thought that, in times like those, it was best to just keep your mouth shut. So, she did.

But she patted his arm. And she said silently wished him peace, love, and understanding.

No matter what she did to keep the facts of this case under wraps, the details were bound to leak out, sooner or later. Sex, violence, and celebrity—media mainstays. When this news hit the tabloids, Dion Zeller was going to need all the compassion and understanding he could get.

CHAPTER TWENTY-FOUR

"I appreciate you taking me out for breakfast like this," Savannah said as she sat next to John Gibson and watched him maneuver the majestic Bentley around the curves of La Palma Drive.

"You'll be eternally grateful when you see where we're going," he replied, a smug grin curving his silver mustache.

Visions of strawberry cheese blintzes danced in Savannah's head, or perhaps Antoine's crêpe Suzette. With John's gourmet taste, anything was possible.

"But there aren't any restaurants in this direction," she said as they headed toward the residential, more rural, hills. "Unless we're going to rob an avocado or lemon grove."

"Better than that, my dear," he told her. "Much better. We're going to be sharing a spot of tea—and with any luck,

a French pastry—with Ford Chesterfield at his marvelous hacienda."

"You got us an interview with Ford Chesterfield? But . . .
but he refused my calls. I've called him at least four times in
the last three days, but he won't come to the phone. He tells
his sister to get rid of me. Of course, she worded it a little
more politely than that, but the bottom line was still the
same."

"I know, love. But, forgive me for saying so, but *you* didn't
attend Oxford at the same time he did, many years ago. And,
since I'm not nearly as charming or beautiful as you, I'm certain
my Oxford affiliation is the only reason I received this invitation. You mustn't take it personally."

"He actually *invited* you for breakfast?"

"Well, I rang him last evening and suggested I knock him
up this morning at half-nine and that he might have a pot of
Earl Grey brewing."

"Knock up . . . ? Half nine . . . ?" She did a quick British/
Californian translation. "Ah, ha . . . you told him you'd drop
by at nine-thirty."

"Of course, dear girl, that's what I said. You *are* happy
about this, aren't you? I distinctly recall at dinner the other
night you were bemoaning the fact that you hadn't had the
opportunity to interrogate him."

"Sure, I am. I'm thrilled. So, he knows I'm coming, too?
He agreed to talk to me?"

"Not at all. It should be a lovely surprise. I simply can't
wait to see the look on the old chap's face. It should prove
most entertaining."

"Me either," Savannah said with subdued enthusiasm.
"Gee . . . just can't wait."

* * *

Savannah sat at a white, glass-topped, wrought-iron table with John Gibson on her right side and Ford Chesterfield to her left. She definitely felt outclassed.

A pot of tea, shaped like a small English cottage, steamed in the center of the table, and each of their cups were filled to the brim with the fragrantly floral-scented Earl Grey.

And Ford Chesterfield had not thrown her out on her ear the moment he saw her. Although he appeared a bit leery, he had certainly been cordial enough when inviting them inside the house, then out to the garden patio.

"Where is Phoebe?" Savannah asked, mildly disappointed that the lady hadn't made an appearance.

"She is attending the monthly meeting of her garden club," Ford replied between small, delicate sips. "I'm afraid the third Wednesday of every month is the only day of peace and quiet I have. Phoebe is . . . well, she's energetic," he added, after an awkward hesitation.

"Yes. I've noticed," Savannah agreed. "Thank you for giving up your one tranquil day a month to see us. I wasn't sure you'd welcome me, after you refused to take my phone calls."

Ford looked embarrassed. He fidgeted briefly with his cup, then refilled it from the pot, and said, "You're here now, so we may as well enjoy our visit."

Savannah thought the sentiment was nice enough, but the look on his face was anything but one of pleasure. In fact, he looked ill at ease to the point of being miserable.

John led the conversation into more shallow waters, reminiscing about their days at merry old Oxford. While John Gibson had been born and raised only a short distance from the university, Ford Chesterfield had been sent to Britain by wealthy parents to complete his Ivy League education. Although their association had been brief, they had shared a few experiences that provided some entertaining anecdotes.

Besides, their chatter gave Savannah time to formulate how she would steer the subject back to Kat Valentina. Thankfully, John did it for her. She would have to remember to kiss him on the cheek once they were back inside the Bentley.

"I understand you and the recently departed Miss Valentina were close friends," John said to Ford as he picked up the silver tongs and dropped a sugar cube into his tea. "A rather cozy arrangement, I hear."

Well, so much for subtle conversation gambits, Savannah thought, listening and watching with acute interest.

Ford cleared his throat and stared down into his tea as though a miniature shark were circling inside the cup. "I'm not certain where you received your information," he told John, "but your source isn't as informed as he or she may have led you to believe."

"Then you weren't . . . close?" Savannah asked.

"We discussed business on a number of occasions. That was the extent of our association."

"Yes," John said smoothly, "I heard you paid a number of visits to the spa, just before Miss Valentina's unfortunate accident."

"I was attempting to buy a section of the Royal Palms property from her. That's all. I've grown tired of hearing my sister complain about all the indiscretions within her viewing. I thought if I could purchase the land and fence it off, I might get some peace."

"Most sensible," John said, nodding solemnly. "Was she interested in your proposition?"

"Not at all. After several attempts to persuade her, I abandoned the idea."

"Mmmmm." Savannah watched him carefully, studying his body language, the movement of his eyes, the way he held himself, the manner in which he handled the teacup in his hand.

Later, when she and John had left the hacienda and were back inside the Bentley, she gave him the kiss she had been saving and asked, "Do you think he was telling the truth about himself and Kat? Was his only interest in her financial?"

"In a pig's eye, my dear girl. I could see it written all over his face. The old chap was smitten with Lady Katarina Valentina . . . positively dizzy over her. And I'd venture to say, he still is."

John shook his head and chuckled. "It was as obvious as the mustache on his face, which, by the way, was trimmed in far too thin a line. For heaven's sake, that style went out of fashion with Errol Flynn. Chesterfield's barber really should tell him how unbecoming it is."

Savannah cut a sideways glance at John's luxurious silver cookie duster with its carefully combed and slightly uptilted ends.

He gave her a grin that made his mustache twitch and her giggle.

She had to agree.

Savannah was halfway back to her dorm room when it occurred to her that even a brief pop-in visit with Dion Zeller might be a good idea. Last night must have been a sleepless one for him, with his life hanging in the balance. Maybe he needed a friend. Everyone needed someone once in a while.

Although he might have been out, running among the daisies, Savannah didn't think so. If she had been in the same circumstances, she would have been holed up in her room, thinking, worrying, deciding. So she stopped by his cottage and rapped softly on the door.

After knocking a second time, she realized the door was slightly ajar. Ordinarily, that fact wouldn't have been particularly noteworthy. But with a suspicious death occurring at the spa only a week or so before, she thought most of the Royal Palm's residents would have been a bit more vigilant about security than usual . . . Dion Zeller included.

"Hello?" she called, pushing the door a few inches wider. "Dion, are you here? It's Savannah Reid. May I come in?"

When she didn't receive an answer, she stuck her head inside and looked around. At first, everything seemed as it had before—neat, tidy, every miniature in its place.

Then she saw something that caused a jolt of adrenaline to hit her bloodstream.

Through the open bedroom door. Legs. Sticking out from behind the bed.

Instantly, she recognized the heavily muscled thighs, the well-rounded calves, and the electric blue running shorts.

"Dion!" She flung the door open and ran to him. "Dion, are you all right?"

Of course, she knew he wasn't, but she couldn't help hoping.

Her heart sank when he didn't respond. She entertained a brief, happy fantasy that he was simply lying on the floor, playing with an electric train set—even though she knew better.

Rounding the end of the bed, she saw he was lying on his back, eyes closed, arms outflung. His face was a sickly white, tinted with blue around his lips. He had vomited profusely.

"No . . ." she whispered as she knelt beside him. "Please, no."

When she pressed her fingers against the inside of his wrist, she could feel a distinct, if weak, pulse. At least he was alive. Maybe not by much, but after thinking she had discovered a corpse, she was thrilled.

He was breathing, but his respiration was rapid and shallow. Laying her palm against his cheek, she shuddered to feel how cold and clammy his skin felt.

"Dion, can you hear me?" she said, glancing over his body, checking for wounds. None were apparent. No blood, no obvious contusions.

Then she saw the three empty pill bottles on the bed, the broken glass, and the water spilled on the floor beside the nightstand.

"Oh shit, Dion," she whispered. "Why did you go and do a stupid thing like that?"

Spotting a telephone on the desk in the corner of the room, she jumped up, ran to it, and dialed the spa's office. Thankfully, Bernadette answered immediately.

"It's Savannah Reid," she told her. "Call Dr. Ross and tell him to get over to Dion's cottage right away. It's an emergency."

Flustered, Bernadette stammered and stuttered for a moment, then she said, "But Dr. Ross isn't here. He's up at the Chesterfield estate. Phoebe called him a while ago and asked him to come up because—"

"Okay, then call 9–1–1 and tell them to send an ambulance. Say we have an unconscious male in his thirties, probable drug overdose. Respiration weak, heart rate thready. Got that?"

"Yeah, but who is it? Is it Dion? Is he—?"

"Just do it, Bernadette!

"But—"

"Damn it! Right now!"

Slamming down the phone, she looked back at Dion, who seemed to be getting whiter and bluer by the second. "Hurry up," she whispered. "Please, hurry."

If that ambulance doesn't get here pretty quick, she thought, *they might as well send the coroner's wagon.*

CHAPTER TWENTY-FIVE

Savannah sat in the hospital lobby, holding Tammy's hand and sending silent comfort to Ryan, who sat across the room beside John. The four of them had been anxiously waiting, jumping every time a professional wearing a white smock had exited the emergency-room door.

A nurse had told them she would bring them a report on Dion's condition in a few minutes. That had been an hour ago, and still no word.

Savannah wanted to believe that Granny Reid's axiom "No news is good news" was applicable in this case. But Dion had looked horrible by the time they had arrived at the hospital, and she had overheard just enough of the conversation between the attending physician and nurses to know he was just as bad as he looked.

Any members of the Royal Palms staff were conspicuously

absent. Bernadette had driven to the hospital along with them, but had left soon with some excuse about having to "take care of Lou." Savannah didn't even want to think what that meant.

After three cups of stale, machine coffee and a Snickers bar, Savannah had practically memorized the burgundy-and-gray tiles on the floor. They matched the burgundy-and-gray tiles on the walls, and the burgundy-and-gray abstract art on the wall.

"Looks like the decorator was into burgundy and gray," she had remarked twenty minutes ago. But the conversational gambit had gone nowhere.

Their little vigil had a somber note about it. Thankfully, somebody you knew didn't try to kill themselves every day.

"When are they going to come out and tell us what's going on?" Tammy asked for the eleventh time. Savannah had been counting . . . along with the tiles.

"I'm sure they'll let us know as soon as they can," Ryan replied with as much calm and grace as when he had answered her the first, second, and third times.

"He's in most capable hands," John said, giving Ryan a compassionate, reassuring look.

"Yes," Ryan replied. "Thank you for asking your private physician to look at him."

"Any friend of yours deserves the best," John said.

Savannah searched John's eyes for any sign of jealousy or resentment. She was certain Ryan had told him that Dion and he had been lovers. Ryan's sense of honesty and openness would have demanded as much. But John seemed perfectly at ease with the situation, other than his concern for Dion and his sympathy for those who cared about him.

"I just don't know why he would do such a thing," Tammy

said, starting to cry again. "He was so handsome and so nice. And he had so much to live for."

Savannah handed her another tissue. Tammy blew noisily into it, then Savannah said, "I think he was afraid."

"Of what?"

Savannah glanced over at Ryan and John, thinking that they might be able to offer Tammy a more insightful answer. But they simply watched and said nothing.

Savannah took a deep breath and plunged ahead. "Of having those he loves and respects think of him differently than before."

"How?"

"Without love and respect."

"Well, I think it's sad," Tammy said, sniffing loudly. "I can't imagine being so afraid and depressed that I wouldn't even want to live anymore."

"Me either." Savannah patted Tammy's hand and sent a silent "Thank you" heavenward that the young woman had an indomitable spirit . . . certainly not someone you had to worry about becoming suicidal.

"I just wish they could give Dion a transfusion of your enthusiasm for life, Tam," she said.

"Wouldn't that be grand," John added. "Perhaps there would be enough for us all to have a pint or so. You *do* seem to have an abundant supply, my dear."

The words that had been intended to make Tammy feel better seemed to have the reverse effect. She only cried that much harder.

Just when Savannah thought she was going to go into hysterics, the door down the hall opened and a white-smocked

Hispanic woman hurried out of the emergency ward. After glancing around the waiting room, she strode over to them.

"Are you Dion Zeller's family?" she asked with a degree of authority that distinguished her as a doctor, even more clearly than the stethoscope slung around her neck or the "Selena Hernandez, M.D." on her name tag.

"Close enough," Savannah said as they all jumped to their feet and rushed toward her.

"How is he?" Ryan asked, reaching the doctor first.

"He's in a coma. Unfortunately, he had ingested most of the drugs before he was found, so pumping his stomach had minimal benefits. Fortunately, he had already regurgitated much of what he took."

Savannah felt a pang of guilt. If only she had stopped by a few hours earlier. . . .

"I understand you were the one who found him," the doctor said to Savannah. Her coffee-colored eyes were searching Savannah's as though reading the guilt ledger written there all too plainly.

"That's right," Savannah admitted. "I—"

"If you hadn't discovered him when you did," the doctor said, cutting off her confession, "he would be dead. So, don't waste your time feeling responsible for his condition."

"Thank you, Dr. Hernandez."

"Will the young man recover fully?" John asked.

"It's too early to tell. We'll know more in a few hours, after his body has processed more of the drugs. And, of course, we're waiting until he comes out of the coma before we make any definitive diagnosis of the damage he's done to himself."

A pager buzzed on the doctor's hip. She reached for it,

peered at the number, and grimaced. "I have to go," she said. "Is there anything else?"

"May we see him?" Ryan asked.

Dr. Hernandez hesitated, studying Ryan's handsome, worried face. When she finally spoke, Savannah could hear the underlying compassion in her voice. "I'm afraid there isn't much to see. Mr. Zeller's coma is quite deep. But, if it would make you feel better, I'll arrange for you to be admitted, one at a time, to the intensive care unit."

"Thank you," Ryan said.

"Only for a couple of minutes each."

"We understand," Savannah told her. "Thank you, Doctor."

Dr. Hernandez hurried away to answer her page and arrange for their brief visits.

"Who goes first?" Tammy asked, suddenly sounding very young and frightened.

"Ryan," Savannah said. She gave John a quick glance.

Graciously, he nodded his silver head. "Absolutely," he said. "Ryan first, and then the ladies. We old fellows have learned to be patient."

When Savannah entered the intensive care unit and saw Dion lying there—his face whiter than the pillow beneath his head—it occurred to her this was more like viewing a corpse in the morgue than visiting a sick friend.

Based upon her past experiences, Savannah held the theory that the average suicide attempt was a cry for help rather than a sincere effort to end a life.

But it appeared Dion Zeller had meant to go all the way, and—from the way he looked, lying pale and motionless on

the bed, hooked to half a dozen, blinking, beeping machines—
he had nearly succeeded.

Savannah walked to his bedside, lifted his cold hand and
folded it between hers, trying to impart some warmth, comfort,
and support . . . at least to his subconscious.

"Dion, can you hear me? It's Savannah," she said, not
that she really expected him to answer, but it never hurt to
ask.

Remembering only several days ago, when this healthy,
vibrant man had been jogging at her side, Savannah was
shocked and horrified by how that vitality could be devastated
by some pills and a streak of self-destructiveness.

She felt a rush of impotent anger at Dion for surrendering
something as precious as himself, his life. She felt rage at society
for forcing some of its dearest and most valuable members into
horrible positions where suicide seemed the best alternative.
And, most of all, she was furious at whoever had murdered
Kat Valentina and started this chain of destruction.

If someone killed Kat, she reminded herself. For all she
knew, she was raging at Fate or Kat's own irresponsibility for
sitting in a hot tub while drinking alcohol.

Either way, her fury seemed pretty pointless. She needed
to spend more of her time and energy thinking about "what"
and "how" this had happened, rather than "why." She was
only a detective, not God.

Hearing a footstep behind her, Savannah turned and saw
the intensive care nurse coming toward her. "I'm sorry, ma'am,"
the RN said, "but you're going to need to leave now. We have
to run some tests on Mr. Zeller."

"Yes, of course. Thank you for letting me see him."

Savannah bent over and placed a kiss on Dion's cheek.

"Don't you *dare* check out," she whispered. "I want to go running in the daisies with you again. I'm counting on it; you hear?"

Still there was no response.

Savannah left the room with a heavy, sinking feeling in the region of her heart. She was afraid she would never know if Dion had heard her or not.

In the hallway between the ICU and the hospital lobby, Savannah ran nearly headlong into Dr. Freeman Ross.

"I just heard," he said, breathless, as he grabbed her by the arm. "How is he?"

"Not so good," she told him. "He's in a coma. But they say he's stabilized; I guess that's good news."

Dr. Ross took off his glasses and rubbed his hand wearily across his eyes. "Man, what a morning! Some days it doesn't pay to get out of bed. Two in one hospital at once! Who would have thought?"

"Two? What do you mean?" Savannah had a bad feeling about this.

He looked confused for a moment. "Oh, I thought you knew. Phoebe Chesterfield called me this morning, frantic over her brother. I went running up to their house and realized he had suffered a stroke."

"This morning? But John Gibson and I were with him this morning. We had tea, and he was fine."

"Apparently she came home shortly after you left and found him lying on the lawn in the backyard. He was incoherent and had lost control of his right side."

"Oh, no! Is he okay?"

"Not really. I'm afraid he suffered substantial brain damage, though we won't know until the test results are in how serious it is. I was consulting with his personal physician when I heard about Dion."

For some reason, Savannah thought of crimson Mr. Lincoln roses and snowy white John F. Kennedy blossoms. "Where is Phoebe?" she said, although she knew the answer.

"By his bedside, of course. Room 4E."

After thanking Dr. Ross and saying a brief good-bye, Savannah hurried toward the elevator, heading for the fourth floor. Of course Phoebe would be by Ford's side. No matter how old he might be, he was still Phoebe's little brother.

And if Savannah knew about anything, it was about the duties of being a big sister.

CHAPTER TWENTY-SIX

Savannah stood outside Room 4E and allowed the feelings of sympathy to wash over her. The emotions quickly turned to liquid and clouded her vision of Phoebe sitting on the edge of her brother's hospital bed, stroking his forehead and weeping softly. As in the garden, Phoebe's hair spilled, unbound, over her shoulders in thick, silver waves. As always, she wore a bright floral-print dress.

But, unlike the dress, the wearer was far from festive.

Savannah knew exactly how Phoebe felt. A few years ago, her own younger brother, Macon, had taken a headfirst tumble off his motorcycle and had ended up in the hospital with a ruptured spleen. And, like any good big sister, Savannah had sat on the side of *his* bed and stroked *his* forehead . . . and, of course, she had wept, too. It was part of the Big-Sister job description.

She knocked softly on the open door. Phoebe jumped, startled, then nodded a curt acknowledgment.

"May I come in?" Savannah asked.

"Ah . . . yes, I suppose so."

Taking note of the fact that Phoebe didn't seem overjoyed to see her, Savannah decided to make her visit short and sweet. Well, at least short. Ford didn't look so good . . . certainly not prepared to receive guests.

He was lying still, eyes open and staring at his sister. The right side of his face drooped like a tragedy mask. The hand Phoebe was holding lay limp and unresponsive in hers.

Savannah thought of the urbane gentleman she had met in the rose garden and wished there were no such things as debilitating strokes that robbed people of their dignity.

"I heard you were here," she said, speaking directly to Ford, though she wasn't sure he understood her. "I wanted to drop by just for a moment and wish you well."

He turned from his sister and fixed his pale blue eyes on her. In spite of the paralytic disfiguration, he seemed moderately alert and aware.

"He can't talk," Phoebe said with a sniff. Savannah reached for a box of tissues on the nightstand and set it on the bed beside her. "And he can't use his right side at all."

"But your condition may well improve," Savannah said, speaking directly to Ford. If she were ever unfortunate enough to be in a similar situation, she hoped people wouldn't speak about her as though she weren't even in the room.

"But what if it doesn't? What if he winds up a vegetable for the rest of his life?" Phoebe wailed. Savannah considered the wisdom of reaching over and slapping some sense into her.

Didn't she have any conception of how frightened her brother was already? She didn't need to add to it by having hysterics.

"Physical therapy is extremely helpful," Savannah said. "I've seen people recuperate from strokes worse than this."

She could have sworn that Ford silently blessed her with his eyes. Yes, he definitely looked grateful.

He opened his mouth and mumbled a few syllables that were severely garbled and unintelligible.

"I think you're upsetting him," Phoebe said. "Maybe you had better leave."

"Do you want me to leave, Mr. Chesterfield?"

He shook his head "no." The movement was feeble, but definite.

"It's almost as though he wants to speak to me," Savannah said.

This time the head nodded vigorously.

Savannah took a step closer to the bed. "Is there something you need to tell me, Mr. Chesterfield?"

Again he nodded. This time he lifted his left hand and made scrawling movements in the air.

"Writing," Savannah said, thinking aloud. "He wants to write something to me."

"You're getting him all upset," Phoebe protested. And Savannah had to agree; she was right. Ford Chesterfield was obviously agitated. And for someone who had just suffered a stroke, that couldn't be a good idea.

Yet, it seemed so important to him that he communicate with her.

"Maybe if we get a pen and paper," she suggested.

But he shook his head again. No, that wasn't what he wanted.

More scrawling in the air. Then he pointed emphatically to himself.

"You want to write something?" Savannah asked, trying to understand. He jabbed a finger in her direction. "You want *me* to write something for you?"

No, that still wasn't it.

Savannah's frustration barometer was rising by the moment.

One more time, he pointed to himself, wrote with his invisible pen, then pointed at her.

"You write me," she said. "You write me . . . oh . . . you *wrote* me. You wrote me already." His head bobbed in assent. "You were the one who wrote me those two notes. You're the one who hired me."

Vigorous nods.

"Okay." Savannah took a deep breath and rearranged her mental notes on this case with her new perspective. "That solves one mystery. But why did you hire me? Why did you think Kat was murdered?"

Even as she spoke, she knew it was ridiculous to expect him to communicate a difficult answer to a complex question. But her curiosity propelled her to ask anyway.

Ford looked at his sister, an expression of helplessness on his face. He muttered some words that Savannah couldn't possibly understand.

"I'm sorry, Ford," Phoebe said. "This must be so difficult for you." To Savannah, she added, "I really wish you wouldn't upset him like this. He has high blood pressure, you know, and the doctor says he has to remain calm."

Savannah understood Phoebe's concern for her younger

brother, and it was obvious he was becoming more agitated by the second.

"Your sister's right," she told him. "I really should go. Maybe if you're feeling better later, I could—"

"Nooo!"

Even though the word was slurred, there was no mistaking the meaning of it. Ford Chesterfield did not want her to leave yet. He still had something to say.

With an effort, he lifted his left hand to his own throat and made a movement as though squeezing it.

"Do you need a drink of water, Ford?" Phoebe asked, scrambling for a nearby pitcher on the nightstand.

"No," Savannah said, "that isn't what he means. I think he's talking about Kat."

He nodded.

"Kat's murder?"

Yes.

"Do you know that she was murdered by someone?"

Yes.

"Do you know how she was killed?"

Yes. He made a movement as though drinking from a glass.

"See," Phoebe said, "he does want some water. He's thirsty."

"No, he means she drank something. Is that what you mean, Mr. Chesterfield?"

Yes.

"Did she drink something that killed her? Something besides the alcohol, that is?"

Yes. Yes. Yes.

"Was it some sort of poison?"

He nodded.

"Do you know who did it?"

"Savannah, stop this immediately!" Phoebe said, grabbing her by the arm and pulling her away from the bed. "Can't you see how red his face is? He's going to have another stroke, and it will be all your fault."

When Savannah turned to look at Phoebe, she saw that Ford wasn't the only one in the room with a flushed face. "What's the matter, Phoebe?" she said evenly. "Are you afraid of what your brother is about to tell me?"

"No, of course not. Why would I be afraid?"

"Then let him tell me what he wants to say. It's obviously very important to him."

She turned back to Ford. "Do you know who killed Kat Valentina, Mr. Chesterfield?"

His head bobbed up and down. Then his finger pointed . . . at himself.

CHAPTER TWENTY-SEVEN

"So, now that you know, what are you going to do about it?" Phoebe said, when she and Savannah had exited Ford's hospital room.

"I'm not sure," Savannah replied, glancing up and down the empty hallway. "Did you know all along that your brother killed Kat?"

Phoebe said nothing, but stared down at the tiled floor and shrugged her shoulders.

"I understand about protecting those you love," Savannah said, "about loyalty and standing up for friends and family, but murder . . . "

"I don't want to discuss Ford with you," Phoebe told her. "I just want to know if you're going to go to the police with what you've found out."

"I'll have to, sooner or later."

Phoebe sighed and, for the first time since Savannah had met her, she looked old. "Then could you make it later? The doctor said Ford may not even pull through. What's the point of causing more problems for him now? It's not as though he's going anywhere."

Savannah gave her what she hoped was a compassionate smile and placed her hand on the older woman's shoulder. "I understand how you feel about your brother, Phoebe. Really, I do. But we're talking about murder here. Someone's life has been taken from her; it doesn't get more serious than that. I have to do something."

"Can you wait until tomorrow morning? Give him a chance to get stronger, please."

Savannah thought of Kat Valentina's body lying beside the mud bath, limp and lifeless. She thought of how Ford had looked when pointing to himself, confessing that he had poisoned her. His eyes had been full of regret and pain. Not that it mattered; Kat Valentina was dead . . . forever.

Part of why Savannah had been a police officer for so many years was because she had a strong sense of justice. If one of society's citizens crossed the legal line and caused someone irreparable harm, they had to pay the price. Retribution was only fair. And having seen so much injustice in the world, Savannah was big on "fair."

But Phoebe was right. Ford Chesterfield wasn't going anywhere until morning. Twenty-four hours wouldn't make that much difference in the end.

Dirk would probably be hightailing it over to the hospital as soon as he got wind of Dion Zeller's overdose. But she wouldn't absolutely, positively *have* to tell him anything . . . at least, not right away.

It didn't seem that much to ask.

"All right," she said. "I'll wait until tomorrow morning. Then I'll need to talk to the police. I'm sure they'll be sensitive in the way they deal with your brother, considering his circumstances. Meanwhile, maybe you should hire a lawyer on his behalf. If he makes it through this present health crisis of his, he's going to need one."

After she left the hospital, Savannah decided to stop by her house before returning to the Royal Palms. In spite of Mrs. Normandy's surrogate care, Diamante and Cleopatra needed a pet from their mistress. And if she were honest, Savannah would have to admit she needed to pet them. It had been the day from hell, and she was looking forward to it ending.

Besides, she had some thoughts churning in the back of her mind, and she thought better at home than anywhere else.

Once inside her house, sitting in her favorite chintz, overstuffed chair, her cats—like sleek, ebony bookends—snuggled on each side of her, Savannah felt a deep sadness steal over her.

Sometimes, there was something worse than not knowing. Knowing could be worse. Much worse.

She needed to talk to her grandmother. She needed to talk about roses and gardens and about what it meant to be the oldest child in a family . . . especially if you were a woman.

Yes, she definitely needed to talk to Gran.

Later, Savannah was filling Tammy in on the details about Dion's condition when Bernadette knocked on their dorm-room door.

"Here it is," Savannah told Tammy. "Just about on time."

Savannah opened the door to find Bernadette standing there, a pink message pad slip in her hand.

She gave it to Savannah. "Phoebe Chesterfield called," she told her. "She wants you to come up there to the house right away, says she has something important to tell you."

"I'm sure she does. Thank you, Bernadette."

"I heard her brother had a stroke," Bernadette said, fishing. "I hope he's all right."

"Me too."

"The hospital called and Dion's doing a little better. They think he's going to be all right."

"That's great. Thanks."

Savannah closed the door and handed Tammy the note.

"How did you know Mrs. Chesterfield would call and invite you up there?" Tammy asked.

Savannah gave a wry chuckle. "Because that's probably what I would do . . . at least, I would *want* to. People are pretty predictable, if you just put yourself in their place."

"Have you got what you need?" Tammy asked as Savannah picked up her purse and sweater.

"Yep. All set." She headed for the door. "Make that phone call for me, okay?"

"You got it," Tammy replied with an eager-to-please smile. "That's why I get paid the big bucks that I don't get paid . . . right?"

"You're absolutely right."

Phoebe Chesterfield met Savannah at the door wearing a long, flowered housedress and a worried look on her face. "They made me go home," she said. "The nurses and doctors wouldn't let me stay with him through the night. Otherwise, I never would have left."

"I know," Savannah said, as Phoebe ushered her inside. "They probably felt you needed your rest. It won't help Ford if you make yourself sick, sitting up with him."

Savannah looked around the house, which was a cluttered, eclectic mix of knickknacks and memorabilia, collected over a lifetime. African tribal masks, china plates, racks of tiny silver spoons, and cases of porcelain dolls lined the walls.

Every era of furniture manufacturing was represented, some Italian turn-of-the-century, early-American, French Provincial, was scattered among some gray, pearlescent and chrome stuff that looked like the Eisenhower administration period.

Phoebe led her through room after room of colorful clutter, until they entered a large, homey kitchen that smelled of freshly baked bread and newly brewed coffee.

"Sit over there," Phoebe said, directing Savannah toward a long, formal table with ladder-back chairs. "I'll get you a cup of coffee. How do you drink it?"

"Black," Savannah said as Phoebe poured.

"It has chicory in it."

"I like chicory . . . reminds me of New Orleans."

"You like New Orleans?"

"I like all the beautiful gardens and flowers."

"Me too." Phoebe shoved the cup under her nose and took a seat across the table, her own cup in her hand. "I'm glad you came," she said. "I wasn't sure if you would or not."

Savannah thought how tired she looked, not at all like the vibrant lady who spent so much time puttering among her roses.

"Your message said it was important," Savannah replied. "Besides, I have some things to tell you, too."

Phoebe's blue eyes glittered briefly in her wan face. "Oh, really? What do you have to say to me?"

"You first."

"Okay." She took a long drink of the coffee. "I want you to know, I don't believe my brother really killed anybody. I don't know what possessed him to do what he did today. But all I can figure is that the stroke messed up his brain, and he isn't thinking right."

"It looked like a confession to me. He seemed in complete control of his faculties."

"Oh, pooh. Ford is male; he's never in full control of his facilities."

Savannah gave her a searching look. "You were there today, and you saw what he did. How can you be so sure he didn't kill her?"

"Because I know my brother. He doesn't have the courage to do something like that. For all of his confident, sophisticated bearing, he's actually quite weak."

"Is that what it takes to commit murder?" Savannah asked. "Courage? I would have thought it took a lack of morality and a disregard for the sanctity of life."

"I think that depends on the circumstances."

"Are you saying some people deserve to be killed?"

Phoebe's right cheek twitched, just a tad. Then she shrugged. "Maybe."

"Maybe . . . under some circumstances . . . murder might be justified. Say, if an adulteress, a woman of ill repute, tried to take advantage of a good man. If she used her feminine wiles to lure him, to make him fall in love with her. And if the man was too foolish to understand that he was being used. After all, he's a man, and we all know how weak and foolish they are."

Savannah waited, and Phoebe said nothing, but her hands began to shake, and her blue eyes filled with tears.

"Men are so stupid about these things," Savannah continued. "They need their women to take care of them. And we older sisters, we're so good at it. After all, we've done it all their lives."

Phoebe's lower lip trembled and a tear rolled down her left cheek as she stared down into her coffee. "I used to change his diapers," she said. "I read him bedtime stories and put iodine on all his cuts and scrapes."

"I'm sure you did."

"And there was that time when he was in college, he got a girl pregnant. She was a piece of trash, that one . . . said she loved him, couldn't live without him. But I paid her off. With her purse full of money, she decided that maybe she *could* live without him after all."

"Did Ford ever know about that?"

Phoebe sniffed. "He didn't need to know. I took care of it, and that's all that mattered."

"I'm sure Ford loves you very much," Savannah said. "I'm sure he's very grateful to you. He would probably even confess to a murder he didn't commit to save you."

Phoebe didn't reply.

"But then," Savannah continued, "he seems to have strong principles. It must have been terribly hard, suspecting his own sister, but not being sure. I suppose, if he hired a private investigator anonymously, he could find out for certain, without actually turning her in."

Still no reply.

"Phoebe, did your brother know for sure that you killed Kat Valentina?"

Phoebe's eyes narrowed. "Who says I killed her?"

"You poisoned her marguerita. I'm not sure how you got hold of her glass or which you used, extract from oleander or azalea. But as soon as they run the special toxicology screens in the San Francisco lab, I'm sure they'll find one or the other. My grandmother says you probably used the oleander, and she's usually right when it comes to her flowers."

"So, you broke your promise to me? You've already talked to the police?"

"No. I told you I wouldn't. And I haven't."

"But you said . . . the toxicology screens. . . . "

"I'll tell them tomorrow morning. That's what we agreed, tomorrow morning, right?"

"Right." Phoebe was visibly relieved. "But even when you do talk to them, these are only suspicions of yours. You don't have any real proof against me or my brother, or anyone else, for that matter."

"I'm still gathering evidence," Savannah said. "That's what I'm doing now, even as we speak."

Savannah saw the split second of panic cross Phoebe's face before she wiped it clean.

Yes, she thought, *not knowing is definitely better, especially when you like the person.*

The two women sat in silence for a long time. Finally, Phoebe said, "Aren't you going to drink your coffee?"

Savannah searched the tired, lined face. "Do you really want me to drink it, Phoebe?"

The facade of bravado slid off the old woman's face as

clearly as one of her African tribal masks falling off the wall. She began to cry—deep, wracking sobs that shook her entire body.

"No," she said. "I don't want you to drink it, Savannah. With Kat Valentina, it seemed like the right thing to do. But with you . . . you're a good person. I'm sorry. I don't know why I . . . "

"You thought you were protecting your brother," Savannah offered, knowing it was a feeble excuse at best.

"And myself." Phoebe sobbed even harder. "I just couldn't imagine myself in jail for the rest of my life. Without my flowers, without the sun and the smell of the soil."

Perhaps it was cruel, but Savannah felt compelled to state the obvious. "Kat Valentina can't feel the sun on her face either, Phoebe. You took that away from her forever. And, even if you didn't approve of the way she led her life, she had the right to live it."

Phoebe pulled a lace-trimmed handkerchief from her pocket and blew into it. "It doesn't matter if I did it or not. I'll deny it," she said. "It will be my word against yours."

"I'll have them run the contents of this cup through the San Francisco lab, along with Kat's blood sample. I'll bet they find the same toxin in both. Besides, I have the tape."

"What tape?"

Savannah pulled back the collar of her sweater, exposing the tiny microphone clipped to her blouse. "Did you get all that, Dirk?" she said.

The gruff, gravelly voice responded in the earpiece hidden in her hair. "Got it all."

Phoebe's tear-wet eyes widened. "You said you didn't call the police."

"I didn't. My assistant, Tammy, did. She's a little ditzy from time to time, but she tries, and she has her moments of efficiency."

"You must be pretty proud of yourself right now," Phoebe said. "You must be feeling pretty smart, tricking a nice old lady like that."

Savannah leaned across the table and fixed her with a level, pointed look. "You killed someone, Phoebe. It was premeditated, cold-blooded murder. If I had been dumb enough to drink your chicory coffee, you would have killed me, too. That's not the sort of thing a nice old lady does to another woman. Especially one who helped her plant flowers in her garden."

She had touched a chord. Phoebe's face crumpled again, and this time her tears seemed to be flowing from genuine remorse.

"Will you check on my Mr. Lincolns and John F. Kennedys from time to time?" she asked, as Dirk walked through the kitchen door, holding a pair of handcuffs. "Even if Ford recovers from his stroke, he doesn't know spit about roses."

"It would be my honor," Savannah replied.

And as she watched Dirk lead Phoebe Chesterfield away, Savannah didn't feel particularly proud or especially smart. More than anything, she just felt tired and sad.

"I have to tell you, I've made more satisfying busts in my day," Dirk said as they entered the all-night diner and took a booth in the back. "Booking an old lady isn't my idea of a good time."

"She's a killer."

"Yeah, yeah. But . . . "

"I know. Think how *I* feel. I actually like her."

"She was gonna kill you."

"I know. But I still liked her. It's a female, flower-planting, bonding thing. You male nongardeners couldn't understand."

"Thank God. I don't want to understand. You're very weird, even for a broad."

"Thank you."

They ordered their coffee, Dirk's donut, and Savannah's cherry pie.

"I guess Lou Hanks will be relieved," Savannah said. "Now he'll get his insurance money and maybe put Royal Palms on its feet again."

"He's not the only one who's relieved. I talked to Dr. Ross at the hospital, and he's glad to be off the hook, too. By the way, I located the market where he rented that rug shampoo machine. He'd just screwed up the name of the place."

"Then why was he paying off Josef Orlet?"

"Because he didn't want to go through all that hassle again, the medical board's investigation, the bad press. He figured it was easier to just fork over the money and hope for the best. But he's decided to file a complaint against Orlet for extortion. Looks like I'll be able to get him for breaking his parole. He'll be back in the slammer where he belongs."

"Good boy. I'll have to buy your donut for you."

Dirk smiled. Free donuts were his favorite.

"Dion's going to be okay?" Savannah asked.

"Last I heard, yes. And Ford Chesterfield will need a lot of rehabilitation therapy, but he'll make it, too." He took a big bite of the pastry and chewed . . . in ecstasy. Dirk was easily pleased. "All's well that ends well, huh?"

Savannah thought of the recently transplanted azalea

bush and knew that the plant would thrive in its new setting. Phoebe wouldn't be so lucky. Prison would destroy her.

"Yeah," she said. "I guess so."

"Heaven ... I'm in heaven," Savannah crooned as the gorgeous Polynesian hunk in the bright orange loincloth finished wrapping her body in the warm, herbal-scented cloths. "Now *this* is my idea of a spa."

"An improvement?" Ryan asked. He lay on the table next to hers, also cocooned in blissful warmth and delicate, floral fragrance.

"No comparison. Absolutely none."

"We wanted you to have a pleasant spa experience," said John, who was lying at her other side. "So, we decided to whisk you away for a few days. After what you endured at the hands of those barbarians, you deserve a little pampering."

"Amen and hallelujah!"

All three were inside a tiny bamboo hut with a tin roof. A light tropical rain was tinkling on the metal, sounding like a hundred miniature jungle drums. Savannah couldn't recall a more delicious moment in her entire life. Unless, maybe, it was the mint scalp massage she had received hours earlier, or the coconut oil, full-body rubdown, skillfully delivered by the same underdressed, overmuscled hunk in the loincloth.

"There's a luau this evening," Ryan said. "The roast pork melts in your mouth."

"Those magnificent pineapple, mango, rum drinks of theirs ... " John sighed. "... and the singing and dancing until dawn. I can hardly wait."

"Heaven, I'm in heaven." Savannah closed her eyes as Ryan and John joined her in three-part harmony.

In two days, she would be back in San Carmelita, paying overdue bills, wondering who her next client might be, scheming about how to keep a floundering detective agency on its feet.

But for now . . . the real world could wait. How often did a woman get to experience pure paradise?

Please turn the page for
an exciting sneak peek of
G. A. McKevett's
newest Savannah Reid mystery
SUGAR AND SPITE
on sale now
wherever hardcover mysteries are sold!

CHAPTER ONE

"I don't quite understand this," Tammy Hart said as she watched Savannah add three eggs to the skillet and several slices of bread to the toaster. "*You* help *him* nab the bad guy and *he* rewards *you* by letting you fix him breakfast?"

The "him" she was referring to was sitting at Savannah's kitchen table, a satisfied smile under his nose. Dirk was always happy when food was imminent. Especially if that food was free. And in keeping with her Southern heritage of hospitality, Savannah made sure that everyone in her presence was stuffed like her Granny Reid's Christmas turkey. Heaven forbid anyone should feel a pang of hunger. It wasn't to be tolerated.

"So I'm a sap for a pretty face," Savannah said.

"And what does that have to do with Dirk?" Tammy shot a contemptuous look toward the table and its occupant, who was still dressed like a street bum.

Savannah chuckled and took a sip of the hot chocolate

she had poured for herself . . . laced with Baileys . . . topped with whipped cream and chocolate shavings. Savannah suffered few hunger pangs herself, as was evidenced by her ample figure.

Tammy, on the other hand, was svelte, golden tanned, golden blond, the quintessential California surfer beach beauty.

Savannah loved her. Anyway.

So the kid was scrawny and ate mostly mineral water, rice cakes, and celery sticks; everyone had their faults.

Savannah retrieved several jars of homemade jams and preserves from the refrigerator and shoved them into Tammy's hands. "Put these on the table," she told her.

The younger woman took the jars and looked at the labels disapprovingly. "Gran's blackberry jam . . . probably full of sugar."

"I'm fresh out of sea-kelp spread," Savannah muttered under her breath, and swigged the hot chocolate.

Tammy sashayed over to the table and plunked the jars in front of Dirk, who gave her a cocky smirk. "Now I have to cook for him, too?" she complained. "It's bad enough that you're his slave, but now I have to—"

"Oh, stop . . . enough already." Savannah snapped her on her teeny-weeny, blue jean-covered rear with a dishtowel. "I'm not Dirk's slave, but you *are* my assistant, so assist. Butter that toast."

"With real butter?"

Savannah sighed. "Yes. Cholesterol-ridden, fat-riddled butter. I'm fresh out of tofu."

"I'll go shopping for you."

"No, thanks."

"Why are you having breakfast at four o'clock in the afternoon, anyway?" Tammy dipped only the tip of the knife into the butter and made a production of spreading the one-eighth of a teaspoon over the slice of bread.

"Because we didn't eat this morning," Dirk replied, watching the meal's progression with the acute attention of a practiced glutton. "We were working, remember?"

"Spraying the genitalia of youthful offenders," Tammy said with a giggle. "That's work?"

"Savannah did that all by herself. Thank God, or I'd be up on charges. You shoulda heard that guy screeching when they were scrubbing him down in the emergency room."

He and Savannah snickered. Tammy shook her head, pretending to be appalled.

"There are advantages to going freelance," Savannah said as she dished the eggs, some link sausages, and thick-sliced bacon onto the plate, then ladled a generous portion of cream gravy beside a scoop of grits. Where she came from, grits might be optional but gravy was considered a beverage.

Dirk's eyes glistened with the light of hedonism as he picked up his fork. "Van, you've outdone yourself. This looks great."

"Yeah," Tammy said as she sat down to a bowl of long-grain rice across the table from him. "She's good at CPR, too. And if that doesn't work, I'm pretty good at angioplasty." She hefted her knife and punctuated her statement with a skewering motion.

Savannah was reaching into the cupboard for a box of marzipan Danish rolls for herself, when she heard a buzzing coming from Dirk's leather coat, which was draped across one of her dining chairs.

"I see you've got it set on VIBRATE again," she said, digging through his pockets and handing him the phone. "Your love life in a slump?"

"Eh ... bite me." He flipped it open and punched a button. "Coulter here."

"He's sure grumpy when somebody gets between him and

his dog dish," Tammy whispered to Savannah. "Reminds me of a pit bull I knew."

Savannah didn't reply. She was watching the play of emotions over Dirk's craggy face: irritation, fading to surprise, softening to . . . she wasn't sure what, but she was fairly certain the party on the other end was female.

"Ah, yeah . . . hi," he was saying. He turned in his chair, his side to her and Tammy. His voice volume dropped a couple of notches. "I'm . . . ah . . . here at Savannah's. No, not like that. We were working together this morning. No, really."

Savannah didn't like the sound of that. Why, she wasn't sure. She and Dirk weren't anything "like that," but she didn't like to hear him saying so . . . so clearly . . . to another woman.

Another woman? *Where did that thought come from?* she wondered. *To hell with that,* she quickly added to her mental argument. *Who is he talking to?*

"Yeah, I was going back home right after . . ." He looked wistfully down at the plate of goodies on the table in front of him. "Actually, I was leaving right now if you want to. . . . Yeah, that's good. Sure. See ya."

He flipped the phone closed and rose from his chair. The look on his face reminded Savannah of a sheep after an embarrassingly bad shearing. "I . . . ah . . . gotta go," he said. "Sorry about the"—he pointed to the food—"ah, breakfast. But I really should—"

"No problem," Savannah said as she snatched the plate out from under him and carried it over to the cabinet. "If you gotta go, you gotta go. Obviously it's an important meeting."

"Ah, yeah, it is . . . kinda." He slipped on his jacket and fished for his keys. "I'll see ya later, okay?"

Savannah nodded curtly.

He grunted a good-bye in Tammy's direction, then headed toward the front of the house.

"Don't let the door slap your backside on your way out," Savannah called after him.

Another grunt. The sound of the door slamming.

"Well," Tammy said, recovering from her shock. "I never thought I'd see the day that Dirk Coulter would walk away from a free meal ... especially one *you* cooked," she told Savannah.

From the kitchen window, Savannah watched his battered old Buick Skylark as it pulled out of her driveway. He was practically spinning gravel.

"Hmm," she said thoughtfully as she took his heavily laden plate from the cabinet and carried it back to the table. She sat down, picked up his fork, and dug in.

"That's all you've got to say?" Tammy asked her. "Hmmm. That's it?"

"I'm thinking."

"And eating." Tammy watched disapprovingly as Savannah shoveled in a mouthful of grits, dripping with butter.

"I think best when I eat."

"That explains your mental prowess," Tammy mumbled.

"Shut up. I've almost got it."

"Got what?"

"The plan of action."

"You've gotta know, huh?"

Savannah snorted. "Only if I intend to sleep tonight."

She downed a few more bites, then jumped up from her chair. "Be back later," she said as she snatched her cell phone off its charger base.

"What's the story?"

"He forgot his phone."

"That's *your* phone."

She shrugged. "We bought them at the same time. They look so much alike. It's an honest mistake."

"Going out there is a mistake," Tammy grumbled as she followed her to the front door. "There's nothing honest about it."

"I don't recall asking for your editorial comments. Go on the Internet while I'm gone. See if you can drum up some business for me so that I can continue to pay you that high, minimum-wage salary you've grown accustomed to."

Tammy sputtered, stood between her and the door, then moved aside with a sigh of resignation. "That's it? The phone story? It's a bit thin."

Savannah grinned and tossed her purse strap over her shoulder. "Yeah, well . . . Dirk's a bit thick. It'll work."

CHAPTER TWO

As Savannah pulled her 1965 Camaro into Dirk's trailer park, she grimaced at the cloud of dust that was settling on her new red paint. There was a nice mobile-home park down by the beach, but Dirk was far too tight to spring for that. He had parked his ten-foot-wide in the Shady Vale Trailer Park fifteen years ago, and once Dirk was parked anywhere, he tended to stay until he rusted.

Shady Vale was inappropriately named. Flat as a flitter, without a tree in sight, the property's picturesque description must have been a figment of some developer's imagination.

Dirk's neighbors were mostly transient, and more than once he had been forced to arrest one of his Shady Vale-ites for everything from armed bank robbery to blowing up half the park while cooking up a nice batch of methamphetamines in one of the trailer's kitchens.

The only residents who had been at Shady Vale longer than Dirk were the Biddles. They were a cantankerous, nosy old couple who watched the comings and goings of everyone in the park, as though they owned the dusty gravel road themselves. From their #1 spot at the entrance, they saw every arrival and had an opinion as to whether that person had legitimate business in Shady Vale.

Their trailer was right next to Dirk's, which was parked in spot #2, and Savannah was hoping she could avoid her usual argument with Mr. Biddle or an interrogation from Mrs. Biddle. If luck were on her side, she might be able to recognize Dirk's mystery visitor's vehicle and find out who his guest was without having to use that ridiculous cell-phone ruse.

But the new silver Lexus parked beside his Buick didn't ring any bells. Since when did Dirk have a girlfriend ... let alone one that could afford to drive a new Lexus?

Looks plumb out of place in this neck of the woods, Savannah thought as she slowed down to see if the car had vanity plates. But the series of random letters and numbers told her nothing.

She saw Harry Biddle sitting in his broken-down lawn chair, swigging a beer, scratching the roll of hairy belly that was protruding from beneath his gray undershirt. As she drove by he watched her with a lascivious gleam in his eye that made her want to crawl out of the car and slap him goofy. Half a slap would probably do the job.

Feeling like an adolescent whose curiosity was about to land her in trouble, Savannah parked her Camaro behind the Lexus and got out. Harry perked up when he saw her walking in his direction, until she turned toward Dirk's trailer.

"Wouldn't go in there right now," he said, his ugly, snaggled grin widening.

"Yeah, why not?" she asked, knowing she wasn't going to like the answer.

"Let's just say, he's already got hisself some company." He waggled one bushy gray eyebrow suggestively. "I think three'd make a crowd, if you catch my drift."

"Well, catch mine, you old coot. Mind your own business."

"Or then . . . maybe you three are into that kinky stuff. . . ."

"And maybe you're a dork with a dirty mind and a grubby undershirt."

Leaving Mr. Biddle behind to mutter obscenities into his beer can, Savannah strode to the door of Dirk's trailer and rapped a shave-and-a-haircut greeting. Might as well be friendly. Might as well be casual. Might as well pretend she wasn't there to snoop.

Dirk might even believe it.

He didn't. She could tell right away by the irritated look on his face when he opened the door. Considering his less than cordial mood, she pushed past him before he could ask her to enter . . . or to leave, which was far more likely.

"Gee, I hate to drop in on you unannounced like this but . . ."

Savannah's voice trailed away when she saw who was sitting on Dirk's 1973 vintage, beige-and-gold-plaid sofa. It was the last person she expected to see.

The former Mrs. Dirk.

The hated and often maligned—though not often enough in Savannah's book—ex-wife who had run away with a shaggy-haired, twentysomething rock-and-roll drummer several years ago.

"Polly!" Savannah replaced her look of shock with a carefully constructed facade of nonchalance. The act probably would have been more convincing if she hadn't been choking on her own spit. "What are you doing . . . I mean . . . what a surprise. I didn't expect to ever see you again."

"You mean, you *hoped* you'd never see me again."

"Yeah, that too."

Polly leaned back and propped her arm along the top of the sofa. She looked as casual as Savannah was pretending to be. Her long legs were stretched out before her, every inch of them bared by her short-short shorts. Savannah noted with just a bit of catty satisfaction that her knees were starting to sag a little.

So was her heavily made-up face. Foundation applied with a trowel, spider eyelashes, red lips that had been painted too far outside the natural lipline to fool anyone . . . except some fool like Dirk. He had admitted to Savannah that he had actually thought Polly was a real blonde for the first year of their relationship. Savannah could spot Golden Sun Frost a mile away . . . especially when it was on a swarthy-skinned woman who, undoubtedly, had been born with dark brown hair.

Like most of the men who had crossed Polly's path, Dirk had been taken in . . . in more ways than one . . . by a used-to-be-pretty face and a not-too-bad body, and lots of skillfully worded female flattery. Those had always been Polly's greatest weapons when hunting.

"Hope I'm not interrupting anything," Savannah said smoothly. She was pretty sure by the frustration on Dirk's face and the way he was pacing the ten foot span of trailer floor that she had. If she hung around long enough, she might just put a stop to this nonsense all together.

Some might call it interference; she called it charity. The guy needed to be saved from himself. On a nearby TV tray lay a single red rose. Probably a pre-Valentine gift from her to him or from him to her. The thought completely irked Savannah . . . either way.

"No problem," Polly said smoothly. "I'm sure you'll be leaving soon. Right? I mean, now that you see Dirk has company . . ."

"And now that you've seen who that company is," Dirk growled as he nodded, not so subtly toward the door.

In her peripheral vision, Savannah could see Dirk's cell phone sitting on top of the television set in the corner. She sauntered across the room in that direction.

"Actually, I had a good reason for dropping by, old pal," she told Dirk. "I brought you something. It's in my car."

She craned her neck to look out the window at her Camaro. As she had hoped, they did the same and she took the opportunity to sweep the cell phone into her jacket pocket.

"What is it?" Dirk said. She could hear the suspicion in his voice. She didn't really expect him to buy this pitch. The best she could hope for was that he would be a gentleman and not call her "liar, liar, pants on fire" to her face.

"Your cell phone," she replied. "You left it at my house. I figured you'd need it."

Dirk shot her a "yeah, right" look and glanced around the room. He didn't see his phone. But that wasn't unusual for Dirk. The guy would lose his rear end if it weren't stapled to his tailbone.

"So where is it?"

"In my car."

"Why didn't you bring it in with you, Savannah?" Polly asked, flipping her lush, golden mane of split ends back behind one shoulder.

"Forgot." Savannah held out her car keys to Dirk. "Why don't you go get it? I think I left it on the passenger's seat."

He grumbled under his breath and headed for the door. "Aren't you coming with me?" he said, not bothering to hide his anger.

"In a minute, darlin'," she said, much too sweetly. "You go ahead. I'll be along shortly."

He looked from her to Polly and back, then shook his head. "I don't think it's a good idea to leave you two broads alone."

"Go on, Dirk," Polly said, stroking one of her legs as though checking for razor stubble. "I'm not afraid of Savannah. We're old friends, right?"

"You may be old," Savannah replied. "I'm barely middle-aged. And just for the record, you and I have never been friends." She tossed the keys to Dirk. "Go get your phone. I'll be right out."

Reluctantly, he exited the trailer, leaving the door ajar. Savannah waited until he was out of earshot. Then she took a few steps closer to Polly.

In spite of what Polly had said, she did look a bit worried, just enough to satisfy Savannah's perverse streak.

"I don't know what you're doing here," Savannah said. "After the number you did on Dirk, I can't imagine why you would come back into his life, or why he would allow you to. But if you use him and hurt him again, like you did before, I swear, I'll beat the tar outta you. And if you think I mean that figuratively, you're wrong."

A flicker of fear crossed Polly's eyes; then she reached for the pack of cigarettes on a nearby TV tray and lit up. She blew a long puff of smoke in Savannah's direction before answering. "Now what is this I hear? Do I detect a note of jealousy? Was I right all those years ago . . . you really do have a thing for Dirk?"

"Yeah, I have a thing for Dirk. It's called friendship. Loyalty. Concern for his well-being . . . all things you wouldn't know about."

"I think you want him all to yourself." Polly released more smoke through her nose.

How perfectly lovely, Savannah thought. *Quintessential femininity. I'd like to snatch her bald.*

Savannah reached over and, before Polly knew what was happening, grabbed the cigarette out of her hand. She crumbled it between her fingers and dropped the remains into a glass of white wine that was sitting next to the ashtray and a bottle of half-drunk beer on the TV tray. Dirk's beer, no doubt. Polly's wine.

"If you hurt Dirk again," Savannah said, using a voice she usually reserved for suspected murderers and child molesters, "I'll hurt you. My interest is not romantic; it's self-preservation. I'm not going to listen to him bellyache for two long, miserable years like he did when you left him before. If I have to pick up the pieces of Dirk, Miss Priss Pot, somebody's going to have to pick up pieces of you. You got that?"

Polly didn't answer. But Savannah could tell by the wideness of her spider eyes and the way her too-lipsticked mouth was hanging open that she had heard and believed . . . at least a little.

Savannah left the trailer, slamming the door behind her, and nearly ran, chest first, into Dirk.

"My cell phone isn't in your car," he said, his nose inches from hers, his voice as low and ominous as hers had been a moment before. "But then, neither one of us really expected it to be, right, Van?"

Savannah reached into her left jacket pocket and took out his phone; hers was still in her right. "Oh, silly me," she said. "Here it is. I guess I remembered to bring it in with me after all."

When she handed it to him, he looked puzzled and apologetic enough to make her feel a little guilty. "Oh, you really . . . oh, thanks, Van."

"No problem. Watch yourself, buddy, with that gal." She nodded toward the trailer. "Remember last time?"

"Yeah, I remember. But it ain't like that this time. She just wants me to help her, to take care of somethin' for her."

"That's all she's ever wanted, Dirk, from anyone. She's a leech. That's the problem."

"Naw. I can take care of it. Don't worry."

Don't worry, yeah sure, she thought as she left him, got in her Camaro, and drove away. Dirk wasn't stupid—not by a long shot. But he had a blind spot where women were concerned . . . especially women he loved.

Why else would he buy a stupid story about a cell phone?

Savannah had no idea what line of bull Polly was going to try to sell him, but she was pretty sure he'd buy it, too.

Savannah had just dropped off to sleep when the telephone rang, exploding in her right ear and sending her pulse racing like a scared rabbit's. She grabbed the receiver, dropped it on the floor, picked it up, and smacked herself on the teeth with the mouthpiece. She could swear she tasted blood.

"What?" she shouted, ready to kill whoever was calling her at—she squinted at the red, glowing numbers on the bedside clock—1:22 A.M.

"Van . . ."

Savannah didn't need Gran's extrasensitive radar to detect the distress in that one word. She sat straight up and flipped on the bedside lamp. "Yeah, Dirk, what's going on?"

"It's Polly."

Savannah had a half a second to utter a quick, silent prayer, one that she instinctively knew was pointless. *God, let her be okay. They just had a fight, right? She's alive, but they just argued and*—

"She's dead."

Let it be natural causes, or . . . "A car accident?"

"Murdered."

ABOUT THE AUTHOR

G. A. McKevett is the author of five Savannah Reid mysteries: *Just Desserts, Bitter Sweets, Killer Calories, Cooked Goose* and *Sugar and Spite.* She loves to hear from readers and you may write to her c/o Zebra Books. Please include a self-addressed stamped envelope if you wish a response.